Attack

He vaulted from the council rise, dashed to intercept his frenzied sire. Before him, Ses and Jah-lila parted, sprang in opposite directions to clear the raging stallion's path. Jan managed to veer ahead of Lell, shield her. Korr plunged past in a dusky blur, a waft of rank air, a snatch of bright teeth and a slash of horn. Jan swung his head with all his might, brought his own weapon down with force enough to knock his assailant's skewer aside. The blow clamored, reverberating in his skull.

He felt the bite upon his neck begin to bleed, the long shallow rent across his chest blaze with pain. Beside him, Lell—scarcely half his size—dodged, trying to get around him, seeking to fall upon their attacker herself. Korr skidded, wheeled. Jan rushed him, mostly to keep himself safely between his young sister and the king. The black prince slapped hard at his sire with the flat of his horn, pounded him with his heels, driving him back, away from Lell and the others. . . .

❋

FIREBIRD
WHERE FANTASY TAKES FLIGHT™

The Son of Summer Stars

Meredith Ann Pierce

FIREBIRD

AN IMPRINT OF PENGUIN GROUP (USA) INC.

For my loving, supportive family.

FIREBIRD
Published by Penguin Group
Penguin Group (USA) Inc., 345 Hudson Street, New York, New York 10014, U.S.A.
Penguin Books Ltd, 80 Strand, London WC2R ORL, England
Penguin Books Australia Ltd, 250 Camberwell Road, Camberwell, Victoria 3124, Australia
Penguin Books Canada Ltd, 10 Alcorn Avenue, Toronto, Ontario, Canada M4V 3B2
Penguin Books (N.Z.) Ltd, 182-190 Wairau Road, Auckland 10, New Zealand

First published in the United States of America by Little, Brown and Company, 1996
Published by Firebird, an imprint of Penguin Group (USA) Inc., 2003

1 3 5 7 9 10 8 6 4 2

LIBRARY OF CONGRESS CATALOGING-IN-PUBLICATION DATA

Pierce, Meredith Ann.
The son of summer stars / Meredith Ann Pierce.
p. cm.
Originally published: Boston: Little, Brown, 1996.
Sequel to: Dark moon.
Summary: Jan, the prince of the unicorns, uses his knowledge of fire to
form a historic alliance between his people and their former enemies
and to return the unicorns to their ancestral homeland.
ISBN 0-14-250074-7
[1. Unicorns—Fiction. 2. Fantasy.] I. Title.
PZ7.P61453So 2003 [Fic]—dc21 2002192889

Printed in the United States of America

Contents

CONTENTS

The Son of Summer Stars

Prelude

For a thousand years, the Hallow Hills had been the homeland
of the unicorns, held in trust to the goddess Alma. As guardians
of her sacred mere, the Well of the Moon, the unicorns called
themselves children-of-the-moon, best belovèd of the Mother-of-
all. Then wyverns came, white poisonous wyrms, who slew the
unicorns' agèd king and fell upon his followers. Proud princess
Halla was one of few to escape that venomous end. She and her
small, beleaguered band fled south across the wide grass Plain till
they found refuge in a broad valley inhabited only by goats and
deer. The unicorns claimed this deserted Vale, and here they dwelt
four hundred years, awaiting one who would end their long exile,
reclaim their lost ancestral lands and drive the hated wyverns out
with the goddess's own empyreal fire.

Zod the dreamer called this warrior-to-come the Firebringer:
black as the dark between Alma's eyes on the coldest of cloudless
midwinter nights. The crescent moon would mark his brow and
a white star one hind heel. Wild Caroc prophesied burning blood,
sparking hooves and a tongue of flame: a colt born at moondark
out of a wyvern's belly and sired by the summer stars. Ellioc, who
followed Caroc, claimed he would be no Ring-born unicorn at all,
but a Renegade outside the Law. He would storm out of heaven in
a torrent of fire, and his advent would mark the ending of the

world. But the unicorns called wild Caroc and Ellioc mad. Their strange visions, though recounted long after their distant passing, were scoffed at. Only Zod was believed true seer of the Firebringer, and he, too, by the time of my tale lay centuries dead.

Two nights past, when we assembled here, I told of how, many years ago, I midwived the birth of the Firebringer. I spoke of Aljan, called son-of-Korr, who, while beardless and callow still, made his way from the Vale to the Hallow Hills on pilgrimage and slew a wyvern there. Her poisoned barb set his blood alight. Companions bore him in her severed hide and cast him into the waters of Alma's mere. The deadly venom fevering his blood cooled then, and he rose weak as a newborn foal from the she-wyrm's bellyskin: hooves and horn tempered to unbreakable hardness, his coat burnt black, a slim crescent moon traced into his brow and a white star marking his heel. Thus completing his initiation into the Ring of Warriors, young Jan returned to the Vale and became his people's battleprince.

Night past, I sang you the second cant of the Lay of the Firebringer, how Jan pledged himself to my daughter, Tek, the pied warrior mare, a bond unshakable in Alma's eyes. I recounted his peacemaking among the goat-leggèd pans, the battle he fought with marauding gryphons by the shores of the Summer Sea and how, in the end, he set enmity aside to befriend the wounded wingcat that had once so fiercely sought his life. I told of his sojourn in the far land of the two-footed firekeepers where, upon the sacred cliffs above their settlement, he learned the secret of the flame that smoldered within him. Before Jan departed, trekking homeward with his gift of fire, his hosts dubbed him Moonbrow, but his name among his own folk means Dark Moon.

This even, which marks the last night of my telling, I sing of how Aljan Moonbrow fulfilled his destiny as Alma's Firebrand, returning with his people to the Hallow Hills and casting the venomous wyverns out. My name is Jah-lila. I am called the Red Mare. A seer and a singer and a traveler am I, a midwife and a magicker — fourth and final prophet of the Firebringer. Of my own small role in his triumph and downfall shall I also speak: how

Aljan broke the Ring of Law and lost his kingship of the unicorns forever, how he hurtled across heaven on pinions of fire and proved every word of my predecessors true — until here at the last, he has kindled the spark unquenchable, which even now as we dance is unmaking the world.

Serpents

★ 1 ★

New grass, green as gryphons' down, covered the dark earth in fine, sparse filaments. Breeze lifted, and the downy strands rippled. Spring sun warmed the hillside's restless air. Jan halted and shook himself. Sod packed the clefts between the toes of his cloven hooves. He bowed his head, used the long, spiral skewer of his brow-horn to pick the clods away. Sparks leapt when the horn's keen tip grated.

With a snort, the black prince of the unicorns straightened, tossed the forelock from his eyes. He bounded up the steep, grassy slope to catch up his twin daughter and son. Aiony, the filly, glanced back at the sudden pounding of his heels. She reared up nickering, limbs fine as a fawn's, her one side pale silver with black stockings and a black-encircled eye, the other side just the opposite: black with silver shanks and eye. Jan nuzzled her as he came alongside. Aiony pranced and whistled to her brother up the slope, the sound high and sweet as panpipes.

"Hey up, Dha! Wait for Jan and me."

The foal Dhattar paused, the same size as his sister but pale as pure cloud. Like her, he sported a nubby horn little more than a promise on his brow. Like hers, his young mane was only beginning to lengthen from its nursling's bristle, the tassel at the end of his ropelike tail barely sprung. He stood picking at the turf with one snow-white heel.

"I *am* waiting," he called.

The prince of the unicorns nickered. Barely weaned, his children already spoke better than most colts half again their age. Jan nibbled his son's withers as he reached him. The white foal shivered happily. Jan snorted, continued moving up the slope.

"Will you tell me what you two are so eager for me to see?" he inquired, for the sixth time.

Chivvying her father's raven-black ribs, Aiony shook her head. Dhattar glanced at her.

"We can't," he answered.

"It's a secret," Aiony insisted.

"A surprise," the white foal concurred.

The prince of the unicorns heaved himself past another slippery place and shook his head. "Well enough, then," he laughed. "Lead on."

The twins bolted, sprinting and chasing as they scrabbled up the rocky hillside. Jan glanced back, startled at how high they had come. The Vale of the Unicorns unfolded below, open meadow hemmed by partially wooded slopes. Far away on the valley floor, Teki the healer stood peering at some medicinal root or herb, his pied black-and-white coloring unmistakable. Around him clustered five or six half-growns — among the few then-colts to have survived the devastating winter that had ravaged the herd barely two years earlier.

The prince of the unicorns gritted his teeth. Half his people had perished in that terrible season of ice and snow — a death toll burgeoned in the prince's absence by one mad usurper's tyranny. A green-tailed, whining fly bit the young stallion's ear, drew blood. Jan rankled and slapped it away with his tail. Korr — his own sire — responsible for so much misery, when a careful policy of scouting and sharing forage would doubtless have saved many who instead had succumbed to hunger and the cold. The prince's ear stung. He shook his head.

"Tell us about the wyvern!"

Aiony came skittering down the hillside. The dark unicorn returned to the present with a start.

"Aye, tell how you slew the wyvern in her den," Dhattar called. "When you were just a colt."

"Like us."

Whickering, Jan shook his head. "Older."

"Lell's age?" Dha ventured.

"Your aunt's only four!" cried Jan. "I was six — three times your age, little goatling kids."

Aiony butted him. Gently, the black unicorn shouldered back. Above him, white Dhattar sneezed amid a swarm of lace-winged flitters. Aiony nipped at her father's flank. Jan shooed her away and began.

"Long ago and many springs past, on pilgrimage . . ."

The tale told itself, unwinding before him like a well-worn path. He hardly listened to his own voice, lost in story, crafting without a thought the internal slant-rhymes and measured cadences of the storyteller's art. His own mate, Tek, was a fine singer of tales, and Teki the healer, her foster sire, one of the best he had ever heard. He had harked the two of them all his life, and never yet dared offer his own recountings to any listeners more critical than his raptly attentive young daughter and son.

"Were you afraid then?" Dhattar broke in, nudged him insistently. "When the wyvern stung, did you fear to die?"

Jan nodded. "Aye."

"But our dam's dam healed you," Aiony was saying. "Jah-lila quelled the she-serpent's poison with the waters of the sacred mere."

Again the black prince nodded, putting his head down, using powerful hindquarters to propel himself up the steepening trail. Dhattar and Aiony spurted ahead as the path led into a dark mass of trees. The black unicorn's skin twitched. View of the Vale behind vanished as firs and cedars closed around him. He glanced at the sky as they emerged once more onto rocky slope, more mindful than ever how they had climbed. The farther from the safety of the valley floor they ventured, the easier prey they made for gryphons.

Yet strangely, for the last two years, not a single wingèd marauder had come. No huge, blue-winged formels — the females — had swooped to steal his people's nurslings, nor had the swifter, lighter tercels struck, their pinions the color of new-sprung grass. The unicorn prince frowned, puzzled, for hunting wingcats would have found ample tender prey. Following that bitterest of winters now two years gone, the Vale had enjoyed early forage, balmy summers, bountiful falls and unseasonably mild winters. *Jah-lila's doing*, the whole herd whispered, *the blessing of Alma's appointed midwife*. The children-of-the-moon had lost no time in getting and bearing new young.

Jan followed his own young, the black-and-silver filly and the snow-white foal, now skirting an outcropping of pale limerock. Truth, he mused, glancing warily at the rocky mass thrusting up from the rich black soil, perhaps the only ill effect of two nearly snowless winters in a row had been a vast increase in the number of serpents: some no thicker than a heron's leg, others stout as a stallion's. The unicorns had begun to watch their tread.

Jan whistled his young. "Aiony! Dha! How much farther?"

Halted on the far side of the outcrop now, the pair whinnied. "We're here."

Jan trotted around the pitted rocks. "When came you here before?"

Dhattar answered, "Never."

Jan turned, perplexed.

"No one brought us," Aiony told him. She and her brother exchanged a glance.

"We came night past," Dhattar continued.

His sister nodded. "Not by hoof. *Looking.*"

Jan cocked his head. "The pair of you slept betwixt your dam and me night past, and never stirred." He turned his gaze from one to another. The twins' eyes watched him with uncanny directness, almost as though they overheard his inmost thoughts. "Are you saying," he ventured, "that you came here, both of you . . . in a dream?"

The white foal nodded, but the black-and-silver filly shook her head. "Not a dream. *Like* dreaming, but . . ."

Her voice trailed off.

"*Looking*," Dhattar finished. "We came looking."

Jan felt his pulse quicken. Might his children, like their grand-dam Jah-lila, possess the dreaming sight?

"Do you see things this way," he asked carefully, "things that are real?"

Aiony had turned away, stood surveying the rocks. This time it was Dhattar who answered. "When we saw this place night past, we knew we must bring you."

"Why?" their father asked.

The white foal fidgeted, silent now.

"To show you the serpent," the filly murmured, standing perfectly still.

"Serpent?" Jan's heart thumped hard between his ribs. Quickly, he scanned again, alert for any sign of snakes. Dhattar cavaled.

"Aye, a great long thing," the white foal continued. "Old and ill-tempered. Snows should have killed it winter past." Jan turned to eye his son as he shifted away from his sister, who stood still gazing off into the rocks. "But no snows have fallen, not these two years running," Dhattar went on. "It's dying now, old wrym, but slow and painfully."

"Here it is," the black-and-silver filly was saying.

Turning again, Jan realized that she had left his side. She was moving forward now, picking her way among the rocks. The prince of the unicorns saw a pale form, seething, blue-speckled, coiled directly in his daughter's path. The nadder rose, hissing, flattening its hood. Above gaping jaws, black-slitted pupils dilated. Milky venom hung at the tip of each long, curved fang. The filly stepped fearlessly within the serpent's range.

"Daughter, no!" shouted Jan, vaulting to come between the nadder and its prey.

The serpent struck. The black unicorn felt a fiery sting along one foreleg as he crowded Aiony aside then spun to crush the sapling-thick viper beneath his forehooves. The dying serpent writhed, struck again, reflexively. Jan felt its spine snap as he trampled it. Moments later, all that remained was a nerveless, twitching tangle. The prince of the unicorns stood swaying, staring down at his bloodied foreshank. The double wound below the joint seared his blood. Dizziness swept over him. His pulse throbbed as the nadder's poison crept upward past the knee.

"Daughter, son," he gasped. "Haste down the hillside and whistle for help. Bring the healer. . . ."

Jan felt fiery venom spreading toward the muscle where his forelimb joined the chest. His whole leg ached, nearly numb.

"Off now," he gasped. "At speed!"

The filly and foal remained rooted, their expressions less frightened than curious. "Peace," Dhattar bade him. Aiony answered at almost the same time, "No need."

Jan stared at the pair of them, his heart hammering. "Children, hark me," he choked. "That was a speckled nadder, fat with poison. Without the healer, I'll die."

"But you won't," the white foal told him. "That's the secret."

"The *surprise*," Aiony insisted. "No wyrm may harm you."

"Not since that other serpent stung you," Dhattar added.

"The wyvern," the filly said.

They both gazed at him calmly, expectantly. Jan stood reeling. He had suffered only one other such sting in all his life, from the wyvern queen four years gone while on pilgrimage in the Hallow Hills. Only the magical waters of the moon's mere had saved him then — but that sacred spring lay half a world away: useless. Unreachable. His vision dimmed. Blood beat like slow thunder through him. The speckled viper's venom had nearly reached his breast — but strangely, its progress slowed, the burning diminished.

"You survived the wyvern's sting," Dhattar was saying. "No serpent can fell you now."

"Nor can their stings harm us, your progeny," said Aiony.

His view began to clear. Jan glimpsed his filly shake her mane, her brother nod. "When we beheld the nadder night past, in our vision, we knew this."

"Its sting only burned you a moment," Aiony went on, "and brought no harm."

Jan's sight returned. His balance steadied. Mute with astonishment, he gazed at his twins. Though his pulse still pounded in his chest, the venom's pain had faded, dissipated like cloud. Feeling returned in a prickling rush to his injured limb. Cautiously, the prince of the unicorns set heel to ground.

"We knew you'd not believe us if we simply told you," Aiony said earnestly.

Nervous, the white foal pranced. "We resolved to show you instead."

"We didn't want you to fear," the filly added. "Did you?"

The prince's injured leg bore his weight easily. He no longer felt any numbness. The clot of blood on the shin was drying, matting the hairs. "Aye, children," he answered truthfully. "Very much."

Aiony nuzzled him. "Are you angry with us?"

The prince of the unicorns bent to caress her. "Nay, little one," he murmured, "but you mustn't keep such things from me."

Clearly relieved, white Dhattar nipped him. "We'll not," he said. "You'll believe us now."

Jan gathered his offspring to him and chivvied them gently. "Come. Let's find your dam."

The twins fell in alongside, frisking and shrugging as he picked their way down the steep, rocky slope. The thought did not occur to him till they were nearly to the trees.

"I wonder," he murmured, as they entered the thicket. "Since I am proof against serpents — you two as well — does a way exist that others also might be made proof?"

The trees thickened, blotting out the sky. The prince of the unicorns shook his head.

"Perhaps if I could somehow sting our fellows, as I have been stung. . . ."

Aiony scrubbed her cheek against his flank. "Scratch them with your blood," she told him.

"We could do it, too," the white foal added, "if we weren't so young."

Aiony sighed. "If we had horns."

Ahead of them the trees were thinning. Grassy slope lay beyond. Jan just barely glimpsed it.

"If the herd could be made proof against poison," he mused, "we'd no longer need fear wyverns' barbs —" The prince of the unicorns stopped in his tracks. "We could win back the Hallow Hills!"

Just paces from the wood's edge, Jan stared at nothing. *Win back the Hills?* The possibility rocked him. He had been waiting years for a sign from Alma that the time at last grew ripe to reclaim his people's homeland. Now the goddess had spoken with the mouth of a serpent, slithering out of his children's dreams to leave a bloodmark on his shank. The black prince of the unicorns shook himself, pressed on downslope. He must speak of this with Tek at once. The moment the thought formed in his mind, Dhattar glanced at him.

"Not our dam," he exclaimed. Beside him, Aiony added eagerly, "Lell's the one you must go to now."

Jan turned at the mention of his younger sibling, barely four, a filly still herself. "Why is that?" he asked, baffled. "Where is Lell?"

"With the great green eagle-thing," the white foal answered. "The . . . the . . ." He frowned, searched for the word. "Catbird?"

"Wingcat," Aiony corrected, then turned to nip at her father's beard. "Lell's below us, just beyond the trees — at parley with a gryphon."

Parley

★ 2 ★

Then Isha, mistress of the sky, turned to Ishi, lord of winds. 'These gryphons, fiercest of all my chicks, shall know a token of my favor.' With one mighty talon, she scratched the earth, creating a valley. With the touch of one wingtip, she brought it life: wooded slopes and grassy meadow. Here the wind god pastured his goats and deer. Here the blue-fletched formels sped each spring to capture first meat for their newly hatched young — until, four hundred winters past, your kind displaced Ishi's sacred flocks. Now the formels find nothing to nourish their squabs but your bitter flesh. *That* is why, little unicorn, this vale belongs to my folk, not yours, no matter how many generations your forebears have trespassed here."

Green-feathered with a golden pelt, the gryphon poised on a jut of rock above the amber filly's head. His coloring clearly marked him a tercel — a male — but so large a one that the young unicorn stood amazed: nearly the size of a blue-winged formel this grass-green raptor crouched. Lell stood motionless, half-mesmerized by the tercel's soft, guttural tone midway between a purr and a growl. The prince's sister started suddenly. Not yet half-grown, her slim, straight horn still unkeened, Lell tossed her head, snorted and stamped. Her dam had warned her of wingcats' charming their prey before they sprang.

"A pretty song!" she cried. "But you must trill a sweeter one to capture me." She shook her dark chestnut coat, shaggy from winter yet, unshed. Her pale mane splashed like milk. "Forty generations have my people defended this vale — we shall guard it forty more if need be. My brother the prince shall hear of your intrusion." She ramped. "Wingcats are forbidden here. Begone!"

One corner of the tercel's mouth twitched in what might have been a smile.

"Little unicorn," he answered mildly, "attend. We gryphons are not the ones who trespass Ishi's Vale. But consider: with the birth of your flock's long-sought Firebringer, does not time at last betide you to depart and reclaim your Hallow Hills?"

Lell felt her jaw loosen with surprise. How could this outlander know her people's sacred prophecies? Green as river stones, the crouching gryphon's cat's eyes watched her.

"Tell Prince Moonbrow," he said, "that his shoulder-friend, Illishar of the Broken Wing, flies emissary from my kindred Malar, now wingleader of all the clans. She would parley a peace if, as your brother claims, you truly mean to relinquish this vale."

"We do! We must. He is Alma's Firebringer!" Lell exclaimed, more than a little impressed at her own bravery in answering the huge raptor without a moment's hesitation. The gryphon shrugged. His pinions flexed. The darkamber filly felt the wind they stirred. The sensation made her skin draw. She demanded, "When would your wingleader treat with my prince?"

The tercel clucked. "When the new-hatched chicks are well grown enough to be left in their fathers' care. Spring's end, or early summer."

Lell frowned, thoughts racing. How would her brother, Jan, have responded? "Solstice falls at Moondance this year. Come then," she called up, "on the night of the full moon marking the advent of summer."

The raptor spread huge, jewel-green wings. "So be it. I fly to bring word to my kin before the hatchlings pip."

Pinions fully extended, he stroked the air. Lell's mane whipped. She stood astonished that he should accept her words so readily in her brother's stead. Her heart quailed. An impulse filled her suddenly to bolt, but she stood her ground.

"Tell Jan that in token of faith," the gryphon said, "Malar will bar the formels from hunting Ishi's Vale again this spring, so sparing your young a third year in a row."

Powerful wingbeats hummed. His voice sounded like a cat's purr still. With a mighty bound and blurred thrashing of wings, the tercel was suddenly airborne. Despite herself, Lell flinched. The sweep of his pinions was startling. His shadow passed over her back and flanks.

"We meet again in three months' time, little unicorn," he called, skimming out from the steep hillside and down.

Had she leapt upward then, Lell realized, she could have grazed him. The rush of air dizzied her. Her horn tingled. The blood in her veins sang. Wheeling, she glimpsed the gryphon's back before his furiously threshing wings gained him lift enough to veer, glide upward toward vale's edge. She wheeled again, following his path with her eyes. The Pan Woods lay beyond the top of the rise.

"Lell!" she cried after him, bounding upslope in his wake. "My name is Lell!"

The gryphon neither checked nor turned. Still seeking altitude, his grass-green pinions winnowed the air. He soared away from her. Lell stumbled to a halt. The bright air seemed to burn where he had been. She wondered what it must be like to sail, free as a hawk, so far above the ground. Her withers tightened unexpectedly, aching almost, longing for wings. Grown small, the tercel passed beyond the hillcrest, disappeared from view. Heart still at full gallop, she realized she had been holding her breath.

A sudden drumming of heels brought Lell's head sharp around. The crack of trampled twigs reached her, and the crashing of brush. From wood's edge, scant paces from her, rang out the battle-whistle of a warrior. A moment later, the black prince of the unicorns burst from the trees. Snorting, ramping, he cast fiercely about as though seeking a foe. Lell whinnied and reared, thrusting her young horn toward the empty sky.

"Jan! Jan! Did you see him?" she cried. "My gryphon! He says his wingleader will come parley with us — at summer solstice, Moondance."

The solstice night fell still and clear, with sky above transforming to the dark, even blue of deep water. The round moon, burning silver as it climbed, paled a heaven pricked with summer stars. Pied Tek, the prince's mate, danced in the great ring of unicorns cantering under the moon. White Dhattar and painted Aiony frisked beside her, pummeling one another with their soft weanlings' hooves. The dancers trampled the thick, fragrant grass, kicking and scattering turf. Night breathed warm with coming summer and the panting and sweating of unicorns.

All around her, Tek watched her fellows bowing and turning their heads to scratch their flanks with keen horntips, then reaching to prick the flanks of their fellows. Each full moon since equinox, they had done the same, ever since her mate had spoken of his battle with Alma's serpent and of the magic in his blood. He had vowed to bestow it upon the entire herd. She herself had been the first. Each Moondance since, those already scratched had mingled their blood with the blood of others until after this night, all — from youngest newborn to most venerable elder — would by Alma's grace stand forever proof against serpents and their stings.

The pied mare shook herself for sheer exuberance and danced. She gazed at her weanling filly and foal traipsing ahead amid the swirling rush to butt at Lell with their blunt, barely sprouted hornnubs. Laughing, the older filly chivvied and nipped at them. They sought refuge behind their granddam Ses. Pale cream with a mane and tail of flame, the mother of Jan and Lell never faltered in her step while the three colts cavorted, playing peekover and tag. Tek whistled Aiony and Dha back to her side.

She spotted Jan ahead of them, emerging from the dancers. He ascended the council rise, a low mass of stone thrusting up from the valley floor. Around it the great moondance circled. Reaching the top of the rock, the young prince halted, his lean stallion's form just entering its prime etched in shadow against the moon-washed hills. *What a wonder I pledged as my mate,* Tek smiled to herself, *scant three years gone, by the Summer Sea.* She admired the crest of his neck, length of his horn, his fine runner's limbs.

Around her, the dance began to subside, moon halfway along its journey to surmount the sky. She halted, gazed about as one by one, unicorns circling her and her offspring strayed to a stop, stood cropping grass or lay down on soft, cushioned earth. Tek, too, lay down with Dha and Ai, not far from Ses and Lell. She sensed the others' expectancy from their skittish prancing, their restive whinnies and snorts. Her own mingled anticipation and trepidation made the pied mare's skin twitch.

On the rise above, her mate tensed suddenly. A ripple passed through the herd. Heads lifted. Necks craned. Gazing into the seamless silver sky, she, too, caught sight: gryphons, a dozen of them in a hollow wedge sailing the moonlit air, dark as cinders, silent as haunts or dreams. Tek's herdmates shifted, jostled, murmured uneasily as the vee descended. A huge wingcat formel occupied the point, the intense blue of her plumage discernible even by moonlight. All were formels, the pied mare realized, save for one flanking the leader's wing, the tips of his green tercel's feathers nearly brushing hers. Scarcely smaller than his fellows, the lone male glided.

Closer they drifted, and closer yet. Their shadows swept the silent herd. Tek felt the hairs of her pelt stiffen and lift. The thud of paws on rippled rock sounded in the stillness as the gryphons alighted on the council rise, first the wingleader, then the tercel beside her, then all the other blue-and-tawny formels of the vee. Tek felt her fellows tense, recoil ever so slightly. Only her mate stood at ease before their enemies, still fanning the air.

The pied mare's ears pricked. "Do you see him, Mother?" she heard Lell whispering. "The green one? My gryphon."

Tek saw the pale mare stroke her daughter once with a motherly tongue. "I see him," Ses murmured. "Be still."

On the rise, the gryphon leader crouched before Jan, her blue feathers sheened with moonlight. Her monstrous wings thrashed vigorously. Tek felt their buffeting even here. The musky odor of raptors and pards reached her, making her flesh draw. Above, Jan stood quiet, waiting until the formel subsided, lashing her lion's tail against one tawny flank. Her feathers roughed, then lay smooth.

"Hail, Jan, prince of unicorns."

The pied mare started. The formel's voice was surprisingly cat-like, throaty and smooth, with none of the raucousness of eagles' cries.

"Hail, Malar, wingleader of the gryphons," the prince replied. "Be welcome in our Vale."

Tek heard him perfectly. His words traveled to the rocky slopes, rang ever so softly there. The formels behind their leader stirred, muttering, their green eyes glinting. Only the tercel remained impassive. The gryphon leader cocked her head, eyeing Jan with one cat-slit eye.

"This was *our* Vale once," she said, "entrusted to us by the sky goddess Isha, fold to the sacred flocks of her consort Ishi. Your kind's coming drove those flocks away."

Again, the formels behind her shifted, snapping bills. Tek thought she heard a low-pitched growl. Her own people moved restlessly. She caught sound of a snort, a stamp, a toss of mane. Dhattar and Aiony leaned sleepily against her. Tek bent to nuzzle them, her eyes still on the rise.

"And at our departure," the prince answered Malar firmly, "it is my hope that your wind god's sheep and deer will abundantly return. My people took refuge in this place centuries past. Driven from our home, we never knew we trespassed here. But now our goddess tells us to reclaim ancestral lands. We must depart, but we would not go as enemies. Hear the tale of our first coming to the Vale. My mate would sing you that lay of our long exile and the treachery of wyverns. Ho, Tek! Will you come?"

Tek felt her heart thump. This was the moment she had awaited all evening and dreaded all spring. The warm odor of wingcats filled her nostrils as she rose. Dhattar and Aiony slept. The pied mare's hooves grated on the hard, worn stone as she ascended the council rise. She and her mate exchanged a glance. Jan pressed his shoulder to hers, but said no word. His presence steadied her. The gryphons' beaks and talons glinted. Their moon-shot eyes gleamed.

"Greetings, Malar, queen of gryphons," Tek hailed them. Her voice sounded even enough. Within her ribs, her heart bucked and churned. "I have met your kind in battle time and again and never dreamed to stand at peaceful parley with you. But my mate assures me that two years past, he and your cousin set aside their enmity."

She glanced toward the green-winged tercel flanking the queen. He acknowledged her gesture with a nod, but spoke no word. His wingleader kept her eyes fixed on Tek.

"I stand ready to make that same peace with you, Queen Malar," the pied mare said, "though we children-of-the-moon have suffered much at the claws of wingcats."

She inclined her head toward her sleeping young, nestled side to side on the grass below, and glimpsed the gryphon leader's headcrest rear, subside. Malar's bill snicked shut. Tek felt her mate's side pressed to hers. He was holding his breath. Behind their queen, the gryphons shifted. One of the formels hissed, but at a sharp glance from the tercel, fell still. Tek felt Jan's breath let out and dared to breathe.

"I would sing you the Lay of the Unicorns," the pied mare told the wingcat queen, "which tells of my people's expulsion from the Hallow Hills. Then the Lay of Exile would I sing, recounting how we found and claimed this unsettled valley, gaining haven from wandering."

Malar seemed to consider, her moonlit eyes half-shut. From the hard clench of Jan's neck beside her, Tek knew his teeth were set. His breath came in little silent spurts. Her own heart thundered.

"In return," the prince's mate continued, "will you sing us your own tales of this vale, that we may learn the whole history of the place we mean soon to leave forever?"

The wingleader of the gryphons glanced furtively at the green-winged tercel beside her. He preened one shoulder, all seeming unconcern. Tek saw one corner of the gryphon queen's mouth quirk momentarily into a smile. Returning her gaze to the pied mare, Malar bowed her great eagle's head and moved back to give the pied mare ground.

"So be it," the gryphon leader purred.

Jan, too, fell back, leaving Tek alone on the center of the rise. All around, her herdmates listened. The gryphons waited with up-pricked ears. She felt her mate's eyes watching her. Tek raised her voice and sang of how, forty generations past, wyverns had invaded the unicorns' rightful lands far to the balmy north. Under guise of friendship, the white wyrmlord Lynex had befriended the unicorns' agèd king, then used sorcery to addle the old stallion's wits, blinding him to the wyverns' schemes.

Only Princess Halla had spied the coming betrayal — but her warnings were ignored. In treacherous ambush, wyverns stung to death most of the unicorn warhost, and slew nearly all the rest with fire. Only Halla and her few, desperate followers escaped, fleeing coldward — south — across the Plain. Coming at last upon a vast, deserted vale, the unicorns gladly claimed it, here to spend long exile awaiting the coming of Alma's appointed, who was to lead them back in triumph to the Hallow Hills.

Tek fell silent, the tale run out. Her words rebounded from the distant slope, hung singing faintly under the round white belly of the pregnant moon now poised high overhead. Below, colts and fillies slept beside their waking sires and dams, all recumbent now. Even some of the gryphons reposed, pard-like, their wings no longer ruffled and half-raised, but folded close. All around burned the thousand thousand summer stars which were the goddess Alma's eyes. The pied mare swallowed, throat dry as dust. Her singer's calm broke then, leaving her stranded on the moonlit council rise, confronting gryphons.

Gryphonsong

★ 3 ★

I am that Firebringer," the black prince of the unicorns said, "which our prophets foretold."

Tek fell back as her mate moved forward. She lay down on the council rise, not far behind Jan. The stone held no warmth. The late spring air had cooled. Her mate and Malar faced one another across a low pile of brush to which the pied mare had paid no heed earlier. Jan's words hung in the motionless air. The gryphon wingleader's eyes seemed never to blink. The prince spoke on.

"Time approaches for my people to end our long exile."

The next instant, in one deft motion, he bowed his head and struck the tip of his horn against one heel. A rain of sparks leapt up. The pile of deadwood crackled and caught. Tek realized then it must have been for this purpose that the brush had been gathered. The gryphons' eyes grew wide at the sight of fire, their cats'-pupils slitting. Behind their leader, panicked formels crowded back. Only Malar's nearest companion, the tercel, held steady. He had seen her mate's firemaking before, the pied mare mused, when they had made their privy peace on the shores of the Summer Sea. Ruffled, Malar herself did not retreat, but peered into the crackling blaze.

"How soon? How soon will you depart?" A purr thrummed in her throat. She leaned closer to the warmth.

"Next spring," Jan answered, "once the grass on the Plain is sprung and last year's nurslings are weaned."

The formel raised one feathered brow.

"Suckling mares cannot join in battle," the prince of the unicorns explained. "And battle there will be, despite our having grown proof against the stings of our foes. The Hallow Hills will not be easily won."

Malar stirred beside the fire, lifting one wing to allow its heat to reach her side. She was silent so long, Tek wondered if she had fallen asleep.

"Like you, prince of unicorns," the formel responded at last, "we gryphons now desire peace. We are wearied of raids and your bitter flesh. If you pledge to relinquish Ishi's Vale to our stewardship, we shall nest content."

Turning her head ever so slightly, she glanced back at her dozen followers crouching or reclining behind her.

"But we, too, have a tale to sing, a chorus of the making of this sacred place, ages past at the pipping of the world. Our singer is blood kin to me — and for all that he is but a green-winged tercel, he holds a heart as brave, talons as keen, and a voice as strong as any formel's. Hark now, I bid you, as he raises our song."

The lone male among the gryphons padded forward, skirting his queen and the fire to come directly before Jan. Tek watched as her prince bowed low.

"Hail, Illishar Mended-wing," Jan greeted him. "When my sister told me who among your folk had carried your leader's offer of parley, my heart leapt."

The tercel's stony countenance eased. Tek saw his ruffled quills settle, the golden fur of his flank grow smooth. His voice, like his queen's, was low and sweet.

"So you remember me, Prince Jan."

The dark stallion shook himself. Tek's own ears pricked. She eyed the green gryphon feather tangled amid her mate's long black hair. "How not," he asked, "when I still wear the gift you gave?" His tone was one of genuine gladness and surprise. "You have grown since last we met."

The tercel chuckled. "You also, prince of unicorns. Two years past I was barely fletched, a gangling squab!"

Jan snorted. "A formidable warrior, by my reck."

With a shudder, Tek glimpsed the scars lacing her mate's shoulder blades, indelible reminders of the mortal combat in which he and this tercel once had joined. She glanced at her sleeping filly and foal and felt the pelt rise along her spine. Despite the feather in his hair, to Tek's mind, Jan's battlescars were only one among a cluster of reasons to mistrust these flesh-eating gryphons. Crouched before the prince, the tercel flexed one magnificent wing.

"I, too, suffered in that fray," he murmured. "But you gave me back my life."

"And what befell after I set your bone?" Jan asked.

Tek peered curiously at the gryphon's broad, green pinion, doubting she could ever have dared approach such a dangerous creature, even one with a shattered limb. She and every other unicorn in the Vale, she knew, would gladly have left the fallen raptor to starve. Illishar shrugged, preened a stray feather back into place.

"As soon as my pinion grew strong enough, I made haste back to the Gryphon Mountains to rejoin my flock."

Tek listened. Her mate tossed his head.

"We heard no word of you," he pressed. "Indeed, we have seen no wingcats since, save for your own brief stop last spring. What kept your folk so far from our Vale?"

Tek tensed as, on the far side of the fire, the gryphon formels suddenly ruffled. Two jostled and paced. Another beat her wings in agitation, so that the fire leapt, flared. Illishar's eyes flicked to them, then to his wingleader. Malar returned his gaze impassively, with the barest hint of a nod. The tercel turned again to Jan.

"The flocks have been at war," he said. "Rival clans sought to conquer Malar, but she triumphed in the end. I, too, soared, winning a perch on the high ledge beside her."

Tek saw another glance pass between the wingcat and his queen. Jan stood listening, offering no word.

"Malar is wearied of war," Illishar resumed. "As are we all. When I returned two years past with word that the unicorns might consent to relinquish Ishi's sacred Vale and return to their own lands across the Plain, she pounced at the chance. Others were not so hungry for peace. They sought to seize the wingleader's place."

The gryphon queen behind him shifted. It seemed to Tek that Malar's eyes, still fixed upon Illishar, now shone with inestimable pride. He continued.

"But with my aid and that of all her loyal flock, she has struck her rivals from the sky and pashed their eggs to shards. Mightiest of wingleaders, she soars, and the clans fly united behind her once more!"

Seated upright behind their queen, pinions poised, the formels uttered shrill cries of assent. Tek saw the herd just below the rise tense in alarm, but just as suddenly, the formels fell silent. Malar demurely nibbled one shoulder, as if ignoring their praise.

"Hear my song," cried Illishar, his wings half-raised. "How Isha laid the clutch that hatched all the creatures of the world, and how we gryphons pleased her best of all."

Again fluting whistles from the formels, but more melodic, rising and falling in a complex harmony to the tercel's words.

"Great Isha created her consort Ishi from greenest grass and most golden seed. But he was lifeless, so she closed him in a silver egg, and he hatched out full grown. Half the mottled shell still turns in heaven. Now full, so we see it end-on, beholding only its outward curving edge. A week hence, when it has pivoted, we will see it in profile, the half moon. And in another week's time, on the night of the new moon, we will discern no silver rim at all but instead gaze into the dark mystery of its inner hollow. Blessèd be the goddess and her consort, Ishi!"

Behind him, the formels raised their voices in intricate, effortless accompaniment, the ever-changing position of their wings seeming to accent his words: now lifted, now folded, now outstretched. Only Malar took no part, still as stone, a moonlit sphinx. Shivers feathered the pied mare's limbs and sides. Tek found herself growing rapt as the herd around her. Jan, too, stood motionless, enthralled.

Illishar sang of Isha's gift of the winds to her consort Ishi, of her creation of the Vale for his sacred flocks, lovingly husbanded as first meat for the newly hatched. The tune pulsed and lilted. Tek's heartbeat sped. Her people had no such sinuous music as these gryphons made, the tercel sometimes speaking or chanting while the formels behind him repeated and ornamented his words.

By the time Illishar recounted how centuries past, unicorns had swarmed into Ishi's Vale, forcing out the delectable sheep and deer, leaving only their own unsavory young as rank pickings for the formel's new-pipped chicks, the pied mare was almost on her feet, ready to shout, *No, no! Drive the intruders out* — until she realized with a start that it was against her own kind she would have railed. Groggy, Tek shook herself, no wingèd gryphon, but a four-leggèd unicorn.

The tercel had fallen silent. The formels, too. Dazed, the prince's mate gazed out over the herd, beheld them coming to themselves, stirring slowly like beasts entranced. She had no doubt now how gryphons managed to bewitch their prey. Shaken and stiff, the pied mare rolled her shoulders, extended her neck. Moon hung low on the other side of a sky paling eastward into dawn.

Below her, Lell reclined beside her mother, the only one of all the colts Tek could see who was not asleep. The amber filly gazed at Illishar, eyes following his every move, ears pricked to the rustle of his quills. Head bowed, the tercel fell back to flank his queen, still crouching beside the dying embers of the fire. Malar rose, stretched, fanning her great blue wings and arching her tawny back like a pard. Before her on the rise, Jan stirred, shifting his limbs. Had he stood the whole night? Tek watched him move forward, gait graceful and loose, unimpeded apparently by any fatigue.

"So, Malar, wingleader of the gryphons," he asked, "are we agreed?"

The mighty formel straightened, nodded. "We are agreed, Jan, prince of unicorns. Henceforth, our folk shall be at peace, and next spring your kind will depart Ishi's Vale, returning to your own ancestral Hills."

The slimmest of morning breezes lifted, died. The formel's feathers riffled, then smoothed.

"We take with us in gratitude your songs," she continued, "and leave you ours. We will not soon forget this night's singing, nor the tales that you have taught us. We trust you will remember ours."

She gave a guttural snort, the meaning of which Tek could not readily discern — supposed it might be a laugh, the first the pied mare had heard the gryphon queen utter.

"I would never have guessed that so hoarse-voiced and whinnying a sort as unicorns could honor the sky with such fetching airs — and from but a single throat. What brave and lonely songs you sing! I salute you."

Tek rose, the muscles of her long legs twinging, and stepped to stand beside her mate. She bowed low to the gryphon queen while Jan replied.

"And I salute you, wingleader of all the clans. Song, to my mind, rings far sweeter than war."

The great blue formel nodded curtly, then half-turned, fanning her massy wings again. Behind her, the other formels did the same.

"We must fly," she said. "Our chicks have nestled their fathers long enough. But know this." Malar turned to face Jan over one shoulder. "In emblem of my goodwill, next spring when you march for the Hallow Hills, I will send my kinsmeet Illishar to accompany you."

Beside Jan, Tek felt his start of pleasure, surprise.

"My thanks to you, Queen Malar," he answered warmly. "Your cousin is a mighty warrior. The ranks of the unicorns will be glad of his strength."

Illishar inclined his head. "I shall be as glad to lend it." His mouth edged into a bare hint of a smile. "My wingleader is most anxious that your war against the wyverns succeed, that hereafter

Ishi's Vale harbor his flocks in peace, untroubled by wandering unicorns."

Tek saw the expression of the gryphon queen almost imperceptibly sour. Jan gave a whickering laugh.

"I, too, share the great Malar's urgency for the success of our endeavor. Your airborne eyes will be of great value to us, Illishar. We welcome you."

The green-winged tercel bowed his head. At a sign from Malar, her formels rose, some rearing to stand on hind legs as if to stretch, others stroking their wings. Jan's forelock lifted. Tek felt her own mane whipped about her neck. The buffeting grew fiercer. Malar moved a few paces from Jan, seeking room to spring into the air. The other gryphons fell back from her. The mighty wingleader sank into a crouch, half opening her wings, when suddenly a voice from among the unicorns broke the stillness.

"Hold!"

Jan reared and wheeled. Cavaling, Tek turned to see Lell spring to her feet. Before her startled dam could move to stay her, the darkamber filly sprinted for the rise. In three strides and a bound, she had gained the summit. Astonished, the pied mare fell back as the prince's sister hastened to his side.

"Brother, a moment," Lell panted. "I would speak! May I speak?"

Tek watched her mate's baffled eyes scanning his sister. Lell's urgency made her prance and sidle beside him. He spoke quietly.

"Sister, you already speak. What would you say?"

Lell seemed to take his response for leave. She spun eagerly to face the green-winged tercel.

"Illishar Brokenwing, do you know me?" she asked.

The tercel nodded gravely. "Could I forget?" he replied. "You are the prince's sister, with whom I set this parley three moons past."

"Lell," the chestnut filly answered. "My name is Lell. I wanted you to have my name."

The tercel's smile was unmistakable now. "Indeed, Lell Darkamber, I already know it. You called it out to me last spring as I departed. I hope that in three-quarters of a year's time, when I return, we may speak again."

"We shall!" exulted Lell, ramping with delight.

Her mother, Ses, had ascended the rise. She nudged her filly with one firm but unobtrusive shoulder. Lell caught her breath, and with a glance at her dam, managed to collect herself. She swallowed.

"That is, I would welcome it," she answered formally. With a deep bow first to Malar, then to Illishar, she added, "I thank you."

The prince's sister fell back with Ses to stand at the far edge of the rise. Malar crouched again and, with one prodigious leap, launched herself into the air. The gryphon queen rose, wings stroking rapidly at first, then locking to glide as she gained sufficient height. In a bound, green-winged Illishar followed. He seemed to have less trouble rising aloft than his larger, heavier companion. One by one, in swift succession, other formels followed, straining for lift in the windless air. None faltered. In another moment, all were airborne, wafting upward in a ragged vee. They headed south toward the valley's nearer slope. The Gryphon Mountains lay a day's flight beyond, across the Pan Woods that bordered the Vale. Tek moved to stand shoulder to shoulder with her mate.

"Do you see, Mother?" Lell behind her whispered excitedly. "How he flies! How he sang. He remembered my name. In under a year's time, he will return to us. My gryphon."

Baffled, the pied mare turned to watch the amber filly gazing after the green-gold tercel. Her eyes shone like those of some moonstruck half-grown. Tek snorted. Nay, ridiculous! It would be a year or more before Lell could join the Ring of Warriors, probably two or three before she pledged a mate by the Summer Sea. Whickering, the pied mare shook her head, convinced she had misconstrued the other's youthful enthusiasm. She leaned against her mate. Above and to the southwest, the tercel's form and those of the formels grew smaller and smaller yet.

"Do you think he would teach me gryphonsong?" she heard the prince's sister breathe. "Mother, what must it be like to fly?"

Wind

★ 4 ★

A puff of breeze played across Jan's face. The young stallion closed his eyes, relishing it. A moment later, when he opened them, the last of the soaring gryphons were just disappearing beyond the edge of the Vale. Dawnlight illuminated the sky, burning it saffron and rose. The few remaining stars winked out. Tek leaned against him. The prince of the unicorns breathed deep, savoring the clean, warm scent of her, pied black as spent night, rosy as the coming dawn. Gently, he nipped her neck and watched his dam, Ses, and sister, Lell, descend the rocky rise. Below, he glimpsed unicorns waking, rolling, rising and shaking off. With a soft whicker, Ses bent to nose Dhattar and Aiony. They stirred. On the rise, his mate beside him murmured.

"Next spring, then."

He nodded. "Aye."

"Good."

He turned, surprised. "You've no fear?"

The warrior mare shrugged, chivvying him. "More relief than fear. Six years have I awaited this trek — since I beheld the Firebringer rush burning from heaven in the vision of my initiation." She nipped playfully at the tassels of his ears till they twitched. "Our folk have waited longer still. Four hundred years."

Her nips grew smarter, more insistent. He half reared, wheeling to fence with her. Laughing, she met him stroke for stroke, their horns clanging loudly in the morning stillness. Breeze lifted, and they broke off, panting. He saw his mate's gaze fall lovingly on Dhattar, up now and harassing Lell. Aiony rolled in the grass at her granddam's forehooves, refusing to get up. Around them, other unicorns frisked and grazed. Tek nudged him.

"My thanks for your waiting till the twins were weaned," she murmured. "I'm no strategist like you, no diplomat. Just a warrior — and a singer of sorts. And now a dam. I could not have borne forgoing the coming fray for the sake of suckling young."

She rested her chin at the crown of his head, lips nibbling the base of his horn, beard tickling his cheek. Jan laughed, sneezing, and shook her off.

"Alma chose the time, not I."

He turned to press his muzzle to her. Doing so, he caught sight of a figure just topping the rise. Two figures, in truth — and then he realized it was three. One had the form of a beardless unicorn deep mallow in color, redder than the dawn. She descended the slope on round, uncloven heels, her black mane standing upright as a newborn's along her neck, her tail silky and full.

Alongside her trotted a very different figure, moving upright on goatlike hind limbs. From the square shoulders of this figure's flattened torso hung two nimble forelimbs, one resting easily upon the withers of the red mare, the other swinging with each stride. A small, round head topped the creature's short, slender neck. Her hairless face held dark, expressive eyes. Curving horns and drooping, goatlike ears sprouted amid a shaggy mane.

A slighter, fairer version sat astride the strange unicorn mare, clinging to her brush, making the third member of the trio. Jan heard his mate beside him give a peal of joy. She reared, flailing the air. All around, on the valley floor below, unicorns turned and took note. Their delighted cries echoed the pied mare's:

"Jah-lila! The midwife! The magicker!"

Reaching the valley floor, the red mare answered, "Well met!"

The herd surged toward her and her goatling companions, who waved upheld forelimbs and whistled in perfect imitation of unicorns. Mares with suckling young especially moved to greet them. Jan glimpsed his own filly and foal sprinting with gleeful shrieks to welcome their maternal granddam. They, like most of the colts in the herd, had been delivered by the red mare and the pan sisters, her acolytes.

"Sismoomnat! Pitipak!" he heard Aiony and Dhattar exclaim. The younger pan slipped from her foster mother's back and joined her sister in frisking with them. The red mare waded on through the press, exchanging greetings with stallions and mares, all of whom fell back respectfully before her, even as fellows behind them crowded forward.

Good fortune, the herd murmured, *to breathe the wych's breath, stand in her shadow, tread her track.*

The half-growns, warriors, and elders were old enough to remember the awe in which the herd had, only a few short years ago, once held her — a fear now turned to reverence. She acknowledged them all but never paused, forging determinedly toward her daughter, the pied mare, still standing beside Jan on the rise. He fell back to let daughter and dam exchange caresses and greetings. Jah-lila nickered and called to him.

"Well met, my daughter's mate," she laughed, her dusky voice a deep, sweet echo of Tek's. "My fosterlings and I spied wingcats overhead as we entered the Vale. They kept their parley as agreed?"

The prince of the unicorns nodded. "Aye. Peace is pledged. We are sworn to depart for the Hills at spring."

The red mare nodded, said firmly, "Good."

"How do my foster sisters fare?" Tek inquired.

Jah-lila nuzzled her affectionately. "As you see. They spend much time in the Pan Woods now, midwiving their own folk's young."

"And our allies there?" Jan asked.

The red mare whickered. "Again, very well. The peace you forged in the Woods has been a lasting one."

Below, at herd's edge, the elder of the pan sisters, Sismoomnat, chased half a dozen wildly fleeing foals while Aiony charged Pitipak, trying to butt her off her feet. Lell laughed and circled. Dhat-tar's coat blazed fire-white among the burning colors of the rest.

"Whence have the three of you come," Tek was asking, "my pan sisters and you?"

The red mare smiled. "From the shores of the Summer Sea," she said. "We watched the narwhals calve. . . ."

Her words were cut short by a long, harsh wail more like a wolf's cry than a unicorn's. Sismoomnat, Pitipak and the foals halted abruptly. Around them, their elders started and wheeled. A haggard figure appeared on the near slope of the Vale, emerging from a dark hollow in the hillside. Jan's heart jolted. He felt Tek beside him sip her breath. Once massy and robust, the tall unicorn at the cavemouth showed sunken flanks, his ribs visible, limbs bony and starved. Black as stormcloud, he loomed in the grotto's entryway. Before him, the herd recoiled.

"Gryphons," the emaciated stallion roared. The cave amplified and echoed the sound. "Wingcats in our midst! First you dance the serpent's dance, then don the quills of our sworn foes. Now you welcome the beardless wych. Traitors!"

He drew nearer, descending the slope half a dozen paces. With shrills of terror, the youngest colts galloped to their dams. The whole herd fell back. Jan spotted Lell standing before young Ai and Dha, pressed close to the pans. He glimpsed Tek's gaze of fury and loathing as she watched the dark figure on the hillside. The prince of the unicorns clenched his teeth and advanced.

"Aye, night past we danced the serpent's dance," he called, "to make ourselves proof against such stings — in honor of That One who made both serpent and the unicorn. We treated with wing-cats to win peace ere we depart this vale. And Jah-lila is our hon-ored guest, dam to my mate and midwife to the herd."

He left unsaid the other, bitter truth: that the skeletal figure above was responsible for the deaths of countless fillies and foals before these. Their elders had not forgotten, could never forget, that terrible winter two years gone when this stallion had seized power in Jan's absence and allowed half the herd to starve to death.

"If Alma stands defiled, it is not by us," the young prince continued. "Cry traitor elsewhere."

Jan heard his people's mutters of assent.

"Poison in your blood!" the haunt on the hillside before him shrieked. "You'll never scratch my flank. No serpent's taint to sully me!"

The rumble from the herd grew louder. Dark clouds appeared above the edges of the Vale. Dawn wind blew stronger, gusting now. Sun flickered and flared, backlighting the shadowy thunderheads that moved to encircle it. Jan's ears pricked at restless snorts and whinnies. He heard a mare's voice call out, "Tyrant!"

A young stallion's echoed: "Murderer!"

"Rout him," another shouted. "Cast him from the Vale."

Jan felt hairs lift along his spine. He spun to face the herd. They shouldered and jostled about the council rise, seething with anger, eyes fixed on the hillside above. The young prince reared, struck the sparking stones of the rise with his hooves till they clanged.

"Hold," he shouted. "Hold! Think you that banishment can heal madness? All the herd ran mad that terrible winter — and those who meekly submitted to Korr's tyranny must share his blame. No ruler reigns without the consent of his folk. Had we not rather seek to drive madness from our own hearts? Only then may the herd know peace."

The unicorns subsided uneasily, eyes cast down and askance, unwilling to face him anymore, or each other, or the figure on the rise. Sires gathered their daughters to their sides and nuzzled them. Dams stroked their tiny foals. Drawing breath, Jan turned once more to the figure on the hillside.

"Father —" but the bony stallion cut him off.

"You are not my son!"

The black prince of the unicorns stopped short. Korr's words tore him like a wolf's jaws. Pulse pounding, Jan fought for calm, dismayed that even now, after all this time, his sire could still spit barbs to rankle him.

"You were never my son!" the mad king snarled. "Wild, unschooled, spurning tradition at every turn. Then you pledged with that strumpet, pied daughter of a wych, and got twin horrors from her womb. I never sired you! You're none of my get —"

"Enough!"

The word burst from Jan, its force bringing the other up short. The young prince of the unicorns shook himself as though to clear a swarm of gnats from his hide. Illishar's feather batted softly against his neck.

"Enough, I say! Two years have you railed against my mate, calling our progeny abomination, yet offered no justification for your charge."

The wind quickened, humming, full of moisture. Stormclouds gusted around the dawn-red sun. Jan snorted.

"Where were you, my sire, when I was but a foal and needed your care? Off ramping with the warriors, haranguing them to endless clashes with gryphons, wyverns, and pans! It was I you shunned then. Not one word or deed of mine was ever worthy of your note."

The old resentment, so long unspoken, roiled up in him now. Jan cavaled.

"Always it was Tek! Her you showered with praise. Tek the warrior, pride of the half-growns, model to all the younger fillies and colts. A stranger would have thought *her* your get and I the fatherless foal. Yet when we pledged, marrying our fates, a bond unshakable under the summer stars — suddenly she was not to be endured, her crimes uncounted, our offspring monstrous. Why?"

The wind blew steadily now, grey clouds obscuring the sun. Jan scarcely heeded it. His smooth summer pelt riffled, teasing his skin. The long hairs of his tail flailed his flank.

"In Alma's name, father, what drives you mad and turns you against me, my mate and young? Speak! If you will but speak, perhaps whatever torments you can be allayed."

The mad king stood gazing at him, eyes wide, rolling.

"Nay," he whispered. "The red wych has cozened you, telling you lies!"

Wind buffeted about them, slapping Jan's forelock into his eyes. The Vale lay in shadow. Thunder growled like a hillcat. Dams and stallions bent over their young, shielding them from the coming rain — but none moved to seek shelter, all eyes fixed on the prince and his sire. Jan glimpsed Jah-lila leaving her daughter's side.

"Korr," she called, "you know as well as I that I have revealed nothing. I have pledged never to speak of the history we share while your silence holds. I honor that pledge still — unlike the oath you once swore me. . . ."

"Never!" the haggard stallion gasped. "You bewitched me there upon the Plain. I was too young to know my own heart —"

"But not too young to give your word." The red mare spoke softly. Her black-green eyes gazed at him without hatred, only sorrow. "Speak of what befell us. Your own silence lies at the root of this madness, not the conduct of any other. Only speak! Be healed."

The gaunt stallion reared, scarcely darker than the stormclouds that towered above. Sudden lightning clashed, followed by deafening thunder. Korr flailed at nothing.

"My mate!" Ses cried. Wind stole her words. "Come back to me. Reveal what troubles you!"

Rain spattered down, stinging as hailstones. Ses moved forward to stand beside the red mare.

"*She* troubles me!" Korr thundered back. "My mate — she is my woe. She stole my heir with her sorcery. Wych!" he shouted above the gale, eyes flicking to Tek's dam, then back to his mate. "You knew. You knew all along. From the time we pledged — you held your tongue and watched. . . ." Again his gaze wavered. "I have no mate, no heir, no son!"

His words had grown so wild Jan could no longer tell to whom the mad king spoke: the red mare or his mate. But the young prince had no time for thought. The king had already launched himself, charging down the rain-slicked slope straight at Ses — or perhaps at Jah-lila. The two mares stood nearly shoulder to shoulder now. Lell cried out and sped forward, as though to fling herself in front of her dam, defend her somehow by coming between her and the mad king's charge.

"No!" shouted Jan.

He vaulted from the council rise, dashed to intercept his frenzied sire. Before him, Ses and Jah-lila parted, sprang in opposite directions to clear the raging stallion's path. Jan managed to veer ahead of Lell, shield her. Korr plunged past in a dusky blur, a waft of rank air, a snatch of bright teeth and a slash of horn. Jan swung his head with all his might, brought his own weapon down with force enough to knock his assailant's skewer aside. The blow clamored, reverberating in his skull.

He felt the bite upon his neck begin to bleed, the long shallow rent across his chest blaze hot with pain. Beside him, Lell — scarcely half his size — dodged, trying to get around him, seeking to fall upon their attacker herself. Korr skidded, wheeled. Jan rushed him, mostly to keep himself safely between his young sister and the king. The black prince slapped hard at his sire with the flat of his horn, pounded him with his heels, driving him back, away from Lell and the others.

At last, with a despairing cry, the mad king shook free, wheeled, fled across the valley floor and up the far hillside. Lightning shattered the sky. Rolling thunder pealed. The wind lashed, flailed. Rain became a downpour. Stunned, the herd broke and scattered, scrambling for haven in the caverns and hollows of the surrounding slopes. Without a moment's hesitation, Jan sprang in pursuit of his sire. Desperately, Tek galloped to intercept him.

"Jan," she cried. "Hold. Forbear!"

The young prince scarcely checked. "Nay," he cried furiously. "Nay, not this time! He'll not evade me more. I'll have the truth if I must chase it to world's edge! Take charge of the herd, Tek — I'll return as soon as may be."

Rain

★ 5 ★

Rain hammered down. Jan's cloven heels bit into the soft hillside, sliding on slippery turf. Thunder crashed. Wind whipped at him. Having long since lost sight of Korr, he gained the trees. Jan shook his head, teeth champed, panting with effort. The downpour was blinding. A glimpse of shadow through the trees ahead. He dodged after it. Treeboles gave way once more to rocky slope. Above, a gaunt figure struggled to the hillcrest and vanished over it. The young prince redoubled his efforts, loose, wet rocks kicking from under his heels. As he topped the rise, rain pummeled him anew. Snorting, he pitched to a halt.

Below him lay the Pan Woods, home to Sismoomnat and Pitipak's folk, the two-leggèd goatlings. Until a few short seasons ago, the pans had been among the unicorns' bitterest foes. Now both peoples enjoyed free forage through one another's lands. Gazing down, the prince's eye met nothing but dark woods, sprawling toward horizon's edge through a grey curtain of rain. He listened, but discerned nothing above the deafening downpour. For all the king's haggard appearance, he made swift quarry.

The young prince cast back over one shoulder at the Vale, lying deserted in the rain. He eyed the council rise, empty and smallseeming, about which he and his fellows had lately parleyed and danced. He marked his own cave on the hillside below, where Tek and the twins now doubtless sheltered, and felt a twinge. Impatiently, he shook it off. He would be returning in a few hours — at most a day or two. Just as soon as he had found his sire and wrested his terrible secret from him. Surely then all could be put to rights. Jan set his teeth. Without another thought or backward glance, he plunged over the hillcrest into the dark Pan Woods.

The trees rose thick around him, dripping with moisture. The morning's deluge had subsided at last to a pattering drizzle. Jan trotted along a streambed, seeking tracks. He had combed for hours in widening circles, hoping to come upon his sire or sign of him, or else to encounter friendly pans from whom to ask news or aid.

Jan splashed to a halt in the middle of the stream and bent his long neck to drink. The water tasted cool in the humid summer air. He shook his sodden coat for perhaps the twentieth time. His head reeled. He had not slept in an evening and a day. It was long past noon. Jan stumbled out of the streambed. He had followed it far enough and found no sign. The young prince felt the hollow ache between his ribs, the weakness in his limbs as he reentered the trees. He would have to feed soon, rest.

A glade opened before him, perfectly round, vegetation carefully cleared from its center. Jan recognized it for a pan place, one of their ceremonial circles. A ring of stones enclosed a heap of ash in the circle's heart. Young oats and rye grass sprouted among the trees bordering the clearing. Inhaling the lush, verdant scent, the dark unicorn bent his head, tearing greedily at the fragrant, juicy stuff. Leaves and buds augmented his fare. The hollow in his belly began to fill.

A thicket of firs stood near the clearing's edge. Their strong, resinous aroma beckoned him. Jan nudged aside a spray of boughs and pressed forward, shouldering past outer branches until he reached the hollow interior. The firs stood so close, their spreading foliage so dense, that despite the morning's rain, the fallen fir needles beneath had remained dry. Only when he had sunk down and folded his limbs under him, did the dark unicorn realize how exhausted he was.

His heart rocked against his ribs. Breathing deep, he settled himself into the soft, fragrant carpet. Jan laid his head along his outstretched forelegs. His eyes closed once, opened, closed again. He thought of Korr and resolved to rest only briefly before going on. The gaunt, dark unicorn fled before him in dreams. Hooded serpents swarmed. The young prince twitched, eyelids fluttering, as a viper rose to strike the king. He who had never danced the serpent's dance, never scratched his flank or received the venom-proof blood, cried out as the dream nadder's fangs pierced him.

Jan felt himself racing, sprinting to fend off the serpent's sting — too late. The haggard stallion reared, screaming, then fell endlessly away from Jan into a yawning crevasse. The speckled serpents attenuated into a tangle of stars. The young prince found himself still running, galloping along through dark emptiness high above the rolling globe below. Cold wind whipped his mane. He was crossing a bridge, a precarious curve that spanned the whole sky, arcing ever more steeply down to horizon's edge. In a rush he realized he could not stop, momentum propelling him, hurtling him swift and inevitably toward the end of the world.

Panpipes woke him, their low, susurrous music fluting through the quiet. Jan stirred, groggy. He lifted his head, felt the closeness of fir boughs. Peering through darkness, he realized it was night. In the clearing, just visible through the trees, graceful, two-leggèd figures crouched or reposed about a flaring fire: young pans and old, full-grown warriors, elders, weanlings and infants. Jan glimpsed roots and other forage passing from forelimb to forelimb, dams suckling their young. The guttural clicks and gestures which were the goatlings' speech made little more than a murmur above the crackling of the blaze.

The gentle trilling of their panpipes wove through the summer air. Halfway around the circle Jan spotted the piper. Beside him sat a grey-bearded male, horns ribbed with age, and a bare-cheeked female, skin wizened as willow bark. A much younger pair rose from the circle and approached with forepaws clasped. They bowed low before their elders and handed them sheaves of grass in exchange for garlands. By their rich, sweet scent, Jan knew the flowers to be night-blooming lilies. Their perfume blended with the tang of woodsmoke and the aroma of the trees.

The young couple embraced, forelimbs entwining, and retired to the far side of the ring. Jan heard glad murmuring among their fellows as, each with a gesture and a word, the two elders rose and cast their sheaves into the fire. Red sparks flared up, subsided. Jan could only conclude he had witnessed some sort of joining, perhaps even the pledging of mates, and was swept suddenly, keenly, by memory of his own pledging to Tek almost three years past, by the shores of the Summer Sea.

The young prince shook himself, struggled free of the firs. Time to make himself known. The panpipes still crooned their haunting soft song amid the cheerful hubbub. The two elders resumed their places beside the piper as Jan reached the edge of the glade.

"*Emwe!*" he hailed them, framing with care the difficult, champing syllables of pan speech. "Tai-shan nau shopucha." *Moonbrow greets you.*

He moved forward slowly, so as not to startle them, until the firelight illumined his dark form.

"Have no fear. I am Jan, prince of unicorns, come in peace to seek your counsel."

The pipe player broke off suddenly as the pan campsite erupted in confusion. Jan heard cries of "Pella! Pell'!" — *Look, behold* — and "Sa'ec so!" *Him! It's him.* Sires and dams caught up their young as though to flee. Others snatched and brandished wooden stakes. He saw children quickly gathering stones. The dark unicorn snorted in bewilderment. Peace with the pans had held these two years running without a whisper of strain.

"*Nanapo:* peace," he exclaimed. "I am no foe. I seek another of my race who has fled and taken shelter here."

The pans hesitated. Jan himself poised, determined to run if he must and shed no blood. With relief, he saw the old male rise from his haunches and hold up one forelimb.

"Bikthitet nau," he heard the greybeard urging: *Calm yourselves.* "This is not the same *ufpútlak* — four-footed walker — we encountered earlier. Though dark as the other, *pella* — observe — he does not have that one's wild, unreasoning air. A great green feather tangles this one's mane. And this *ufpútlak* speaks our tongue."

Jan's heart seized at the other's words. He moved a half pace nearer. The pans twitched, pulled back, but did not flee. The greybeard held his ground.

"Elder, have you seen another of my kind this day?" Jan asked urgently. "A night-dark stallion such as I, but lawless, gaunt — it is he I seek."

Carefully, the bearded male nodded. Around him, the goatlings murmured, uneasily. The agèd female, now risen to stand beside her mate, answered, "Such a one came upon us near noon this day. What can you tell us of him?"

Jan drew a deep breath. "He is Korr, king of the unicorns."

Gasps, angry cries rose again from the goatling band. The furrows in the brows of the two elders deepened.

"If he is Korr," the greybeard said evenly, "do you, Jan, prince of *ufpútlaki*, now come to revel in your broken truce?"

The young prince's ribs constricted. "I come seeking him," he answered slowly, carefully. "He is my sire, and he is mad. Having fled our Vale this day, he now imperils not only himself and his folk, but our allies as well. I must find him and return him to the Vale, that his madness may be healed."

More murmuring from the pans. They eyed him, suspicious still. He sensed a slight — if only very slight — easing in the two elders. The fire crackled. The young prince waited. No one spoke. Finally he broke the silence.

"Tell me, I implore you, where I may find him. What deeds of his have made you so wary and put our peoples' hard-won truce in jeopardy?"

Glancing at one another, the elders considered. The rest of the goatlings held silent, watching. At last, the wizened female spoke.

"This midday," she said, "while we rested in the shade of the brittle-blossom trees, this mad *ufpútlak* stampeded among us, cursing us — so we surmise — in his own tongue. None were spared: not elders nor suckling young." Her tone grew hard. "Even children he would eagerly have trampled, had fathers and mothers not snatched them from his path."

Jan felt the blood drain from him at the thought of the mad king charging unchecked among these slight, retiring goatlings, only lately come to trust unicorns. "Did he harm any of you?" the young prince breathed, praying to Alma his worst fears might not prove true.

"Nay," the greybeard replied, and Jan's heart eased. "To our relief, your king drew no blood. We fled and dodged. Our warriors drove him off with volleys of stones — as we shall drive away all unicorns from this day forward! Your king is well-bruised. He fled toward the grassy land that borders our Woods. What do you call it? The Plain."

Jan's breath caught in dismay. The Plain was far more dangerous than the Woods: rife with grass pards that ambushed their prey. Sharp-toothed dogs that hunted in packs. Unicorns, too, roamed the Plain — wild wanderers outside the Ring of Law, of a tribe other than Jan's own. Korr had sworn eternal enmity toward these so-called Renegades. If he were reckless enough to attack Plainsdwellers as he had this goatling band, he would do so at his peril. The Free Folk of the Plain were as dauntless in their own defense as any Ringborn unicorn. Jan set his teeth. He must fly with all speed to intercept his sire.

"My heart grieves with you that this outlaw from my Vale has caused you such alarm," he answered, bowing deeply before the two elders of the goatling band. "My own tribe as well has suffered such inexplicable acts of his madness. A terrible secret haunts his mind. I mean to discover it."

He scanned the pans, gauging their mood, hoping desperately

that the damage Korr had done the newborn alliance was not truly beyond repair.

"Meanwhile, I beg you not to let his trespass spoil our peoples' long-sought peace." Jan turned his eyes back to the elder pair. "Korr will be stopped. That I vow. Even now I hasten to call him to account. I ask only that you send runners to my Vale. There you will find my mate, the regent Tek, with her foster sisters, Sismoomnat and Pitipak, and their dam, Jah-lila. Treat with them before you decide to abandon the peace. Tell them I seek my sire upon the Plain and will not rest until I find him."

Silently, the pans deliberated. The elders' eyes roved over the rest of the band, seeking consensus. Jan felt his heartbeats pulsing one by one, his muscles growing taut. At last, the agèd goatlings nodded.

"Very well, Moonbrow," the greybeard replied. "We will do as you ask. The newfound friendship between our two peoples is indeed too precious to be lightly shed."

His mate beside him echoed, "Find your sire, Prince Jan. Our goodwill speed you."

The prince of the unicorns bowed low before them. Their fire, untended, had dwindled to a feeble glow. Jan turned and launched himself, galloping away through the moonlit trees. Alma's daughter, waning now, illumined his path. Behind, he sensed the glow of coals newly stoked and fanned to life again, heard the panpipes resume their plaintive song. He headed west through the still, dark wood, sprinting in the direction of the Great Grass Plain.

Summer

★ 6 ★

Tek stood in the entry to the cave. Moonless night breathed warm around her. Above, a myriad of summer stars flocked the heavens like thistledown. Still discernibly blue, the early evening sky held onto the set sun's light. Nine weeks. The pied mare shook her head. Most of summer flown since the serpent's dance, since peacemaking with the gryphons and, a few days following, goatling envoys.

Snorting, the warrior mare marveled. No diplomat, she had had no fine phrases such as her mate always used to win his enemies' trust. Instead, she had employed her storier's art, reciting the tale of how, two winters past, Korr's derangement had slaughtered nearly half her own people, driven her from the Vale, and imperiled her unborn young. Only intervention by Sismoomnat and Pitipak had enabled Tek and her twins to survive. That seemed to mollify the pans.

She spoke with loathing of Korr and of how, were it not for her faith in Jan, she and others would have fallen upon the mad stallion years ago and driven him from the Vale. In the end, the peace held — but Tek knew it could shatter in a moment if Jan proved unable to capture his sire. Korr had, so the envoys averred, now fled the Pan Woods for the Plain.

Tek gazed up at the summer stars, gradually brightening as

evening deepened. Breeze lifted her forelock, and she breathed in the scents of yellowing grass and distant evergreens. The breath became a sigh. She longed for her mate, knew the twins missed him sorely. Where could mad Korr have hidden that Jan must spend moons hunting him? Twice Tek had sent search parties after her mate. Each time they had returned without success.

Night sky grew jet black, its white stars fabulously bright: legend called them Alma's eyes. The piping cry of a mourning-will sounded, high and sweet, from the Vale's far slope. Moments later, its mate answered. Tek turned from the night, back into the cave. Luminous mushrooms clung fan-shaped to the grotto's walls and ceiling, intermingled with phosphorescent lichens. Pale yellow or white, some blue, plum, amber, even rose and brassy green, they cast a glow that was warm and steady.

She did not see the twins and realized they must be in the little alcove at the back of the cave. There a tiny spring welled up. Tek peered around the bend into the dark alcove. Only a scattering of mushrooms here. She spotted the twins. They stood side to side, gazing intently into the black, mirror-smooth water. Their dam moved closer.

"What see you, children," she whispered. "A cavefish?" Neither took eyes from the water. Tek, too, peered down. Painted Aiony leaned against her.

"Nay, Mother," Dhattar replied. "We watch for Jan."

The pied mare laughed. "Watch for Jan — in a cavepool? Your father's leagues distant, on the Plain."

Aiony nodded. "We know. But we find him sometimes, when we watch."

"Water is best," Dhattar continued, "but we see him in clouds and moving grass as well."

His sister shrugged against Tek's chest. "Night is a better time than day, especially when you are wishing for him. That helps us."

Puzzled, Tek bent to nuzzle her. "How do you mean?"

"Stand between us," Dhattar was saying. "Then you'll see him, too."

Still frowning, Tek shifted to bring herself between her twin filly and foal. They pressed against her.

"Look deep," Aiony said.

Eerie sensations flitted through Tek. The pool lay far from still, she realized. Currents swirled below its glassy surface, rippling the image of the stone bottom. The reflected glow of the lichens shifted, trembled.

"Think of him," Dhattar murmured. "He is never far from your mind — or ours — but think of him directly now. School your thoughts."

The pied mare's pulse began, slowly, to pound. Her image in the water before her seemed to grow distant and fade. She felt the twins' warmth, their young heartbeats, more rapid than hers, perfectly synchronized.

"Be at ease," Aiony soothed. "Naught is to fear."

A gathering sense of motion. Tek's heart hammered, then seemed to stop. Time hung suspended as a strong, invisible current began to sweep her more and more swiftly along. She was aware of standing still within the cave beside her young — yet at the same time, some other part of her was galloping free, infinitely swift, like the Mare of the World, who had matched the sun in his race and won her heart's desire. Images of lichenlight in the dark water brightened and shrank, becoming stars. The Vale lay below. Wind buffeted. The Pan Woods raced by, and then the Plain.

Renegades loped across its grassy, rolling back. Starlit grass pards crouched and sprang. In the distance, she caught a glimpse of one who might have been Korr, dark as shadow, but only a glimpse. More Plainsdwellers thundered by, leaping and prancing in a long, snaking dance such as Tek had never before seen. Drawing closer, she heard their snorts and whinnies, felt the drumming of their hooves, caught the scent of their manes and sweat. They vanished over horizon's edge.

The Plain lay empty but for starlit grass. Clear, hornlike notes sounded in the distance, from the throats of thickset, square-nosed oncs grazing unseen. A banded pard prowled by, gave its low, coughing cry. Jan lay in a hollow not twenty paces from it, Tek saw with a start. The prince's eyes were closed. His ears twitched to the sound, but the wind was with him. The pard, never scenting him, padded on.

"Jan," Tek murmured. "Jan. . . ."

Again he stirred.

"Hist. Don't wake him," Dhattar beside her whispered. "Ordeals undreamed of lie ahead."

Aiony nodded. "To find his sire sooner than he knows."

Dhattar sighed. "And chase him longer than he need."

"Ordeals?" the pied mare breathed.

"Fear and anger," the white foal hissed. "Grief and loss. Loneliness. A wound so great it alters time."

Tek's motionless heart started again with a thump. "When will he return . . . ?" she began, baffled.

"Never," the painted filly replied.

A waft of terror swept over Tek. Dhattar nipped her gently. "No fear. You will see him again, but not here. He will never return here. In the Hallow Hills will you behold him, when he scours the wyverns' dens with the fire of the end of the world."

The cool of morning woke him. Dawn, not far from breaking, barely paled the sky. The thousand thousand summer stars, winding across the dark like a river of milk, were fading. Jan lifted his head, inhaling the scent of earth and grass that was the Plain, a vast rolling veldt that sprawled from the cool south, where the Summer Sea lapped, northward past the Pan Woods and the Vale to the warmer Hallow Hills and beyond. Somewhere to the eastern south, so rumor claimed, rose the Smoking Hills, home to red dragons.

Still couched, Jan stretched his leg, craned his neck and shook himself. He nibbled at the dew-drenched grass. His throat ached with thirst. He had not come upon water since before yesterday. Food, of course, was plentiful. But danger abounded, too. The rolling land hid many hollows where grass pards might lie. Thrice the sandy-colored predators had sprung at him from the haycorn. Each time he had shied, taken to his heels unscathed. More than once, he had found the bones of unicorns. He kept his ears pricked, avoided places above which kites circled, traveled into the wind whenever he could.

Tracking Korr had proved daunting. The mad king meandered and doubled back. At best, Jan found himself forever a day behind the haggard king. Evidence of struggles scattered Korr's path: two with predators — one in which the pard had lost its life, the other in which the wounded cat had retreated, trailing blood. Worse still were the ambush sites. Jan had found tracks clearly showing where the mad king had charged among small bands of Plains-dwelling unicorns — a stallion and two mares, or a mare with both her half-grown and suckling foals — and scattered them, fencing with those he could catch. Perhaps inflicting other harm which did not show in the tracks.

Sickened, Jan rolled to scrub his back against the loamy ground. He had spent most of the summer chasing Korr all over the Mare's Back, and not once had he spoken to a free-ranging unicorn of the Plain. Often enough he had seen them in the distance, but one glimpse of him and always they fled. He had given up pursuing them. They were fleet as wind and seemed to regard him with a terror better deserved by Korr.

Jan felt the beat of hooves before he heard them, vibrating up through the earth. Three sets of larger heels: warriors, one of whom sounded lighter than the other two — probably a mare. The fourth set was tiny, doubtless a filly or foal. All four headed in his direction at a trot. Jan rolled to get his limbs under him, but did not rise. The sound of their approach drew nearer and nearer yet. Jan waited until they were almost upon him, before he rose from the long grass, calling, "Peace! I am no enemy, but a stranger seeking water. Can you tell me where I may drink?"

With snorts of alarm, the Plainsdwellers halted. The wind was wrong for them. They had not scented him. One of their number nearly bolted, but Jan called again.

"Peace! I need your aid."

The party did indeed consist of a mare, two stallions, and a suckling filly. Feathers of birds entangled their manes. The mare was brilliant crimson, her filly palest blue. The younger and slighter of the two stallions was fair gold, his companion brindled grey. The pair circled forward to protect the mare, who stood to shield her foal.

"Look! Look!" The gold stallion whistled. "'Tis he of whom Calydor warned: the black Moondancer. Flee!"

Wide-eyed, the grey looked half persuaded, but the mare held her ground.

"Nay," she muttered. "'T cannot be. Calydor described a haggard stallion of middle years. . . ."

"I am not he," Jan broke in swiftly. "It is he I seek. He has wronged my folk and our allies. I must capture him ere he harms others. . . ."

"Already he has wronged others," the grey snorted. "Pursued, even injured some. Calydor foresaw and warned us from his path. By your speech, you are Vale-born, your hue jet black. What assures us you are not the mad destroyer?"

Jan turned his head so that the green gryphon feather might come into their view. He remembered from a brief encounter on his initiation pilgrimage years ago that unlike his own folk, who dipped only the neck, Plainsdwellers bowed by going down on one knee. The prince of the unicorns now did the same.

"Free People of the Plain," he answered, "I am Aljan Moonbrow, prince of my folk. The one I seek is Korr, our king, though he no longer rules us. For years we contained his madness within our Vale, but now he has broken free. He must be found. This I am come to do."

The golden stallion frowned, suspicious still. The grey seemed somewhat less so, but the crimson mare nodded. The brown and the white feather, each tethered in the long strands of her hair, bobbed.

"Aye, Korr," she murmured. "The one whose name means thunder. . . . All sooth, you are not he," she said suddenly. "I know you now — for I have seen you ere time. Recall you this? You were but a colt half grown, and I a filly about the same age. You had slipped away from your pilgrim band to sing the dead rites for a mare of ours killed by a pard. My dam and I and our companion came upon you. You told us your name. 'Twas — 'twas . . ."

She paused, searching.

"Aljan, the Dark Moon!" she exclaimed, triumphant. "We later heard you succeeded Korr. You are now called Aljan-with-the-Moon-upon-his-Brow, are you not? A Moondancer, but fair-spoken, aye. And honorable."

Jan drew back, astonished. Memory washed him — of his initiation pilgrimage four years before, and the Renegades he had met upon that journey — at the end of which had lain the wyvern in her den. The young mare — had she been the filly he had met? She looked so much older now, a mated mare. "I am Aljan," he murmured, still struggling to recall, "though I never knew your name."

"Crimson," she told him, whickering, as though the answer were obvious. She nodded toward the other three. "And these, who were not with me when first we met, are Ashbrindle, my sire." The grey-and-white nodded. "My brother-beloved, Goldenhair." The younger stallion tossed his head. "And my filly, called Bluewater Sky till she grow wit enough to choose her own name."

Jan bowed his head to each in turn, even Sky, before returning his gaze to the mare.

"Will you aid me, Crimson?" he implored. "I intend no ill against the Free People of the Plain, only to find my sire. Do you know where I may discover him?"

Before him, the three warriors exchanged a glance, seemed to reach agreement. The suckling filly began to nurse.

"Calydor will know," the grey stallion replied, coming forward now. "Ask of him."

Jan looked at him. "Calydor," he mused. "Who is this Calydor?"

"Our prophet," the golden stallion declared. "He recks much and dreams more. He will judge if your words sing true."

"Hist, belovèd," the crimson mare broke in. "Let us speak this stranger fair." She turned to Jan. "Calydor is a farseer. Many call him Alma's Eyes. Were he not our close kin, we might do the same."

The dark unicorn felt his spirits lift. "Where may I find this seer?" he asked. "You say he can scry my lost sire? Will you guide me to him?"

"Water first," the grey brindle replied. "Let us quench our thirst on it." Turning, he whistled his companions to follow. "Come, daughter, filly, and daughter's kin. Time enough to ponder my brother's whereabouts once we have drunk."

Stars

★ 7 ★

Jan trotted beside the crimson mare. Her pale-blue filly pranced alongside. The mare's sire, the brindled grey, led them over grassy, rolling hills, with the mare's brother-belovèd — what did the term mean, Jan wondered: foster brother, half brother? — pale gold, bringing up the rear. The grey-and-white trotted briskly, with hardly a glance behind. He seemed to have accepted Jan, for the present at least, though the younger stallion watched him carefully still.

Only the crimson mare seemed wholly at ease. She had spoken little during their five miles' journey to where a slender brook meandered between two slopes. There they had lingered, savoring the creek's coolness, dipping their heads for a second draft as the young sun cleared the horizon and floated free, turning the morning sky from misty white to deeper and deeper blue as it climbed toward zenith. At last, the grey brindle spoke.

"'Tis well," he said. "You seem no mad raver. I would lead you to my brother, if my companions assent."

The mare and the other stallion both nodded, the pale gold grudgingly, barely dipping his chin. So it was the crimson mare the young prince now found himself pacing: the grey ahead, the gold at rearguard, the pale-blue filly frisking and teasing. Morning had grown late, warm, the sun high overhead. White clouds gathered, their shadows slipping over the Plain.

"Tell me of your life here, upon Alma's Back," he bade the crimson mare.

She cocked an eye and replied, "Gladly — but first speak of yours within your Vale. My dam's dam came from there. She said 'twas all proud princes, rules and Law, so she fled to the Mare's Back to win freedom. You call yourself prince, Aljan, yet you seem fairspoken still, not ruled by pride."

He laughed. As they trotted through the long, warm noon and lay up in the shade of steep banks for the hottest part of the day, he spoke of Moondance, of new warriors initiated upon spring pilgrimage, of the yearly trek by those unpaired to find and pledge their mates by the Summer Sea. He spoke of autumn feasting and spring birthing. Of Kindling and Quenching, the herd's winter ceremonies of fire. Crimson listened intently, interrupting from time to time. Jan knew by their silence the grey and the gold were listening, too.

Not until midway into the afternoon had Crimson heard enough. She told then of the Free People, a scattered, far-traveled folk who ranged at will across the Plain. Though some were loners, most traveled in small bands. Plainsdwellers dodged pards, encountered each other at waterholes, whistled greetings to those sighted at distance, and followed one another's spoor to meet and trade news. Alliances formed, endured awhile, then just as easily and amicably dissolved.

The impermanence of such an existence struck Jan as both utterly foreign and oddly alluring. Unbound by any sovereign or herd, each Plainsdweller was completely free — but at what cost? Danger from pards. A life spent in constant motion, rather than settled in a sheltered Vale. *Friendships must be difficult to sustain,* Jan mused. He wondered how mates fared in the rearing of their young.

Yet Crimson seemed to regard the Vale as unbearably confining, circumscribed by rules of every kind. Plainsdwellers had customs, but no Law and no way of enforcing Law had they had any.

Far from admiring his status as prince, the crimson mare pronounced Jan's position an unspeakable burden, imposed without consent, to be shaken off at the earliest chance. Who, after all, would not wish to be free as was she? All Moondancers must be mad, she exclaimed, only half in jest, to forgo the liberty of Alma's Back for a rocky, gryphon-haunted Vale.

Six days they roved in search of Calydor, traveling northwest. The Plain became hillier, its terrain more broken. Thunderheads brought showers in the late afternoons. White towers of cloud were building now, Jan noticed as they loped: but too scattered and far to coalesce into a storm. Jan listened to distant thunder growl as the setting sun declined. The wind still smelled dry. Sometimes thunder made the ground tremble — Jan came aware all at once that the tremor he felt was not thunder.

Hoofbeats, he realized. The stamping, tramping cadence of hard heels drumming the Plain, but neither approaching nor receding. It was he and his companions, the dark unicorn decided, who were drawing nearer to the unseen source of that low, rhythmic mutter. With sun just down and sky now a fiery blaze, flushing the scattered thunderheads all shades of melon and rose, the broken landscape of the Plain had grown dusky. His companions' ears pricked, heads lifted and nostrils flared. Their pace quickened.

"What is it?" he asked. "What do we near?"

Crimson tossed her head. "A Gather — 't can only be that! Calydor has called a Gather. I hear them dancing the longdance by water's edge."

Jan caught sound of snorts and whinnies. Evening breeze brought him the warm, unmistakable scent of unicorns. Ahead, the grey-and-white brindle rounded a hillside and halted. Jan and the crimson mare did the same, followed by the others. The prince drew in his breath. Before him, a dark green river snaked through rolling hills. On the far side, in the broad, inner bend of one meandering curve, moved twelve score Plainsdwellers, perhaps more. Their sinuous line recurved and doubled back upon itself, wending and swirling, veering, unwinding, sometimes at nearly full gallop, sometimes in a complicated stamping pattern.

All ages joined in the winding dance. Jan saw elders, mares and stallions in their prime, half-growns, colts and fillies, foals. The Plainsdwellers, Jan saw, were more variegated than his own folk, who were mostly red or blue with occasional greys. Gold and other shades only rarely appeared in the Vale. Among the Free Folk of the Plain, too, hot reds and cool blues cantered by in abundance, but greys and golds seemed nearly as numerous, with a generous sprinkling of dapples and roans, even spotted coats. Feathers adorned the manes of many.

One figure in particular caught Jan's eye — that of the one leading the dance: tall and lank-limbed, with a long neck and horn and a slim, straight muzzle, easily the best dancer, a stallion in his prime. His coat was indigo. Three white feathers tossed in his mane, which was silver, as were his hooves and horn. The evening darkness of his coat was spattered with hoary flecks. They wound upward past one eye before spilling down his neck. Turning at the shoulder, the widening runnel of tiny frosted spots flowed diagonally across his back and meandered down one flank. Pale socks washed three pasterns. The rest of him, almost wholly dark, sported only slight speckling, like stray pricks of light in a summer sky.

Jan studied the other. Twilight was fading, the sun well and truly set. A pale sliver of moon floated amid a river of stars just beginning to become visible. The astral path wandered overhead, arching like a bridge from one to the other end of the world. Scattered to all four quarters, tall thunderheads floated motionless in the distance. Occasionally their thunder growled above the thrumming beat of the dancers' hooves. Lightning illuminated the clouds' interiors, like the diffuse, rosy radiance of cave lichens. Beside him, Crimson suddenly reared.

"'Tis Calydor," she cried joyously. "I see him there!"

She sprinted down the long, gentle slope toward the river below, her pale-blue filly flying after. Jan sprang in pursuit, heard the grey and the gold coming hard on his heels. Crimson plunged into the smooth green river. Her filly leapt to follow, fording the slow, calm waters with a will. As her dam reached the far bank,

Sky clambered out, shook. The mare nuzzled her, then trotted toward the dancers, her filly close behind. Jan swam in their wake, reaching shore half a length in front of Goldenhair and the grey. He paused to shake off, and the other stallions sprang past and up the bank to join their fellows thundering by.

The dark prince bounded after, merged into the long, winding train full of sudden eddies and shifts. Caught up in its wild tempo, he struggled to decipher the intricate patterns of stamping. Eventually he realized that whatever step the dancers executed was chosen by the one leading the line. That one chose the pattern, demonstrated it, and the others repeated it until their leader chose anew. Dancing, Jan noted with relief that though some eyed him with curiosity, none reacted with alarm. Perhaps because of Illishar's feather, he was certain none took him for a Moondancer. Perhaps, too, in the settling dusk, the black of his coat was not so evident.

Evening deepened. The slender crescent moon declined, throwing long shadows. Its pale light glided along the backs and faces of the dancers. At length, their stamping ceased. Halted, the dance's participants stood blowing, shifting to loosen their limbs in the sudden, ringing silence. Panting, Jan heard the distant yip and hoot of Plains dogs scrapping over scavenge. The dance's leader trotted to an open space before the crowd. Behind him, the bend in the river gleamed. Beyond, the Plain sloped moonsheened to horizon's edge. Above, stars burned. The evening blue with the starlight pattern in his coat shook his pale feathered mane.

"Hail, my fellows!" His voice sounded oddly familiar, though Jan was certain he had never encountered this striking stallion before. "Tonight we gather," he cried, "to foot the longdance, for the dark destroyer roves no more among us. We are free of him. He has fled."

Trepidation seized Jan. Korr no longer upon the Plain? The black prince cast about for his companions. If so, he had no time to lose. He needed one of them to point out who among this press was the seer Calydor. A moment later, Jan spotted Crimson

and her filly standing very near the speaker. Ashbrindle stood back
a few paces. He did not spy the gold.

"So we celebrate," the star-marked stallion continued, "now
that danger is past. Soon our longdance will run its course, praising Álm'harat and her endless Cycle."

Around him, Jan glimpsed half-growns rubbing shoulders,
mares nipping after stallions' flanks. Colts and fillies lay down,
other, younger ones already asleep. Heat rose in wisps from the
Plainsdwellers' backs. The evening-blue unicorn with the starpath
markings spoke on.

"But first, respite. I'll sing you a tale. The dark one who lately
ramped among us hailed from the distant Vale of Moondance. All
our lives have we heard of its warrior Ring, glimpsed its members
pilgriming upon the Plain, learnt of half-growns initiated into its
warhost — in the name of Álm'harat, yet! Aye, Moondancers do
battle to honor The One who makes all life.

"These Valedwellers spare us no love, kick dust on our customs,
harry us as Renegades — yet we eschew this witless conflict. The
Mare's Back is broad, and we have always found room to dodge
them. Until the dark destroyer came, black as a night without
moon or stars. He called himself a king. Yet he ruled no one, not
even himself. He fell upon us wherever he found us and sought
the lives even of fillies and foals in his madness to make war.

"Yet we slipped his grasp. Our ears were keen, our limbs fleet.
Dreams gave warning, and we scented him in the wind. We traveled in larger bands, avoiding those places he had last been seen.
At length, we drove him from our midst — and, having survived
this ordeal, we have begun to think all Moondancers fiends.

"Such is not so. Some of us have sires or dams born to the
Ring, who later fled to freedom here. Others have aided such refu-
gees. True, these Ringbreakers disparage the Vale. I little blame
them. To speak of it is painful to them. But I will tell you of one
I met, many years ago, who was of the Vale and who returned to
the Vale, and was no monster, no mad maker of war."

All around, Plainsdwellers shifted and swayed, now pricking

their ears, their murmurs quieting. Despite his urgency, Jan found himself listening as the other spoke.

"Many seasons past, when I was a youth with a young beard on my chin, I dreamt one summer under Alma's eyes of a mare: pale as cloud newly warmed by sunset's glow, with a mane and tail brilliant red-orange as the poppy flower."

The dark prince heard sighs, contented murmurs among the crowd, as though the tale were well known, a favorite. Reluctantly, he settled himself, aware that making his way unobtrusively to Crimson or Ashbrindle now through the hush might prove well-nigh impossible.

"She, too, was young," the singer continued. His way of turning, of lifting his head nipped at Jan like a gnat, reminding him of someone he could not quite recall. The star-marked stallion continued. "Gazing upon her in my dream, I sensed that like me, she had never danced the longdance to its end.

"She lay far to the south, I knew, where the wind blows cool. I set out alone across the Plain. For days I traveled, until I drew near the southern sea that spills green against a golden shore. Tasting salt upon the wind, I halted, knowing Moondancers summer upon that strand. I had no wish to clash with any of that warlike tribe.

"Night fell, and I saw my love, coming by moondark — yet the light of Álm'harat's eyes blazed so, I saw her as well as by day. She moved with caution and with speed, casting about as she traveled, ears pricked, scenting the breeze. She was all my dream had promised: dancer's grace and runner's gait.

"With a joyous cry, I leapt to meet her as one would a long-lost friend, unguarded — and nearly lost my life. She screamed and shied, wholly surprised, then met me with a pummeling of hooves and a slashing of horn. I broke off, bewildered. She sprang back, stiff-legged, horn at the ready.

"'Stand off! Stand off, wild Renegade,' she shouted. 'I seek no enmity with you, but I am a warrior born and versed and can defend myself at need.'

"We both stood wild-eyed, panting, stunned. She, from what must have seemed an ambuscade — I, from the dawning that though she was indeed my vision's mare, she herself had dreamt no such dream. She knew me not, and sooth, what knew I of her? Until that moment I had not even suspected what now stood clear: she was no Plainsdweller as was I, but a Moondancer strayed from her folk. If she searched for another upon the Plain, that other was not I.

"I stammered some halting amends. 'I cry your pardon. I mistook you for a . . . a friend and meant no harm.'

"She eyed me warily. At length she said, 'I, too, seek . . . a certain friend.' She hesitated. Then, 'Perhaps you have news of her.'

"Carefully at first, then with growing ease, she told me of a belovèd companion who had deserted the Vale. Now each night, she said, she slipped away from her band, ventured onto the Plain, intent upon finding her missing companion and persuading her to return. I listened, lost at times. She assumed I knew all concerning her folk, that I had once been one of them, and that I, too, like her friend, had run away.

"I told her I knew naught of her friend, that I, like most of my folk, had been foaled upon the Mare's Back and wist little of her reclusive, warring clan. But I pledged to search and bring word if she would await me nightly on this spot. She was grateful, relieved beyond measure. Venturing the Plain entailed great risk for her. Besides danger from dogs and pards, if discovered, she might have been cast from her band. Simply conversing with me was counted treason.

"The harshness of her people's lives astonished me: hidebound by tradition, imprisoned by Law. How, I wondered, could one raised within such strictures have even conceived this defiance: to dare to follow her own heart rather than the dictates of capricious kings? For all her people's warlike bent, they seemed to my mind to be cowards all, afraid to think and do for themselves.

"This young mare's plan to return her friend to what she believed the safe haven of her Vale was surely bold. Yet in truth, my sympathies were all for the other, the one who had leapt the confines of the Vale and fled to the open Plain. In the space of a heartbeat, I envisioned a plan: that if I could indeed find my love's lost companion, perhaps I and that one together might convince her to remain at liberty upon the Plain.

"She and I parted ere the paling of the stars: she — hopeful but wary still — to return to her summering band; I flush with determination. I scoured the Plain, importuning every passerby for news, imploring those I met to search upon their travels for my belovèd's friend and send me word. Always I returned by nightfall to meet with the poppy-maned mare, bring her what news I had gleaned — maddeningly little, most days.

"She never seemed disappointed, as at first I had feared, only sad, and hopeful still, and patient, ready to wait as long as need be. After we spoke each night, she appeared reluctant to go. So we spoke on, I telling her of my life and my people's ways, she telling me of hers. I learnt more of them from her than ever I could have dreamt.

"Slowly, she warmed to me. I sensed she kept our meetings for more than just the chance of news. I sensed she began to look to me for companionship, that she enjoyed my company more and more. I sang her songs of our folk — I was a young singer then, and my store of stories small. She recited for me those of her own folk's lays that she could recall. Our friendship deepened with each waning night.

"Then at last, word came. A passing band knew of the mare I sought. Another wayfarer spoke of a Gather. The mare for whom I searched would likely gather with the rest to dance the longdance. Excitedly, I told my friend from the Vale. We struck off across the Plain, flying like the wind, and reached the milling celebrants just at dusk. My friend spotted her comrade and ran to her, calling gladly.

"My love's fellow at first mistook her for a new Renegade like herself and welcomed her eagerly to the Plain. Soon, however, my love's intentions became clear. The two mares quarreled, cajoled, discussed and reconciled, each seeking to convince the other to join her. I hung back, uncertain, avid to support the other mare's arguments, yet fearing to intrude. Meanwhile, all around us, the longdance began, its rhythm swelling, ebbing, and rising again.

"At last, my love's friend turned from her and disappeared into the quickening rush. My heart beat hard. Before me, my love stood shaken, confused. Clearly, she had believed persuasion would be easy after the difficult trial of finding her friend. Instead, her comrade had refused to return to the Vale and pressed my love hard to remain. She had spoken convincingly, I saw, touting her newfound freedom. My belovèd wavered. Made bold, I, too, now spoke, declaring my passionate love.

"All around us, our fellows coursed, snorting and plunging, stamping and swirling. Their throb, the tow of their motion overwhelmed us both. She followed me as one lost in a daze. We entered the dance. 'T swept us along, two dreamers caught in currents too swift to swim, too powerful to wake, and we danced the longdance to its end, under the summer stars.

"Briefly, I think, she cast off her Vale and its Ring of Law, entering wholeheartedly into our joyous rite. Perhaps I delude myself. When dawn broke, blinding the stars, our companions scattered, her lost friend among them. She stood unable to follow, and my hopes ended. She must return to her seaside band, she said. She could not go with me.

"I stood speechless, realizing at last why Álm'harat's vision of this mare had never gone beyond the dance. Last eve, which I had thought the dawn of our sweet fellowship upon the Plain, marked its conclusion instead. In dreams the goddess speaks, had spoken true. 'Twas I who had been too lovestruck witless to comprehend. I felt I might die then, the land beneath my heels heave upward, the air became dust, and darkness swallow me.

"Shaking with sorrow, she bade me farewell, and told me that among her folk, mates pledge for life. I had never heard of such a thing. We have all known a few such blessèd pairs, yet I could scarce conceive how one dared hope for such a fortuitous outcome from every tryst, every dancing of the dance. Valedwellers, I learnt, *expect* to pair for life. Yet she had cast even that most venerated custom aside to join with me for but a night.

"And night was done. We could not prolong it, though from that day on, both would be forever changed. She would not skip home to put me coldly from her mind. No day would pass that she would not think of me, just as no hour since passes for me that I do not think of her, dream and desire her. Though that moment filled me with unbearable sadness, never once in all my years have I felt regret. The goddess led me to my love for some purpose as yet hidden.

"Never after have I looked upon all Moondancers as monsters. Warlike and arrogant as a people, perhaps, but this mare that I so briefly loved, and still love, and will love all the days of my life, was not. She was witty, warm, courageous, shy, all traits I can only admire. I trust she, too, has never again thought evil of my folk. Surely the myth that we are all outlaws from the Vale is dispelled from her heart. Perhaps from the hearts of her children. I cannot say, but if Álm'harat joined us for this alone — that we might cast off our peoples' long enmity — it is enough.

"I charge you now as you finish the dance: remember my love. For every dark destroyer, other southlanders abide who are honorable and bear us no ill will. Above all, love one another wisely and well, for what you may hope to be a lifelong pledge under Álm'harat's eyes may endure but an hour. The goddess's ways do baffle us. The night is brief, but the dance is long. So join and accomplish her rite, all you who so desire. It is part of the Mare's great Cycle, which turns all the world and the stars."

As the singer fell silent, bowing his head, the throng surrounding Jan roused themselves. With sudden snorts and wild whinnies, they reared and pranced. Mares and stallions paired off, mock-battling. Small bands of friends cavorted seemingly for sheer pleasure. Yawning colts and young half-growns cropped grass or dozed, oblivious to their elders' energetic frolic. Some pairs had already struck off into the long grass surrounding the clearing. Most still chased and chivvied in the river bend.

In mounting dismay, Jan cast about, aware suddenly that he must find the one named Calydor before he, too, slipped away in this joyous frenzy. Yet, the young prince realized belatedly, he had no inkling where to begin. He could have kicked himself for never having asked Crimson to describe her uncle's coloring. He spotted the crimson mare suddenly, approaching the star-spotted singer, who stood surveying the crowd. He, apparently, did not intend to join his fellows in completing the dance. Jan trotted toward them.

"Hail, my child, daughter to my sib," the dark-blue stallion cried as the young mare shouldered against him with an affectionate nip. "Well met."

"Hail, Calydor," the crimson mare replied above her filly's delighted squeals, "brother to my sire. I bring you greetings."

Jan halted in his tracks.

"More than greetings alone, I see," the singer laughed as he nuzzled her sky-blue foal. "You bring a young Moondancer. Turn and acquaint us, if you will, for he stands not three paces from your flank."

Night

★ 8 ★

Jan came forward. The thin crescent slip of moon was just setting, sinking curve-downward into distant horizon's edge. Soon only summer stars would remain to illuminate the dark. The crimson mare turned with a whicker of surprise.

"There you are, my moondancing friend," she exclaimed. "I sprang ahead to bring word of you to Calydor, but could not catch him ere his tale. Nor could I spot you afterwards. Behold Calydor, brother to my sire."

"Hail, my son, guest to my brother's get," the star-strewn unicorn greeted him.

Jan was struck again by the odd familiarity he felt in the presence of this stallion he had never met before. He and the seer stood the same height, very similar in heft and build. Long-leggèd and lithe, each had a lean, hard dancer's frame. The dark prince bowed in the way of the Vale, dipping his neck.

"Hail, Calydor," he replied. "I seek one of my folk who runs amok, him you call the dark destroyer."

The deep-blue and silver unicorn nodded. "Sooth. Be welcome here. Come, let us retire to the riverbank, and leave the dancers to their sport."

Dozens of unicorns galloped by, some engaged in nothing more than high-spirited games. Others slept, still others lost in the teasing lead-and-follow of mates at play. Jan spotted the brindled grey stallion loping past, following a mare who whistled at him over one shoulder and plunged away into the grass. The crimson mare stood poised, eyeing her fellows. Jan spied the pale gold stallion standing at Plain's edge, watching expectantly. Calydor whickered.

"Go, my child. Enjoy the dance. I will see to Sky. In Álm'harat's keeping, love wisely and well."

With a whistle of gratitude, the crimson mare bowed on one knee and sped away. Her filly hung back uncertain, until the indigo stallion called her. She trotted alongside him as Calydor turned, headed across the trampled grass toward the river's bank. Jan fell into step. The sound of cool, green waters murmured in his ears. Their dark, wet fragrance filled his nostrils. The seer chose a spot at the crest of the bend. The bank here was steep, the river reeds low.

"I dreamt your coming, my son," the starry other said. They stood looking out over the river, the little filly in between. "And well I know of the one you seek."

"Your niece says you are a seer," the young prince replied, "that your folk call you 'Alma's Eyes.'"

The blue-and-silver stallion laughed. "No compliment to my powers, I vow. Only a play upon my name."

"'Calydor'?" Jan asked. The name was not used in the Vale. "What does it mean?"

"'Stars in summer,'" the seer replied. "My folk call the stars 'Álm'harat's eyes.'"

Jan nodded. "And mine. But I did not know you for a singer as well. I am honored, having heard your song."

He fell silent, choosing his words. The singer's tale had moved him strangely, though it had told of a mare breaking the herd's Law to run wild renegade. He himself had never seen the wisdom of many of his people's most rigid strictures. Since becoming prince, he had relaxed or discarded a fair number of the oldest and harshest laws. And he had never subscribed to his herd's ill will against the folk of the Plain: another old hatred that made no sense to him.

"My mate is a singer," Jan continued. "Her name is Tek. When I return to her, I will recount your tale."

Calydor bowed his head. "Then 'tis you who honor me. But tell me of the one you seek. Though my dreams speak true, rarely do they reveal all. Much mazes me still about that one, who for two moons trampled the Mare's Back, terrorizing whomever he met."

Jan dug into the riverbank with one cloven heel. The sky-blue filly's head drooped as she leaned against her great-uncle. The young prince gazed off across river and Plain. Images of stars scattered the water's dark, smooth surface so that it looked like a river of night sky threading the grassy hills. The moon had slipped below horizon's edge. Its silver gleam faded.

"I come seeking my sire," the younger stallion replied. "My herd acclaims me their warleader, and Korr was once accounted our king. Three winters past, in my absence, he seized power, leading a mad crusade that cost many their lives. At last his fanaticism was condemned for what it was. He has been outcast since, shrieking curses upon my mate and her dam, upon his own mate and child, and calling Tek's and my offspring abomination. Lately, he railed of some past deed upon the Plain. Now he has fled here, as though so doing can dispel whatever memory from his youth haunts him still. It is time his rampage ceased. This years-long silence must end. It is his silence that has maddened him. If I can but persuade him to reveal this secret he holds, I am convinced he will know peace."

The star-strewn unicorn listened in thoughtful reserve. The little filly leaning against him had closed her eyes.

"I judge you to be sincere," he answered quietly. "No deception shades your voice. Your folk and mine share a long history of enmity, but I see no reason for you and me to perpetuate it. Ask of me what you will."

Jan sighed deeply, and then drew breath, hopeful yet cautious still. "Has Korr harmed any of your folk?"

"Frightened, mostly," the other replied, tossing his head. "By and large, the injuries he dealt were flesh wounds. We are a fleet and wary folk."

Jan nodded, relieved. "Did those who brought news of him to you recount any of Korr's words?"

Sadly, the star-specked unicorn sighed. "Only curses and threats. Those who encountered him called him crazed: violent and inconsolable. Who proffered peace and strove to reason with him suffered worst."

Jan watched the river flowing, swirling the reflected stars. He felt as though Alma's eyes watched him both from heaven and from below. He said to Calydor, "Do I glean rightly that your folk have driven him from the Plain?"

The other nodded. "Dream reached me four days past that a band of young stallions and mares came upon him at a watering place near Plain's edge. He flew at them. At length, they succeeded in driving him from their midst. He struck off into the Salt Waste bordering our grasslands."

Inwardly Jan groaned. Pursuit of his sire, which had seemed at first a matter of mere hours or days, now promised to stretch on from weeks and months into a season or more. His heart ached to be reunited with his mate and young, but he could not turn back. Korr must be halted and, if at all possible, healed.

"Where may I find the spot at which he left the Plain?" the young prince asked.

Beside him, the blue-and-silver stallion nodded. "'T lies to north and east, ten days' journey from this spot."

The little filly beside him had lain down on the riverbank. Calydor joined her. Jan folded limb and couched himself as well. His ears swiveled to the snorts and playful whistles of the Plainsdwellers. The drum of heels and their romping cries told him the games and impromptu contests continued. The younger voices were dying down. Other sets of heels, always in pairs, beat away through the grass, accompanied by breathless laughter. Jan was reminded of his own courting rite with Tek beside the Summer Sea.

And yet, so it seemed, these celebrants had no thought of pledging themselves for all eternity under Alma's eyes. Whatever vows they spoke would last but the night, to lapse or renew daily, exactly as they pleased. This baffling custom troubled Jan. How could young know their sires if their parents parted after a tryst? Nonetheless, he realized, Crimson knew her sire. Her brother, the pale golden stallion, knew his sire as well — at least, so Jan had gathered, that his differed from the crimson mare's.

That, too, astonished him, that brother and sister might share but a single parent. Though he could scarce conceive not being pledged to Tek or — more unimaginable still — breaking that pledge, the freedom the Plainsdwellers knew was breathtaking. He could hardly envision such lives as theirs, forever free of the constancy of kings and Law, the touchstone of eternal vows. With a start, Jan woke from his thoughts. The blue-and-silver stallion was speaking.

"Rest here the night, my son. You are weary, having pressed hard these many weeks in pursuit of your sire."

Jan nodded heavily, head drooping, eyes slipping shut. His limbs ached. His ribs throbbed, his spine sore where it flexed. He was weary, but less in body than in spirit. He wanted this business with Korr to be done. He wanted to learn the dark secret that drove Korr mad. Only then, he was sure, might he and his mate and young be free of it. Korr, too, and all the Vale. The young stallion roused himself and reached to taste the rushes at the riverside, aware only now that in his haste to reach the Gather, he had not eaten since noon. The stallion beside him watched.

"You wear a feather in your hair," he remarked at length, "as many of my people do. I have never seen a Valedweller so adorned. Does it signify your rank?"

Jan tossed his head and felt Illishar's green feather slap gently against his neck. In the years since he and the gryphon had sealed their first, tentative truce, it had never worked free. He took it for a good sign. The tender rushes filled his belly, warm and sweet. He turned to Calydor.

"Nay," he laughed. "It commemorates a peace."

The seer's eyes widened, then smiled. The little filly slept slumped against him, limbs folded, chin tucked. She reminded Jan intensely of his twins before they had been weaned. Their horns must have sprouted by this time, breaking the skin and spiraling up. They would be butting into everything now, scrubbing their foreheads against bark and stone to quell the itch young horns always suffered. Beside him, the singer gazed at his grand-niece with the fond absorption Jan recognized in himself for his own young.

"The mare of which you sang," he began, uncertain quite why he was asking — and yet the singer's tale had stirred his curiosity, piquant and strong. "You never forgot her?"

The star-strewn stallion whickered softly, as though thinking back on a memory both rueful and dear.

"How could I?" he breathed. "She was extraordinary. Never after have I been able to view your folk simply as savage warmongers, suppressed by tyrants and imprisoned by laws — but as a tribe not wholly unlike my own, despite very different ways."

Jan snorted. "High time my folk abandoned the worst of our old ways," he remarked, "and adopted new."

Calydor laughed. "How strange you are. A warleader who celebrates peace. A Moondancer who eyes tradition askance."

The dark prince shrugged. He had long since left off wondering at himself.

"But the mare," he continued, "who consorted with you, then returned to the Vale — I have not heard of her. She must have guarded her daring well. In Korr's time, and his father's time, and the time of the queen before him, such a mare would have been cast out had her deeds been discovered."

The older stallion nodded. "I named that very danger in urging her to remain with me, to no avail." He sighed. "Had any way existed for me to go with her and join her folk, I would have. But I could not. Your Law barred me."

Again he sighed, more deeply now, as though resigned.

"Well, 'tis done. One cannot walk another's path, nor halt the turning of the stars, only live and seize what joys one may. I loved this mare. I would do so again, even knowing the outcome."

Jan felt an inexplicable sadness rise up in his breast. He thought of Tek. Could he ever have so resigned himself to part from her for the rest of his days? The wound was deep enough simply being parted from her for the present.

"You never saw your love again?" he asked Calydor. The other shook his head. "Perhaps she dwells yet within the Vale." Jan frowned, calculating. "She would be about the age of my dam."

"Aye," the star-thrown stallion murmured. "Sometimes I wonder if she will ever break free and return to the Plain, as she vowed to do, when the unnamed task that called her back to the Vale was done. She bade me dismiss her from my thoughts and not to wait for her. Yet I have never forgotten and have waited the years, in hope that one day we once more may meet and dance the long-dance to its end."

"The wait may not be much," Jan suggested, unsure why the matter should concern him so. "If she lives, this poppy-maned mare will travel among us when we leave the Vale next spring and trek to the Hallow Hills."

The seer glanced at him. "I have not dreamed of that," he whispered. The night breeze stirred. "Your Vale is hidden from me. The goddess conceals it. I know not why."

Calydor fell silent, gazing off across the river of stars that flowed below them. The soft lowing of far-off oncs haunted the air. The singer's ears pricked, listening. He remained still so long that Jan began to wonder if their conversation were at end. At last the other drew breath.

"After I lost my love, after she turned from me and struck out for the distant sea, I dreamed of her one final time. Álm'harat granted me that. I saw her not as she had once appeared, but older, a mare in prime rather than one just entering the first blush of her youth, still hale and fair, but one who has borne her young and seen them grown. I beheld my belovèd traversing the Mare's Back. I dare to hope therefore that I will see her again, that the promise of our first love may yet be fulfilled, to run shoulder to shoulder all the rest of our days across the wide and rolling Plain."

The broad veldt had quieted, the sound of revelers long stilled. No more contests or further sport occupied the dancing ground.

Many of the Plainsdwellers had returned to lie beside their young. Even those yet roving the long grass had hushed. Jan caught only an occasional rustle, a snort or stamp, a breathless whicker. A breeze sprang up, combing the grass, its touch pleasantly light along Jan's back.

He felt at peace, no longer stiff and sore. He turned toward Calydor, drowsing now by his tiny grand-niece, his silhouette against the star-sheened grass so familiar that Jan pondered anew. Of whom did this stranger remind him? The young prince shook his head. His eyes slipped shut. He drifted into dreams only half aware.

He dreamed he saw his dam profiled by starlight. She stood on the lookout knoll high above the Vale, gazing off toward the Plain. The twins stood beside her, horn-buds sprouted, blunt thorns upon their brows. Tek kept watch below them on the slope. All four stood silent. Jan wondered how often they held this vigil, forgetting that he dreamed. Ses murmured to his mate, then turned back to the twins. The wind lifted her forelock, fanning her magnificent mane, washed of all color by the faint light of stars.

"Can you sense him yet?"

Painted Aiony nodded. "Aye."

"Is he safe?"

White Dhattar nodded in turn. "He sleeps."

Tek climbed the slope to join them. "Where is he?"

"At riverside," her filly replied. "Among companions."

"Renegades?" the pied mare asked quickly, forgetting and using the old term for the people of the Plains.

"Plainsdwellers," Ses murmured. Tek nodded.

"A dark-blue stallion all spattered with stars," Dhattar replied. "A river of them flows overhead, and another below. Alma's eyes are everywhere."

Beside them, Ses gave a little snort. "Dark blue?" she asked quietly. "How dark?"

Dhattar butted her. "Like indigo."

Gently, she shouldered back. "And the stars?"

"Silver," Aiony told her. "His mane and tail as well. Three hooves wear silver socks."

Her brother scrubbed his chin against his granddam's shoulder. "A seer and a singer and a dancer, like Jan."

Tek shook herself. "Jan is no singer."

Dhattar and Aiony exchanged a glance. Ses said nothing.

"He knows where Korr may be found," Dhattar whispered at Tek, "or where to begin the search."

His black-and-silver sister nodded, shrugging him away from Ses. "He'll lead Jan there."

The pale mare seemed not to hear them. Her expression was distant, deep in thought, eyes gazing toward the Plain. Tek gathered her filly and foal.

"When will he return?" she asked, nuzzling them.

White Dhattar raised his eyes, blue as summer sky, with pupils black and deep as wells. "We said before. He will not return. We will not see him again till the fire from heaven falls."

Tek glanced away, rolling one shoulderblade. She could make nothing of their talk. Their granddam stirred.

"And Korr?" she asked.

The twins turned to her, their faces solemn. They said nothing. Night breeze lifted. The pied mare sighed, missing her mate. League upon league away across the Plain, the sleeping prince shifted and then lay still. He dreamed of traversing a wasteland toward distant thunder. Nearby, a tiny filly's legs twitched, flexed, dancing in dreams. The blue-and-silver stallion beside which she lay nodded over his knees. He dreamed of a mare pale as cloud at first dusk, older now, but still graceful fair, her mane red as sunset, as poppies, as flame, lifted and thrown by the freshening breeze.

Jan stirred. Dawn air held still, sky fading into grey. The summer stars had faded from bright beacons to mere specks. The dancing ground lay largely deserted. A few foals and fillies still dozed. Their sires and dams stood by. Others were just emerging from the long grass, mares leading, stallions trotting behind. Many shouldered and chivvied one another fondly, like newly pledged mates. Jan longed for Tek powerfully, and for their twins.

"Good dawn," the blue-and-silver stallion nearby him murmured. Nestled beside him, the sky-blue filly slept on.

"Good dawn," Jan murmured in reply.

Sky above brightened. Those on the dancing ground rose, shook off, some bidding companions farewell. Jan listened to hoofbeats heading off in all directions. Dawn blush touched the horizon, infusing the sky. Crimson loped from the tall Plains grass. Behind her, Goldenhair halted at grass's edge. Farther back, Jan spied others, evidently part of this new-formed group. The pale gold whinnied and stamped. Crimson approached her uncle, bowed low to one knee.

"Good dawn, my child," he greeted her.

She answered him, "Good dawn."

"So you travel with Goldenhair again," he observed.

She laughed. "Always."

"And two companions."

Glancing past the pale gold to the russet mare and the middle-blue half-grown beyond, Crimson nodded. "Newly met. We'll share the way awhile and see if friendship grows."

"Love wisely and well, my child," the seer replied. He nuzzled her filly, already half roused. "Wake, my little child. Fare gently till next we meet."

Sky shivered and stretched, rose unsteadily to her feet then shook off like a wolf cub. Her mother whickered. The filly leapt to her with a glad whistle and began to nurse.

"Ashbrindle fares not with you?" the singer observed.

The crimson mare shook her head. "He has found an old comrade and will not range with us this round." Calydor nodded. Crimson turned to her young. "Come, Bluewater Sky," she said gently. "You fed long and well, night past. We must do a little running this morn before we rest. Then I will show you how to eat grass."

The blue filly stopped suckling and looked up. "'Rass?" she

said, in a small voice, distinctly. It was the first word Jan had heard her utter. Her dam nodded, laughing.

"Aye, grass. How well you speak! Goldenhair will be delighted. Come, let us tell him your new word." She turned, and the filly trotted after her.

Calydor exclaimed, "She will be weaned and hornsprung before you know."

Crimson laughed again, tossing over one shoulder, "Then bearded and grown, as was I!"

"Fare safe, daughter," the star-flecked stallion called after his niece.

"And you, Calydor," she cried. "Fare you well, Aljan Moonbrow. May you Valefolk regain your homeland soon and cease tramping our Plain in a wartroop each spring."

Her voice was light, no malice in it. Jan saw Crimson rejoin Goldenhair and the other two. They stood consulting while the filly suckled. Most of the others had already quit the dancing ground, cantering across the Plain. The sky's rose blush had blanched to white, its stars unseen, but burning still. Sun broke horizon's edge and floated up into the sky. Calydor rose and shook himself. Jan did the same, flexing the stiffness from his legs. He joined the other in tearing a few quick mouthfuls of grass.

"Time to be off," the star-patterned stallion said, "if we mean to catch the cool of the day."

Jan nodded. Pards prowled at dawn, he knew. The two of them kicked into a lope, heading north and east across the Plain.

Calydor

★ 9 ★

At the start of all things, when time was young, Álm'harat fashioned the world and the stars and the dark between. Maker of everything, mother of all, Álm'harat walks among us in mortal shape. Sometimes she appears as a unicorn, a beautiful stallion or a fleet-footed mare, or assumes the guise of a pard in the grass, or wears the wings of a kite upon the air. Life and death she deals, each in its season, advancing her great Cycle that turns all the world and the stars.

"Once she sojourned in these parts as a mare pale as moonlight, who ranged the broad Plain and allowed none to stay her. Such a traveler was she, bearing tales from far lands, that companions dubbed her the Mare of the World. This Mare of the World fell in love with the sun, whose golden mane is burning fire. Feeling that heat, she was smitten and called out to him, but far above, he galloped on. Sprinting the Plain below, she sought to draw his gaze, but still he paid her no heed. So planting herself on the tallest rise, she whistled his name — only to see him race past overhead, aloof and unanswering.

"Undaunted, the Mare of the World asked her fellows, the birds, to fly to the sun and press her suit. They did so, but the sun stallion only flared with laughter, so hotly that some of her envoys' feathers singed and fell fluttering to earth far, far below.

The burning sun proclaimed himself too high and fair to return any meager mortal's favor — never suspecting the one who proffered was Álm'harat disguised. He would return her love, he scoffed, only if she proved herself his match.

"'He means me to fail,' the Mare of the World exclaimed when the birds flew back with their news. 'But I do not concede defeat. Mortal I am —'

"She had forgotten, of course, that she was Álm'harat, for when the goddess dons mortal flesh, she sets aside all remembrance of her true nature, that she may ken the world of her creations as they themselves do. Carefully, she gathered the fallen feathers of her friends.

"'Weave these into my hair,' she bade. The birds complied. 'Though but mortal born,' she vowed, 'a little of Alma lives in me.' So much is true. The goddess burns within us all, even the kite and the pard. 'Your feathers, my fellows, shall speed me like wings.'

"She bade the birds take strands from her mane and tail and wait. Then she traveled east through moonless night with only the light of the stars for a guide. That is why we call them Alma's eyes, for they limned her path through the dark. All night she sped until she reached the rim of the world, where daily the bright sun launches skyward, traversing the arc of stars which spans the vast ether above. There she lay in the long grass like a pard.

"Soon she saw him, the splendid sun, his brilliant fire paling the sky. Night faded. The starpath sparked under his galloping hooves. All heaven caught fire, his radiance infusing the air as he rounded horizon's rim where the starpath ascended. Then the Mare of the World sprang, flying before him, stealing his course. Her shadow fell upon the Plain, racing before the sun. He cried out that any mortal — so he thought — would dare eclipse his light.

"'Catch me if ever you can, proud sun,' she taunted.

"The pinions in her mane lifted to lend her speed. Higher she climbed throughout the morn, as the starpath swelled toward its crest at the apex of the sky. Some stars, by her heels kicked free, fell burning to the earth below. The sun called at her to halt, but she only laughed, her shadow sweeping the Plain. She reached sky's zenith barely ahead of him, her morning's slender lead slipping. As they began the long afternoon's descent down the star-path's arc, Álm'harat whistled to her birds.

"'Time to do as I have asked! Aid me if you love me, friends, for only should I best him shall I win him.'

"The birds rose, carrying the silken strands of the Mare's mane and tail. These they wove into misty nets to hinder the sun. His anger flashed. He sought to sear the billowing webs from the air, but they only melted into rain, damping his fires, despite all shouts and rumbling. All afternoon the birds played cloud-catch with the sun. Unaware still that she was Álm'harat — but feeling the goddess's power within — the Mare of the World ran on, barely two paces ahead of the sun.

"At dusk he caught her, just as they reached the starpath's terminus at the other end of the world. Far from raging now, the sun had calmed, his fires mellowed. No longer white with heat, they simmered yellow, then rosy, then amber. His temper, too, had cooled in the afternoon rains, for during his pursuit, he had deigned to gaze — truly gaze — upon this seeming mortal for the first time.

"The toss of her mane and the long curve of her throat, the plain of her back and roundness of her ribs intrigued him. Her sinewy legs and flashing heels dazzled. Her laugh, when she called, had begun to beguile him, so that when he captured her at last, 'twas no longer anger he felt, but another passion, just as ardent, but no cause for fear. His nips upon her flank were gentle, his words inviting, his touch a caress.

"Yet when he fell upon her, just where the starpath meets the earth and merges with the netherpath — which is also stars, bridging the underside of the world — she ran on. She felt the weight of his belly against her back, the heave and fall of his panting sides, the heat of him infusing her. Her skin glowed, throwing back a cooler radiance borrowed from his. She bore the heft and the heat and the light of him all along the netherpath that curves below, through darkness, seeking dawn.

"All night they sped mated. All night she carried him, and the sacred children of that union are still being born into this world. The Mare reached dawnpoint again, whence their long race had started a full day before. There the netherpath turns upward to touch easternmost horizon's rim and the starpath begins its ascent into daylit heaven. Here the sun at long last, conceding defeat, set her free.

"'You win, wild mare,' he gasped, breathless. 'Both this race and my heart. Let us pledge forever, body and soul, and never be parted.'

"The Mare of the World smiled, for she had remembered now her nature and her name. 'I am already yours,' she answered. 'I am Álm'harat. You are part of me and of my making. We have never been sundered and never can be, for I am you, and you are I, and the long dance we have been footing circles without end.'

"Álm'harat became herself again, wide as the world and the stars beyond. She became everything that was ever made or has ever been or will be. When the sun no longer saw her as the alluring, willful mare he had chased heaven and underearth to win, he cried out, desolate. But the mother of all things whispered, 'Do not fear.'

"She made an image of herself to be the sun's mate, the same compass as he and filled with his borrowed light. This new creation she called the moon, which strives to travel the starpath ahead of the sun. He must gallop his hardest to catch her up. As he gains, she wanes, spending more and more of her light. When he seizes her, by the dark of the moon, both moon and sun tread the netherpath as one, a time of miracles and strange tidings, when the world sees by the light of Álm'harat's eyes alone.

"Thus has it been for time out of mind. We of the Plain yet wear feathers in her memory. Birds take strands from our manes and tails in payment for their fletch. When Álm'harat created us, she skimmed from the moon some of her shining stuff and poured it into our hooves and horns, into the hearts and minds of all unicorns. Moondancers of the Vale commemorate the goddess at fullmoon, when she fares brightest and farthest from the sun.

"But we of the Plain honor her at moondark, when she and her mate run joined in joy, dancing the longdance to its end. This is the Great Dance, the Cycle unending. Let us live as the maker of all things invites us, as she herself has always done, withholding herself never, sharing favor with all, preferring none of her creatures above any other, loving all wisely and well."

The tales Jan heard and the days he spent in the company of the one the Plainsdwellers called Alma's Eyes were like none he had ever known. The grass grew thinner, shorter, paler, the farther north and east they strove. The green, once so savory upon the young prince's tongue, began yellowing, its sweetness soured. Waterholes became scarce. Once he and his guide sipped from a spring no bigger than a puddle — one they had searched half a morn to find. The soil grew poorer, looser, drier. Dust increased, rimming Jan's nostrils red. As the land grew hillier and grass sparser, he saw scant trace of other unicorns. Calydor's fellows, it seemed, avoided these parts.

The seer spoke of his far-traveled folk, how widely they ranged and seldom they met. He sang of pards and the heroes who had dodged them, of summer storms, flash floods, droughts. The one thing he did not speak of, Jan learned in time, was war. The folk of the Plain had no use for it. Here, those who quarreled either settled their dispute, ignored one another, or parted. Each free-born unicorn was his own ruler: Plainsdwellers attached little merit to following others and viewed obedience with varying degrees of amusement or disdain.

It occurred to Jan at length that the Vale's lore told mostly of battle: mighty warriors and contests, all struggles ended by force. The Plainsdwellers, he saw, praised heroes who turned foes into friends or averted strife. Keenly aware how Korr's violence must embody for Calydor and his folk all the worst of the Vale, the young prince strove to offer another side, recounting the end of centuries-long feuds with the gryphons and the pans. He held out hope for treaties with the seer's tribe as well. Telling of the herd's anticipated return to the Hallow Hills, he pledged his folk would harry no Plainsdwellers while passing through their lands.

"My son, your herd will not even see us unless we mean you to do so," the other replied. "We will not allow you to bait us. At your approach, we will simply vanish, returning only after you have passed."

The pair of them lay in the long grass near a tiny waterhole they had come across just at noon and there resolved to rest an hour in the heat of midday. Though the year was fast rounding toward summer's end, noon sun could still beat fierce. The young prince turned to Calydor.

"I beg you," he countered, "do not remove yourselves from us. My herd is ready for change. Warlike ways united us during our first, long years of exile. But that exile is soon to end. We must custom ourselves anew to peace."

"Peace which is to follow your war," the seer reminded him. "You mean to wrest the Hills by force, my son."

"As once they were wrested from us!" Jan found himself exclaiming. He stopped, confused, then stammered, "Thus has it been prophesied, by Alma's will. . . ."

The words trailed off. Never before had Jan realized how vainglorious the boast sounded. And yet he knew it to be true — he knew! Calmly, the star-scattered stallion gazed at him. Mirrored in the other's eyes, Jan saw himself for the first time as one seized by war, enthralled by it: ever pondering strategy and measuring potential foes while smugly spouting the goddess's permission for it all. Doubt teased at him, brought him up short.

"My son, none but Álm'harat truly knows the will of Álm'harat," Calydor quietly replied. "But this I do know: the goddess wills much that is beyond our ken. And she is both the maker and the unmaker of the world."

Jan learned much from Calydor of the singer's elusive,

wandering folk. By night, the star-marked stallion recited his people's legends, with heroes and heroines all grander than life. Wild paeans to the goddess Álm'harat he chanted, too, as well as passionate ballads extolling the joys of the longdance. The Plains-dwellers, Jan discovered, gathered for such dancing not just in late summer or early fall, but whenever they pleased. The north-ernmost reach of the Plain, which lay beyond the Hallow Hills, was warm enough, Calydor informed him, for mares to bear their young in any season.

That unicorns might know such freedom astonished Jan. Among the herd, mares conceived only during that season which yielded a spring delivery. No stallion dreamed of asking his mate to do otherwise. Had he and Tek been born upon the Plain, Jan concluded, stunned, he and she might partake of the longdance as often as they chose. Was it really nearly three years since he and his mate had pledged eternal fidelity in their courting by the Summer Sea?

The memory made his blood beat hot — but mates always took care to space their young at least two years apart. Whatever Tek's charms, the young prince would never have considered their danc-ing again until the twins were weaned — as by now they must be, he realized with a jolt. Fury and longing rose in his breast. Instead of chasing his elusive sire halfway across the Plain, he might have sported the summer beside his mate, renewing their vows.

In exchange for Calydor's godtales and ballads, Jan recited as best he could his own folk's ancient lays — until, on the fourth night, the singer gently told him he much preferred to hear of Jan's own life. The young prince blushed beneath the black hairs of his hide, certain his unpolished rendition must be the cause. Truth, he was no singer: that he knew. Yet here Calydor contra-dicted him with vehemence and surprise, insisting he had all the makings of a fine singer — timing, cadence, ear — but a heart that clearly joyed far more in spontaneous recounting than rote recitation of histories long past.

At last Jan relented, relating his battle with the wyvern queen, his sojourn among the two-footed firekeepers, his truce with the gryphon Illishar, his pact with the pans, the herd's ordeal during the usurpation of mad Korr, and of Tek, his mate, whose many trials had brought their young safe into the world. Deeply absorbed, the star-flecked seer listened.

"I have no mate, no young," he said at last. "I envy you, my son. Though life upon the Plain allows great liberty, I will say for your Vale that it lends a continuity unknown among my kind. You have friends whom you encounter every day. You do not spend your waking hours trekking from one waterhole to the next. You do not sleep each night in a newfound spot, one ear cocked for pards."

Hearing this, Jan felt a secret triumph, savoring his companion's admission that the Vale might have its merits. The young prince had liked Calydor on sight, sensed his admiration returned. He experienced the oddest camaraderie with the seer, a natural familiarity. Plainly, the older stallion enjoyed his company as well. Jan had never encountered such easy kinship before. It felt uncannily like something he ought to recognize, ought to have known in his colthood but missed somehow.

At last the Plain gave out. A great rift cleft the land as though the whole earth had pulled asunder. A steep slope led down to a flatter, nearly barren expanse, its soil a pale, poor alkaline color. Rounded hills and worn mesas surfaced here and there, slopes striated, alternating bands of soot and light. A chafing breeze blew, smelling of salt and dust. Below, Jan saw only patches of dying grass and leafless thornbriars.

"Behold, my son," the star-strewn seer told him, "the Salt Waste. According to my dreams, 'twas here my folk put the dark destroyer to flight. Legends say that this was once a vast, shallow sea. Some claim seashells and the bones of great fishes can still be found here. I do not know. I have never ventured this place, nor have I any wish. My people call this a realm of haunts, where those who can find no peace withdraw to die."

Jan stared in dismay at the vast wasteland before him, into which his mad king had fled. "How am I to find him?" he murmured. "What hope have I now?"

Calydor turned to him. "See you those mountains far, far to the east?"

The young prince peered through the wavering salt haze, barely discerned a jagged mountain range, white crags nearly fading into the paleness of dusty sky. It hovered before him, almost a dream, resembled a line of great, ridged lizards lying at rest. He nodded.

"See you where the two highest peaks pierce the sky, and the gap plunging between?"

Again, the young prince nodded. "Aye."

"My visions promise that if you keep them ever before you as you go," Calydor told him, "you will catch this dark other whom you seek long before you reach the peaks."

Almost fearing to ask, Jan breathed, "Will I succeed? Will I wrest from Korr the secret that drives him mad?"

The seer's look turned inward. "Yes, my son," he answered softly. "You will see his madness end — but may wonder after if the news you learn be worth the cost."

Gazing off toward the distant mountains, Jan scarcely heard the last of what his companion said. They were not real, he knew, these summits: merely an illusion that floated at the limit of his vision. The true peaks lay beyond horizon's rim, hidden by the curve of the world. This far-off range existed much farther away even than it seemed. Jan gritted his teeth, determined to start at once.

"Little that is edible grows upon the Salt Waste," Calydor was saying. "When you need sustenance, dash open one of the fleshy prickle-plants and take care to avoid the spines. The inside is succulent and sweet."

Jan nodded absently, storing the other's words, his thoughts fixed upon the far horizon still. He came to himself a moment later with a start and turned.

"I can never repay your aid and kindness, Calydor."

The blue-and-silver stallion tossed his head. "It was little enough. Until next we meet, my son, I bid you in Álm'harat's name, love wisely and well."

Jan felt a great sadness stab his breast, could not say whence it came. He felt desolate suddenly, as though parting from a lifelong friend. The seer seemed similarly stricken. Jan bowed low to one knee after the fashion of the Plain. The older stallion did the same. Looking one last time into the indigo darkness of the other's coat, the dance of stars that wound across, it almost seemed to Jan that he could see himself lost upon that path of stars. The young prince blinked. The illusion broke.

"Fare well," Jan bade him. "May we meet again."

He turned and began his descent down the soft, crumbling slope to the Salt Waste below.

Salt

★ 10 ★

Jan traveled across the barren waste, threading his way through banded hills. His last glimpse of Calydor had come hours earlier. Atop the slope where the Plain began, the other had reared up, whistling a long wild cry of farewell. Halting, Jan had done the same. He had not looked back again, faring on toward the gap in the far mountains, but he sensed the stallion of the summer stars watching him out of sight.

The Salt Waste stretched on and on, its monotony numbing. His eyes reddened, ears filled with blown dust, coat caked with it. Whenever he felt his throat parching and empty belly grinding, he dashed open the nearest spiny plant to taste its sour flesh. Eventually he discovered that outcroppings of what he had mistaken for pebbles were actually plants, their waxy, grey-green surfaces concealing a sweet, juicy pulp. Whenever he found these, Jan ate greedily.

Three days he trekked, sleeping only briefly. Little sting-tailed insects crept out at night. Other animals, too, apparently inhabited this desolate place. Diminutive lizard tracks scampered away over the alkaline dust. Slithering trails of serpents or worms snaked through the sand. Once he came across delicate traces of some sort of minute pig or deer. The little creatures had been feeding on wax-rinds. Their tracks fled northward, the pawprints of some predator, equally tiny, pursuing. The young prince doubted a creature his own size could long survive here.

When, on the fourth day, he encountered Korr's tracks, he nearly stumbled on past, so mesmerized had he become. The wind had fallen the night before, leaving the traces of the night creatures intact. Haze hung in the air. Jan came across a line of cloven-hoofed impressions leading east. He stopped. The imprints were large, unmistakably the king's. They staggered, sometimes curving in great circles, their maker moving little faster than a shamble.

Heart quickening, the young prince started to trot. Crumbling mounds obscured his vision. The dream of white-maned mountains floated coolly before him on horizon's edge. He found where Korr had paused to feed, tearing at thorns. He passed a spot where the king had rested, disturbing the sand beneath the scant shade of a spindly tree. Eagerly, Jan pressed on. Morning hours crept away. The sun was a fever-blaze dead overhead. He cast no shadow. The tracks wove through a meandering maze of mesas and hills.

Abruptly, his ears pricked. He heard slow hoofbeats ahead, much muffled by dust. Jan broke into a lope. He rounded a hill-mound, another. The tracks snaked on through the maze. In the stillness, the thud of his hooves, his own breathing, sounded impossibly loud. He rounded more curves. Suddenly the hoofbeats ahead of him faltered. A shrill whistle of surprise reached him, then the hard, random thumps of a warrior leaping and shying.

Jan's heart kicked against his ribs. He bolted into a run. The shrills ahead of him continued, more peals of fury now than alarm. Whistling his own warcry, the dark prince skidded around an embankment to see emaciated Korr, rearing and plunging at a thing that writhed and whipped on the ground before him. Sand flew. Fine dust floated, a smoky curtain on the air. Jan caught a glimpse of long coils pale as salt. Korr charged it. Turning, it massed itself, hood flattened, fangs bared and ready to strike.

"No!" the prince of the Vale shouted. He dashed to interpose himself between the serpent and the king. The hissing creature lunged. The mad king struck at it. "Run," Jan cried. "It's poison!"

Again the viper lashed. The young prince felt its fangs click and slide against his horn as he swept it back. Seething, it gathered itself. Jan gauged himself at the edge of the serpent's range. Korr behind him stood safe.

"Wyrm!" the mad king raved. "Would you impede me?"

Without warning, he plunged past the younger stallion and rushed at the serpent again. Jan leapt after with a cry, threw one shoulder against him. Korr shook him off with a whinny of rage. Black hooves and pale sand flew. Jan saw the viper strike. The dark king ramped and dodged.

"Stop!" Jan exclaimed, colliding with him again. "You've no proof against its sting. Let me!"

With an effort, the young prince managed to shove the older stallion aside. He pinned the serpent's body between one forehoof and the opposite hind heel, then struck its head off with his razor-edged horn. The dead thing continued to flop and bow upward even after he leapt free. Jan turned to Korr. The king stood staring at his own foreshank. Blood ran from a double wound.

"I'm stung," he said.

The prince felt the strength drain from him. His knees trembled. He could not seem to catch his breath.

"No," he whispered. "No. A flesh wound. A scratch, the venom already spent."

The king shook his head, still gazing at the wound. "Deep," he answered. "To the bone." His voice sounded petulant, perturbed. "It smarts and burns." He flexed his leg, then shook it. Blood trickled down.

"Don't," Jan gasped. Dust filled his lungs. He could get no air. Everything tasted of salt. "Stand still. Don't help the poison spread."

Korr tried to put his hoof down, but stumbled. Jan shied, his reflexes strung tauter than a deer's. The king's foreleg seemed unable to bear his weight. He stood three-leggèd, frowning. He muttered, "Numb."

"Cut the wound," Jan cried. "Bleed the poison out!"

He sprang to rake the tip of his horn across the swelling gash. Runnels of red spattered. The other stallion shook his head, staggered again.

"Late," he remarked. "Too late."

Jan felt a scream tear from his breast as Korr's legs folded. He pitched forward. A grey puff of dust welled up, swirling. The king lay struggling to rise. Jan smote the ground for lack of any serpent left to strike.

"Why?" he cried. "Why did you fly at it? What harm to have let it go?"

Korr's forehooves dug at the sand, uselessly. "It thwarted me," he mumbled.

Jan heard himself railing, unable to stop. "Why did you not let me fend it off? You've no defense from serpent stings —"

The king tossed his haggard shoulders weakly, gave up trying to rise. He murmured, "I needn't listen to you."

"You do!" Jan burst out. The landscape around him reeled. "If not because I am your son, Korr, then because I am your prince! Even a king must obey the battleprince in time of war...."

"Prince," the dark king snorted, refusing to look at him. "You're no prince. I should have let your sib have the office. I should have acknowledged her at the start."

"Lell?" Jan demanded. His sister had been but newly born when Jan had become warleader. "Lell's barely five years old, still unbearded, not yet a warrior. She's not even been initiated...."

Korr's sudden glare cut short the absurd laugh rising in his throat. "Not Lell," he snapped. "Your other sib. My firstborn. Tek's twice the warrior you'll ever be."

The king's words made no sense to him. Nothing made sense. Time stopped. Jan stood staring at the dark other. Nothing happened. Nothing moved save the airborne dust, which all around them, very slowly, was beginning to settle. The murky air gradually cleared. Jan heard his own ragged, labored breath. His lips and teeth and tongue were numb. He could not speak. Korr rambled on.

"Small matter she was born outside the Vale and by that red wych. She was an heir any prince could be proud of — until you sullied her. I warned you against courting! The pair of you pledged against my will and got your vile get. Ruined now. She'll never lead the unicorns."

The taste of salt swelled, closing Jan's throat. His gorge rose. Pale dust made the other grey as a haunt. Himself, too. "What are you saying?" he managed, barely able to whisper. "What are you saying of Tek?"

Korr examined the sand-caked wound on his leg. It barely bled. "Corrupted," he murmured. "Like all the herd. Jah-lila's to blame. And you. Weanling sop, what have *you* ever done but nuzzle up to gryphons, Renegades, and pans? As though the world were a courtship! You and your peace have betrayed Halla's legacy: eternal vengeance and war till the day we regain our rightful Hills. . . ."

Jan scarcely heard, hardly able to follow the gist of his words. "Are you saying Tek is your daughter?" he gasped. "Your firstborn — my elder sister? Out of Jah-lila? You got foals on two different mares, and the first mare still living?"

The king's head lolled. Roaring filled Jan's ears as he realized the other was nodding. He felt as though lightning had seared him. The agony was uncontainable. Boundless wasteland swallowed his cry.

"Why did you never tell me? Why?"

The king's head, dragging with weariness, lifted once more. The hollow eyes looked at him.

"I tried," he whispered. "When you went with her to the Summer Sea, I warned you against courting. . . ."

"You gave no clear warnings!" Jan shouted. "Only veiled threats that meant nothing. You urged me to choose a mare my own age — you never said Tek was your daughter! Never called her my sister."

The dark king shook his head feebly. "I couldn't. I meant never to speak of it, to . . . to spare her. . . ."

"To spare yourself!" Jan choked. "To spare yourself the shame.

You pledged yourself to Jah-lila long before you ever danced the courting dance with Ses by the Summer Sea. You raised me and Lell all our lives without telling us we had a sib . . . a sib by a different mare."

Strength returned momentarily to the withered king. His nostrils flared. "She beguiled me, that wych. No beard, round hooves, mane standing in a brush. She was not even a unicorn! I made no pledge to any unicorn mare. Our sacred pool may have given her a horn, but it could not make her one of us. I left her and returned to the Vale, telling no one that, in my folly, I had consorted with a Renegade. I bade her not to follow me. . . ."

Furiously, Jan cut off the other's storm of words. "Jah-lila is no Renegade. She comes of a different tribe, the *daya* whom the two-footed firekeepers enslave. When she escaped and fled to the Plain, she asked your succor. Drinking of our sacred mere in the heart of wyvern-infested Hallow Hills, she became a unicorn. She is one of us now, and the mother of your heir."

"I never intended —" dying Korr shrilled. "I gave my word to a mere Renegade, to no one. . . ."

"It was still your word," retorted Jan, "the word of a prince's son, the prince-to-be, grandson to the reigning queen. You pledged yourself to Jah-lila, a bond unshakable in Alma's eyes, and then deserted her."

Korr laughed, a dry, wheezing sound. His body tremored as though with cold. The sun overhead blazed shadowless. "Aye, but she found me. Tracked me all the way to the Vale. Who would have thought it? Arrived in foal for all the world to see. Yet she never shamed me, never named her unborn filly's sire. Hoping to tempt me to acknowledge her! Fool. I pretended not to know her."

Again the horrible, airless laugh. Jan's hide crawled. The king continued.

"When Teki sheltered her, all assumed him to be her unborn's sire. Neither he nor she spoke a word of denial. Teki could easily shoulder my blame — he is the herd's only healer, immune to censure. He could sire a dozen foals on a dozen dams and the herd would never cast him out. They need him — far more, it seems, than they needed me."

Korr's voice grew bitter. He sneered.

"Jah-lila haunted the Vale for months, seeking acceptance, striving to lure me back to her side. But the herd never accepted her. I saw to that."

"They accept her now," Jan breathed. He doubted the other heard. "They welcome and honor her."

"At last she departed, self-exiled to the wilderness beyond the Vale. I thought me done with her and heaved a prayer of thanks. Alma had forgiven me. My granddam the queen had died, my father Khraa become king. I was prince now. I devoted my reign to serving Alma and the Law."

"You served neither," Jan growled. "What you called Law was tyranny; what you named Alma, madness."

Korr ignored him, spoke on, gasping now.

"That very year by the Summer Sea I pledged your dam. She bore you to me the following spring. I reared you sternly, that you might never stray, as had I in my youth. I sought to keep you safe. . . ."

"To keep me ignorant!" Jan cried. "How is it, my sire, you loathe all Renegades so? Did you not once long to be one? Did you not, in your youth, once strike out across the Plain, make promises you spurned to keep — only to think better of your flight and return to the Vale?"

Korr shuddered. The dust on his coat rose and settled. "And if I did?" he muttered sullenly. "I came to my senses with none the wiser. Would you condemn me for mere folly?"

"Not for folly, but for deceit," Jan answered hotly. "You told me I was prince-to-be and deprived a princess of her birthright."

"Aye," the dark king snarled. "The red wych bore her filly in the wild, reared her there two years till she was weaned — then brought her back to the Vale and left her in Teki's care. To shame me! And never a word of who her filly's father was. I made her swear never to tell what had passed between us. All these years, her silence has tortured me, chasing my reason!"

"It is your own silence," cried Jan. "Your own silence that has maddened you."

The other sank, sagged. "But I am dying now. My silence is broken." Salt covered him. He turned glazed eyes toward Jan. His bony head looked like a skull. "So, my son," he grated, "you have wrested my secret at last." His voice was a rasp and a rattle of bones. "Has it been worth the trek?"

Jan stood unable to move, to think. The Waste all around him lay utterly lifeless, motionless, still. He groaned. "How am I to tell Tek?" he wondered, desperate, only half aware he spoke aloud. "How do I dare?"

The haggard king rolled onto his side. His frail head touched the dust, then rose with momentary strength.

"Speak of this to no one," he hissed. "Carry my secret to the end of your days. Jah-lila will hold silent. Her daughter will never rule. The herd will not dream they stand duped by a second son. Tell them, and you destroy them! They will cast you out, strip you of power. If not their prince, what are you? Who are you, if not my son?"

Jan stared at nothing, the words of the dark king still ringing in his mind. Wind hissed about his fetlocks, lifting the sand, stinging him. He had not felt it rise. It hummed, moaning. The mad king of the unicorns laid down his head. His body shuddered, tremored, stilled. His stark ribs rose, subsided, his breathing growing shallower, more labored. Jan stood fixed, swaying. The wind gusted and whipped. Salt grit beat at his ears, his eyes and nostrils. His mane and tail thrashed, lashing him.

His fallen sire lay at his feet, unmoving now. Jan scarcely recognized him, so thin and fleshless had he become. Korr's lifeless form lay like a shadow, a deep pool in the sand. Gazing down at him, Jan felt oddly disoriented, as though he were beholding a great chasm, a darkness reft of moon or stars. He had no notion how long he stood gazing into this void. The wind increased, lifting clouds of pale, bitter sand.

Jan stirred, though whether his trance had lasted a heartbeat or an age, he could not say. He felt numb. His sire was dead. He must complete the burial ritual. The prince of the unicorns bent his horntip to the sand and drew a circle around the fallen king. Wind blew the shallow depression in the sand away. Jan tried again, and yet again, to close the circle, but the wind prevented him. He tried to fill his lungs, to sing the endingsong:

"Fate has unspoken,   one of the Circle. . . ."

Rising tempest stole the words from his teeth. Salt blinded him, smothered him. Wind battered and deafened him. The world tilted, steeped in the bitter redolence of ashes and dust. Jan teetered away from the fallen king, afraid somehow that if he remained, he might fall into endless, bottomless nothingness. He tried to turn, but the wind drove him on. He managed one backward glance, and saw fine sand drifted high against Korr's side. It spilled over, pale grains streaking across the blackness of him like hurtling stars.

Jan's hooves sank, grit rising to pull him down. He struggled, aware he must keep moving or be buried in salt. The storm, coming out of the west, drove him eastward, away from the Plain. Blindly, reluctantly, he stumbled on toward the dreaming mountains — invisible now — that bounded unseen horizon's rim and bordered the end of the world.

King's Mate

★ 11 ★

Wind howled. The salt grit stung. He could move no direction other than toward the sandstorm's lee. A weight like that of the world crushed him. How many leagues had he already traveled, one torturous step at a time? Thirst tormented him. He could hardly breathe. His empty belly ached. He tried to halt, to rest, but the gale harried him. Whenever he lay down, dust drifts overtook him within moments, threatening to bury him. He rose and stumbled on.

Time proved impossible to gauge. He had no notion of night or day. The way seemed to be rising, becoming more solid. Fatigue stupefied him. He dared not stop. The ground grew firmer, its shifting granules coarser underfoot. Cold wind cut through his numbness. He felt as though his pelt had been scoured from his hide.

What woke him to himself at last was the sound of his own footfalls. He was walking, slowly, step by step, must have been doing so in a daze for he knew not how long. Numb still from the hours or days that it had flailed him, he realized the wind had ceased. He felt indescribably light. His mouth still tasted of salt. He dared not even try to swallow. But he could breathe. Pitch dark surrounded him. Night, he reasoned: moonless night.

No sound met his ears other than that of his own hooves,

scrunching loudly. Each step sank into something loose and rough and pebble-sized, but irregular in shape, and much lighter than riverstones. He felt as though he were treading great piles of cracked acorn shells. He felt muffled, dusty, caked with grit.

Jan halted and shook himself. Sand flew from his coat and mane. He twitched his ears furiously to clear them. The smell of dust rose. He felt light enough to be treading sky, not earth. He became aware of stars, not sure whether they had emerged suddenly or slowly, or whether, perhaps, he had been walking with his eyes shut.

He gazed up, lost in their brightness, trying to recognize a pattern there. They dazzled him, many more than he had ever seen. Too stunned by hunger, thirst, and fatigue, he could find no familiar constellation. He gave up. The scrunch under his hooves gave way to solid stone, rippled and hard. His hoofbeats scuffed, rang, at times struck sparks. Moonless night lasted forever.

After a while, he perceived an utter darkness to one side of him, dividing the night. A faint echo rang from that quarter. To his other side, stars blazed, filling that half of the sky as far above him as he could crane, and as far below as he could peer. The air from that direction felt empty and unimpeded. No echoes rang. A hint of breeze wafted thence, lifting his mane.

Suddenly the starless darkness fell away. He heard a quiet, continuous rushing sound, very familiar to him, but in his daze, he could not think what it was. The susurrous murmur soothed him. He had heard it many times before, he knew, though not for a very long while. A slight pressure lapped against his hooves, a cool ripple, a gentle rill.

Stars burned all around now, above and below. Those beneath him were in motion, winking and wavering, moving past him to a point seemingly only a few paces distant where, converging slightly, they simply vanished. Other stars continuously replaced them, gliding forward from behind, their fixed companions above burning steadily.

Walking among the stars, Jan reached the place where those in motion vanished, and stepped beyond it. Every heavenly light before him hung motionless. The plashing whisper continued behind, quiet, lulling. The coolness streaming against his hooves had ceased. He could not go another step. His eyes slid closed. He realized that he had just lain down. A vast, illumined void surrounded him. He had no idea where he lay. A breath of starwind sighed across him, thin and slight and very cold. He slept.

Jah-lila stood looking down at the dark pool. Though it was daylight outside the cave, here at the grotto's innermost chamber, no sunlight reached. The phosphorescent lichens from the larger, outward chamber cast little light. Few grew on the smooth ceiling above the spring. The little chamber was dim. Jah-lila gazed into the spring's dark pool. Its surface stirred, but did not break.

She saw the Salt Waste, two dark figures, widely separated and very small, converging. As though she were a kite, she watched, suspended high above. The tiny figures reflected in the pool met. She moved closer, saw the maze of low canyons, a white serpent coiled to strike. She saw the haggard king fly at it, the young prince desperate to save him. The serpent struck. The prince dispatched it. The king stood staring at his shank.

The red mare felt her breast tighten. It was the moment she had feared all the years since she had first sipped of the Hallow Hills' magical mere and become a unicorn. It was the fate she had fought so hard to stay — that the first and only love she had ever known should die of a serpent's sting. She wished then that she might halt, withdraw, end the vision here, but she forced herself on.

Jah-lila gazed deeper into the pool. The image rippled. She heard the words Korr and the one he called second-born exchanged, heard the younger stallion's cries of horror and disbelief. She saw the king collapse, saw the one he had raised from colthood standing stunned. In the dark pool before her, a colorless cave fish slipped through the lifeless form of the king. Korr's image wavered, broke, re-formed. The red mare saw the young prince trying to draw a circle in the dust.

She bent her own horn to the dark pool's bank and traced the semblance of the fallen king into the sand. Completing a circle around it, she scraped dirt onto the likeness with one round, uncloven heel, obliterating it. In the pool before her, wind lifted. Sand began to fly. The burial song rose in her throat. Jah-lila breathed upon the water. She watched the dark prince stagger away.

Softly, painfully, she hummed the endingsong through, then closed her eyes and bent to where the form of fallen Korr reflected. The water felt cool upon her tongue, quenching the song, soothing the parched ache in her throat. She drank a long time, deep, then raised her head. No image lay upon the water. Something brushed her side. Jah-lila turned. Painted Aiony stood nearby, Dhattar peering into the chamber. He came to join them.

"What saw you, Granddam?" Aiony asked her. Dha echoed her. "What did you see?"

"Your father, little ones," she answered.

"He was well?" asked Dhattar.

Jah-lila nodded. "Aye."

The filly spoke. "We've not seen him since he left the Plain."

"He's very far now," the white foal added.

Jah-lila said nothing, lost in thought.

Aiony asked her, "Is our father in the Salt Waste still?"

The red mare shook her head.

Dha's voice was hopeful. "When will we see him?"

Their granddam bent to nuzzle first him, then his sister. "You know well enough," she answered. "Hist now, or your dam will come looking."

She herded them away from the spring, into the outer chamber. Her daughter, Tek, was just coming in the entryway. "There you are," the pied mare exclaimed. "I sought you everywhere. Off, now. Outside. Your granddam has work, and Lell wants to show you the rueberries she found."

She chivvied each gently and scooted them toward the grotto's egress. Beyond it, the daylight shone. Whickering and giggling, they went. The red mare watched them disappear, heard Lell's whistle of greeting, the twins' answering calls. Tek turned to her dam.

"You found him," she said, voice low, urgent with certainty.

Jah-lila nodded. The pied mare closed her eyes, gave an out-breath of relief.

"At last," she murmured. "Safe?"

"Aye."

Her daughter studied her by flickering lichenlight. "Korr," she said softly. "You found him as well."

Again the red mare nodded. She heard the wariness in her off-spring's voice, the loathing and dread.

"So Jan has found his sire," she breathed.

"Found and lost him," Jah-lila replied, heart heavy as stone. The lichenlight was far too bright.

Tek stepped directly into her path. "And?"

"And Korr has spoken."

"Then Korr's madness is healed?" The pied mare's words held sudden hope.

"His madness is over," the red mare replied wearily.

"Then Jan will be returning —" Tek cried, full of gladness now. Jah-lila cut her off.

"Nay. Not at once."

Tek stared at her, outraged. "Why not?" she demanded. "What can Korr do to keep him from us still?"

The red mare drew a great breath, spent to the bone. She felt fragile as a bird's egg.

"Daughter," she said. "Jan will return to you; I have promised. In time. I beg you now, let it rest. Farseeing drains me. Let us go outside."

Her daughter pressed against her, instantly contrite. "Forgive my impatience," she murmured. "I miss him so."

The red mare leaned into her daughter's warmth, then nipped her gently and nosed her out the grotto's egress ahead of her. Jah-lila waited until her daughter's shadow passed, muffled hooffalls ringing out on the slope below, heading down. The light of mid-day stabbed the red mare's eyes as she rounded the bend to stand in the cave's entryway. Lell and the twins' whistles and whickering drifting from far upslope as Lell shouted, "This way!" and the twins insisted, "Hey up!"

Much nearer, on the hillside below, Jah-lila spotted her daughter trotting toward Ryhenna and Dagg. The coppery mare was, like the red mare herself, a runaway from the city of two-footed firekeepers. With Jan's help, she had come to live within the Vale. Drinking of the moon's sacred pool in the Hallow Hills, as the red mare once had done, had given Ryhenna her spiral horn. The pied warrior Dagg, Jan's shoulder-friend, had pledged with her little over two years gone, and their tiny foal, Culu, suckled at her flank.

Idly, Jah-lila watched her daughter converge on the trio down-slope as she blinked the sunlight from her eyes. Another unicorn stood by, coat palest cream in the noonday sun, her mane like burning poppies. Jah-lila turned and the chestnut eyes of Ses, Korr's mate and the prince's dam, found her own black-green ones. She whispered, "Jan?"

The red mare murmured, "Alive."

A long pause. Very long. "And Korr?"

Jah-lila gazed at her. "A serpent."

The pale mare started. Her eyes winced shut, her whole frame rigid. She stood racked with a recurrent trembling that might have been suppressed sobs. When she spoke, the red mare scarcely heard. "I feared it."

Silence. The sun beat down.

"I should have told him," Ses gasped suddenly, her voice strangled. "He never knew I knew. So many times I longed to tell Korr all. If I had. . . ."

Jah-lila cut her off quickly, firmly. "No word of yours, however well meant, could have spared him."

The pale mare choked back tears. "I am to blame . . . ," she started.

Jah-lila touched her withers. "Never! Do not shoulder a burden that is Korr's alone. It has lain within his power all these years to speak out, free himself — but always he refused, afraid to confront his past. Till now, at the very end, too late."

At last, the pale mare spoke: "He confided to Jan? Told him of Tek?"

Jah-lila nodded. "Everything. All that he knew."

The pale mare gathered herself, fighting for breath.

"Do not fear," the red mare bade her, "for he will weather it."

Ses set her teeth. "Should we tell the others?"

"Not until your son returns."

The prince's dam opened her eyes. "Should we announce Korr's death?"

Again, the red wych shook her head. "The elders would only declare Jan king. Let us wait. When he returns, he will bring that news with all the rest."

Ses blinked hard. "It will tear the herd apart."

"The herd is stronger than you think," Jah-lila answered, "and primed for change. Your son has seen to that. It was why he had to be their prince, though he can never now become their king."

The pale mare snorted. "Jan's never wanted to be king." Her gaze wandered. "And Lell growing up so reckless wild. . . . All this time you and I have kept our peace. Both held our tongues, praying for Korr to speak, save himself, be healed."

"Can you doubt that had you opened your heart, spoken freely to him, he would have cast you out, and Jan, and your youngest never have been born?"

Ses shook her head and whispered bitterly, "No doubt. But forebearing has been hard. So very hard."

Gently, Jah-lila shouldered against her, as much for her own comfort as to lend the other strength. "Never forget that Tek, Jan, and Lell all have their part to play in winning the Hallow Hills."

The red mare stood silent. Above, Lell and the twins were almost out of sight. Below, Tek had reached the other three. The pale mare's sigh was painful, deep.

"He was not so cruel in his youth," she said. "He was

magnificent, magnanimous. It was only later, when bitterness consumed him that I could bear him no more. When he grew so cold toward Jan, so heartless of Lell. Before that, for many years, I loved him well."

Jah-lila nodded. "As did I. It is all lost now. Undone by a serpent's sting." Her heart ached. Resolutely, she turned her thoughts ahead. "Let us mourn and ready ourselves," she murmured to Ses. "The end of all is soon to be, and your young Jan-with-the-Moon-upon-his-Brow must lead us there."

World's End

★ 12 ★

Dawn woke him, its greyness paling the air with the first light he had seen in an eternity. Heavy-headed, half-sleeping still, Jan watched the sun emerge from dark caverns housing the netherpath. The fiery stallion leapt onto the steep incline of the starpath, his radiance blazing around him in a burning sphere. Full tilt, he galloped up the endless bowed and rocky path of stars.

The dream passed. Jan found himself lying on a rocky promontory. Sun's featureless disc, inflamed by dawn, floated at eye-level dead ahead. No horizon lay before him, only sky above and mist below. Disoriented, Jan stared. The flat, limitless Salt Waste had vanished, along with its sweltering heat. A cold tang to the air told him he was now much higher.

Sky ahead shone white where the sun burned, paling the stars, but overhead was darkly, intensely blue, almost evening's shade. The trickle of breeze felt thin, the air oddly bodiless. Jan found himself breathing deeply, despite lack of exertion. Below and before him lay nothing but cloud. The narrow promontory on which he lay jutted out into the empty air.

The rock itself was barren black, of a sort he had not seen before. Fused and burned, it appeared as though it had once been thickly liquid, like oozing pitch, then hardened. It felt heavy, utterly solid beneath him, like the substance of skycinders. It echoed faintly, subtly amplifying a low, gentle rustling behind him. Jan realized he had heard it all night as he slept.

Turning his head, the dark unicorn saw the jut on which he lay sloped steeply down to a broad ledge adjoining a sheer cliff face. The ledge narrowed and curved around the cliff on either side. Jan could not see where it led. Down the escarpment's face from above streamed a curtain of water, the stone's featureless blackness visible beneath the swiftly moving glaze.

Reaching the spacious ledge, the transparent fall fanned out, rippling and murmuring, before spilling in wafts of pale spray to the white clouds below. The sheet of water drenching the ledge was less than hoof deep. Jan realized he had felt its coolness against his heels the night before, seen the stars reflected there, slipping over the rim into emptiness below.

Understanding gripped him then that one step farther, or to either side, would have taken him, too, over the edge. He lay on the promontory, breathless, staring at the colorless flow of water washing the cliff. The darkness behind its gleam seemed not solid but empty, holding nothing, not even stars. A pulsebeat or a millennium later, Tek's likeness formed itself before him.

Mottled like the moon she stood, sad seeming, poised as though watching for something beyond her sight. Longing rose in him, and then a tide of nausea. He remembered Korr's words. They clung to him. Salt welled in his throat, choking him. Tek's filmy image rippled in the evermoving glints and shadows of the dark waterfall.

She is my mate! The silent cry rang through his mind. *She cannot be my sister!* His heart knotted. He felt as though it might burst. *The herd will cast me out. And her* . . . His belly lurched. The sky above wheeled. Cold tremors shook him. *What will become of our young?*

For a moment, Tek's image seemed to look straight into him. Brow furrowed, ears up-pricked, she appeared to be listening. Jan flinched and turned away. Shaky with hunger and thirst and the thin air's chill, he gathered his limbs, managed to rise. Despair enveloped him. Before him plunged the abyss.

He stared at the mist swirling far, far below, caught glimpses of dark ridges, all blanketed with the same. When had the Salt Waste given way? He had no idea, no notion how he had come here. It was as though he had stepped from the earth, walked among stars, then crossed back into the world here, among the clouds.

He stood swaying. His shifting weight dislodged a stone. Silently, it plummeted. He found himself thinking, *How effortless, simply to fall* . . .

The clang of hooves roused him. Distinct but distant, they moved at a walk: half a dozen sets, coming from below and around the bend of the broad, wet ledge. The dark unicorn turned, careful, suddenly, of the perilous drop-off. On the black escarpment before him, Tek's image had disappeared. Only darkness loomed behind the falling water.

Above the murmur of the waterfall, sound carried undistorted. Underlying the hooves' faint, rhythmic tramp, the young stallion detected a thrum of voices. The hard, black rock hummed with the sound, vibrating ever so slightly. Jan felt the sensation as a whisper in his bones. The hoofbeats neared, climbing toward his level, and the voices clarified. He distinguished words, a chant:

> "Red Halla's royal scouts roved forth,
> Explored the Plain's edge east and north,
> Sought scarlet dragons' Smoking Hills
> Beyond bare Saltlands' bitter rills.
> Four scouts fared forth, fast shoulder-friends,
> Climbed clouded cliffs where world ends,
> And, ragged ranks reduced to three,
> Were warned of wyvern treachery
> By Mélintélinas, lithe queen
> Of dragons languid, long, and lean.
> One scout sped south, strove to return,
> Lest Halla, herd, and homeland burn.
> His fellows fallen, stranded here,
> Have heard no word four hundred year.

Their daughters' sons bide, yearning yet
For news of Halla's offspring's get
That wyrms lie vanquished, Hallows freed
By valiant victors' distant deed.
Come outlander with tidings and
His name shall be the Firebrand.
More swart than midnight swept of stars,
The moon athwart his brow bescars.
One heel whicked white by wyvern stings,
His flame the final firefall brings.
We dragons' denmates must remain
Till Firebrand fetch us home again. . . ."

A line of unicorns appeared around the bend. They were all
smallish, stocky, with shag thick as the dead of winter. Their
beards were bristling, their fetlocks thickly feathered. Their manes
stood up an inch or two before flouncing to one side. Perhaps
half a dozen filed onto the black, water-washed ledge, all darkish:
charcoals, deep blues, an earthen red. Most were roans, Jan noticed, with a dapple, two brindles.

As they caught sight of him, their words abruptly ceased. Only
the lead unicorn had chanted, the others sounding a harmonious
drone. He was a young stallion, his coat berry-colored, almost
maroon, and frosted with paler hairs. He and his little band stared
up at Jan, balanced above them on his slender jut of rock.

"Hail," their leader called up, eyeing him curiously. "Who be
you? Be you come for the Congeries?"

The dark prince stared in turn. The last creatures he had expected to encounter so far from home were unicorns.

"Jan," he managed, voice a gluey mumble. Bowing his head
made the world reel. "My people call me —"

The words caught in his throat — for he realized that no matter
how the herd might hail him, he was not their prince. By rights,
Tek should be princess, she who was Korr's secret, firstborn child,
his own belovèd mate and the mother of his young. Cold sickness
surged in Jan.

"Care!" He heard the other's cry only faintly. "Come down!" As through haze, he saw the maroon start nearer. "Why stand you on the brink?"

The dark unicorn felt his balance right, grasped only then how close to falling he had just come. Unsteadily he picked his way down the rocky slant to the broad, drenched ledge. The young maroon gazed frankly at his flowing mane, lightly fringed heels, at his midnight coat and silky beard. Behind, the others murmured and stared. Jan realized only then that the frayed remnants of Illishar's feather still hung amid his hair.

"I be Oro," his hosts' leader was telling him, bowing in turn, "come for the Congeries. But what manner of unicorn be you, with a falling mane and pelt so dark and fine? What people be these of whom you speak? Whence hail you?"

"I —" Again, Jan faltered. Never before had he hesitated to declare himself Korrson, born of the Vale. Now such an admission appalled him. "Storm drove me across the Salt Waste," he stammered, "from the Plain. . . ."

Not a lie exactly. His head throbbed. The world receded. His knees felt dangerously weak.

"The Plain?" Oro's voice vibrated with sudden urgency. "You hail not of here but from beyond?"

The others buzzed excitedly. Jan could not discern their words above the plash of running water.

"What is this place?" he gasped, locking his legs to keep from falling. "Where have I come?"

Oro cocked his head. "Dragonsholm — or, as those in the time of Halla called it, the Smoking Hills."

Jan raised his head, turned to gaze at the small, shaggy unicorns before him.

"What do you know of Halla," he panted, "ancestral princess of my folk?"

He saw the maroon unicorn's eyes widen.

"The Hallows!" those behind Oro exclaimed. "An he claim ancient Halla, then he hail of the Hallow Hills."

Jan shook his head, careful not to unbalance himself. "Nay,

though I have pilgrimmed there. I am from the Vale," he said slowly, "many leagues to the south. There my people settled after Halla's defeat."

Again the hubbub, mixed with cries of consternation. "Defeat? Halla defeated — slain?"

"Not slain," he explained, "but forced to flee." His forelock had fallen into his eyes. He tossed it back. "Within the year, my folk intend . . ."

The sudden hush that fell was deafening. Most of the party started and drew back, some nearly touching the clear curtain of water behind. Only Oro held his ground, staring up wide-eyed at the dark unicorn's brow. Jan saw others' anxious glances, heard excited whispers:

"Come outlander with tidings, and/His name shall be . . ."

"Firebringer," Jan murmured, "so my folk call me."

Still staring, Oro drew near. He quoted softly, "More swart than midnight swept of stars,/The moon athwart his brow be-scars. . . ."

He seemed to come to himself, bowed deeply before Jan. His voice, at first uncertain, gained in strength.

"Be most welcome among us, swart Firebrand, outland born, moon-browed. Come below! Sing at our Congeries, whither we, already overdue, now hasten."

To the rear of him, his fellows began ducking hurriedly into the flat darkness behind the shallow waterfall. Jan blinked, stared, unable at first to comprehend what he was seeing. Swiftly, one by one, Oro's band walked straight into the dark, sheer stone — over which the clear watercurtain streamed rippling — and disappeared. The roan maroon was the last to go, backing away from Jan. His joyous words rang ghostly above the water's patter.

"All Dragonsholm must hear your news! Four hundred year have we awaited it, and you."

The Netherpath

★ 13 ★

W e ourselves hail of the Hallow Hills," Oro was saying, "four hundred summer ago."

He trotted alongside Jan. Moments earlier, as the dark stallion had followed the mountain unicorns from the ledge, he had found himself passing not into solid rockface, but through falling water, which sluiced the dust from his pelt, into the narrow opening of a steeply slanting cavern. Promising rest and sustenance below, Oro and his fellows sprang with careless agility along the dim, rocky path — at times less a tunnel than a shaft. Jan followed as nimbly as he could.

"We be the Scouts of Halla," the young maroon continued, "descendants of the original four dispatched to gather news of wyrms when that verminous race first squirmed its way with honey-tongued lies into our own far Hallows. One of the four died, and another departed again to bring word to our waiting princess. We do not know if he succeeded, or what befell if indeed he managed to warn her of wyvern treachery in Dragonsholm before their flight to the Hallow Hills. You say the wyrms defeated Halla? That she fled north to some place called the Vale?"

Jan nodded, weariness weighing him. It was nearly all he could manage simply to stay on his feet.

"Each winter at Congeries we sing of Halla's deeds," Oro

informed him, "and of the tragedy which parted our ancestors from her so long ago. We honor the line of Halla yet and hail the far Hallows our true home."

Jan looked at the shaggy maroon trotting just ahead, negotiating the treacherous terrain with ease. "Did neither of your two forebears ever depart?"

Oro shook his head.

"What held them here?"

The other snorted. "Wounds," he answered. "Exhaustion. Then young. Then age." He sighed. "None of us born after have ever seen the far Hallows."

"Have your folk never traveled thither since?" A furrow creased the dark unicorn's brow. "Did none ever seek to find the Hallow Hills?"

"The Saltlands form a daunting barrier," the young maroon replied. "After our progenitors died, none knew the way. Moreover, the shifting steeps to western south be at times impassable."

"Only at times?" Jan felt the furrow on his brow deepen. Though till now too few in number to reoccupy the Hallow Hills, forty generations of his own folk had pilgrimmed there. The resignation of Halla's Scouts to remain so long from their ancestral lands puzzled him. "Then what keeps you here?"

"Our hosts keep us," his escort replied, clearly misunderstanding his meaning entirely. "They have sheltered us since our first forebears came. They subsist a rare long while. Many who greeted Halla's original scouts be living still."

"Hosts?" Jan inquired.

"The red dragons," the maroon-colored roan answered, "who settle these steeps, which be drenched in swirling clouds of their slumbering breath. By their grace, peaks hereabouts hold stable and still, that we need not fear."

The dark unicorn shook his head, not understanding. His companion chatted on.

"All summer we forage the lower scarps, where the bristlepine and the rock lichens green. Each winter we climb to the cave-mouth and take the netherpath to a Congeries, where we feed upon the cave straw, the waternuts and milky white mushrooms that flourish below. Many pass the time in the Hall of Whispers, singing of Halla and of other heroes for our own and dragons' ears."

"The red dragons," Jan murmured. Hunger and thirst had fogged his memory. Slowly, he recalled. "They who once cherished our enemies the wyverns before those wyrms rebelled and fled, seeking refuge in our Hallow Hills, which they overran. Before that battle, Halla sent her scouts to consult the dragons' queen, Mélin . . . Mélintél . . ."

"Yea, Queen Mélintélinas," Oro exclaimed. "You do wit of our red dragons, then."

"Too little," the dark prince of the Vale replied. His mouth tasted of cobwebs and dust. "Tell me of them."

"They be vast," the young maroon responded, "and spend their lives underground, lost in what we deem slumber, but they call contemplation. Betimes they wake, but only rarely do they stir."

Jan turned to study his comrade. "Will I see them?"

Oro sighed and shook his head. "Unlikely. Most of my kind live whole lives without setting eyes on them, so deep do our dragons lie. No unicorn could pass into these mountains' fiery heart unscathed."

The dark unicorn considered. "How do you know of them, then?" he asked his shaggy guide. "And they of you?"

"We hear them," the young stallion replied. "They speak to us at Congeries. Their words reach us in the Hall of Whispers. All winter they hark our songs, our tales, while they meditate and dream."

Jan found himself scarcely able to take in his companion's words, so far had thirst and hunger dulled him. The maroon-colored scout rattled on, and the dark unicorn of the Vale heeded as much as he could. This descent by what Oro called the netherpath was often precipitous. The tunnels themselves looked like gigantic worm hollows eaten into the dense black rock. Lightwells provided illumination. From time to time, the tunnels passed beside breaks in the outer wall, allowing views either of sheer canyons or drifting cloud. Once from such a view, Jan spied distant fountains of steaming water shooting skyward, accompanied by rumbles like thunder. The tunnels themselves occasionally shook. As Jan and his companions descended deeper, the lightwells grew rarer, then altogether ceased. Soon the only light came from cave lichens, glowing pale shades of blue and amber, yellow and mauve. In places, small luminous creatures like crickets meandered the walls.

Though Jan frequently heard the soft plash of water, the tunnels themselves were warm and dry. A gentle heat radiated from the black rock itself, which carried sounds softly yet distinctly — over great distances, it seemed. Several times, the party passed cavernous cracks lit by a shifting, reddish glow. Gazing down into one, Jan saw very far below a sluggish river of fiery stuff. When he asked what it was, Oro responded, "Dragonsflood."

The path they traveled, though steep, was well worn. Generations of hooves had smoothed even so hard a surface as the ringing black stone. Other tunnels beside which they passed seemed long abandoned, coated along their interiors with pale, smooth, crystalline stuff. Lichens did not grow there, nor cave crickets crawl, but the iridescent crystal conducted light, providing a ghostly glimmer along such tunnels' length. Passing the first of many, Oro snorted as if catching wind of something foul.

"Those hollows once were wyvern ways, before our dragons cast them out. Slithery wyrmskin contains a volatile oil which rubs off as wyverns glide, leaving behind a shining trail which hardens over time."

Jan nodded, little needing the other to tell him so. He had discovered as much during his first pilgrimage, when a wyvern queen had lured him underground and tempted him to betray his folk. The wyvern dens underlying the Hallow Hills were thickly coated with such shimmering crystal.

"We do not tread there," Oro added, hurrying past along their own dark, winding path. "Wyrmsoil be flammable, the hardened residue as well. During their sojourn here, the wyrms lay ever in danger of fire."

Jan stumbled, sluggish. The trail led endlessly down and down. Unlike the pliant heels of Oro and his fellows, his own fire-hardened hooves clanged and sparked against the ringing black rock. He marveled at these small unicorns' deft maneuvering along the rocky steeps. They seemed more shaggy, curl-horned sheep than unicorns. He himself had to place each step with utmost care lest he plummet into crags the bottom of which he could not see but which sounded, from the echo of falling scree, interminably deep.

At last the trail leveled off. Before them lay a great cavern, vast in its expanse. Entering, Jan could not discern whence the dusky illumination came. Much of the dimly lit chamber was shrouded in darkness. Oro's companions hurried to either side where, the prince of the Vale realized, a large assembly of other unicorns waited expectantly among the shadows. All faced inward, toward the chamber's heart, and all, so far as Jan was able to discern in the murky light, resembled one another as closely as Oro and his band: small, dark, shaggy brindles, dapples, and roans with half-standing manes.

His maroon-colored guide was leading him forward, out onto the chamber's wide floor, which, Jan saw, was littered with great pebbles, all roughly round, some smooth as riverstones, some faceted as bees' eyes. Of many colors they gleamed — deep amber, darkest blue, violet so pure it was nearly black, swarthy gold — but reds predominated. Most, especially the larger stones, ranged in hue from dark crimson to wine red, from russet and ocher to vermilion and scarlet. They reminded Jan of the dim, smoldering coals of a fire long perished.

Among the stones lay crystalline pillars, smoothly irregular in shape, all fallen on their sides, some with bulbous knobs at either end. Other crystal forms resembled rotted treestumps, overturned. These squat, pearlescent masses were full of openings. A long trail of them wound snakelike across the chamber's length, most nested one against another, others lying askew. Large, semitransparent leaves or shells lay everywhere, brittle as fanclams and more numerous than the jewels. They, too, were mostly red, looked almost like enormous fish scales. Blearily, Jan's eyes swept the trove, unable to take it in.

"What place is this?" he mumbled, stumbling to a stop as Oro halted at the chamber's heart.

Magnified, the echo of his voice leapt away from him on every side, less jarring than a shout, but just as penetrating. Jolted, Jan listened to the sudden sound's reverberations, already dying. Leaning near, the maroon stallion scarcely breathed, though the prince of the Vale heard him distinctly as mothwings beating against a leaf.

"The queen's vault," he answered, "known as the Hall of Whispers. Peace, now. I must announce you."

They stood among the jewels and shards and crystal boles, very near a massive oblong boulder. One end formed a great flattened dome. The other tapered to a ragged, broken point. Two smooth, symmetrical hollows gaped from the translucent dome, one on either side of the tapering cone. At dome's crest, between the hollows, dipped an oval depression. It was filled with clear fluid, sparkling though absolutely still, its dark, reflective surface smooth as skin. Jan gazed longingly at the well-spring. His parched throat burned.

"Hail," Oro beside him said, without so much as raising his voice. Nevertheless, his words filled the chamber. Those assembled at the chamber's periphery responded, "Hail."

Each must have spoken no louder than a murmur, yet the collective ring was strong and clear. Jan thought he detected other voices, too — deeper and more resonant than unicorns' — lost among the rest.

"I beg you forbear our latecoming," the young maroon continued. "Rockfall day past delayed our climb. Then, just as my fellows and I reached Streaming Ledge hard by the veiled ingress to the netherpath, we met a stranger on the brink of dawn."

Again the echoing murmur, curious, even excited now. The ranks ranging the vast hall's edge shifted and stirred. This time Jan could not distinguish words, but once more he sensed, blended amongst the others, strangely timbred voices which were not of his own kind.

"By me he stands," Oro announced, his timing and cadence clearly that of a singer, "an outlander called Firebrand, with the moon-marked brow. He comes from beyond, over Saltland and Plain, bearing news of lost Halla, our sovereign princess, and the wretched wyverns who wrested from her the Hallow Hills."

The uproar that greeted these words was deafening: shouts of surprise, exclamations, disbelief, calls for Oro to explain. Jan flattened his ears, overwhelmed by the rolling waves of sound. Beside him, the young maroon stood calmly, undismayed — perhaps even a little pleased — by the upheaval his news had occasioned. An instant later, the tumult vanished as voices infinitely fuller and stronger than any unicorn's spoke, extinguishing all other clamor.

"Welcome," the first of these new, resonant voices said, and others echoed it. "Welcome. Welcome . . ."

The words seemed to come from all directions. Casting his gaze, the dark unicorn strove to locate their source.

"Welcome to Dragonsholm, Firebrand." A fourth voice spoke. Others chorused, "Firebrand. Firebrand . . ."

Their pure, even tones filled the hall like the calling of oncs or the belling of hounds, richly pleasurable to harken. Jan felt no fear of these unseen speakers, wherever they might be. All were female, he sensed. The timbre of their voices, so much more powerful than those of his own folk, somehow told him so. He sensed, too, that regardless of how near they sounded, in reality they lay many leagues distant, the black rock carrying their words to him and his to them.

"Hail, red dragons," he answered, "holders of the Smoking Hills, hosts to the Scouts of Halla, my people's long-lost kin."

Around him, the hushed unicorns stirred, ears up-pricked, listening. Oro stood no longer at his side, Jan realized. He glimpsed him just joining the edge of the crowd. The prince of the Vale stood alone by the great crystalline boulder with the pool in its crown.

"You are called Firebrand," a dragon voice said.

Another, speaking just on the heels of the first, asked, "Are you the one?"

"The one of whom the Scouts have spoken," still another voice continued, "destined to lead them back to their Hallow Hills?"

"You have traveled far," still others added. "You must be weary."

"I am Aljan," the dark unicorn answered, and indeed, he felt nearly mazed with weariness, unsure how many hours or days he had gone without water and food. "My folk call me Firebringer, and Moonbrow." But not prince. He would not tell them the folk of the Vale called him prince. "It is they I mean to lead in retaking the Hallow Hills. As for the Scouts of Halla, I cannot say."

"Tell us this tale," the dragon voices responded.

"The tale of you."

"The tale of your journey."

"All season lies before us."

"It must be a wondrous tale."

Jan felt his knees growing weak. The dark room spun. He heard murmurs of concern from those in the shadows, saw Oro start toward him.

"But sip first," the voices of dragons invited. The maroon stallion halted, hesitated. The dragons lilted on.

"Sip."

"Sip of the queen's pool beside you."

"Turning, Jan tried to focus on the natural basin of water in the huge white boulder's crown. Oddly, though its surface lay perfectly still, it seemed to bend and shift somehow, as though currents beneath its surface created eddies. As he bent to drink, the depression's shallow bottom appeared to recede from him. He caught glimpses of comets and suns, of unicorns hurtling across a field of stars — or was it a starlit Plain?

Jan shook his head. He closed his eyes, sure that fatigue was causing him to dream. His mouth touched the water, and he was surprised to find it warm, not cool. As the water filled his mouth, the fantastic notion came to him that he was drinking stars. He swallowed once. The pleasantly tepid fluid seemed slightly thicker than water, its taste mildly acerbic, yet at the same time like balm. He had prepared to draw in long drafts, but strangely, after the first sip, he felt entirely satisfied.

He had been speaking, he knew, for a very long time. Jan felt wholly detached, free of hunger, thirst, and fatigue. Time seemed suspended. The sea of figures before him shifted and changed, Oro's the only one he was able to distinguish with certainty. His own voice, filling the vast, dimly lit chamber, sounded unlike himself, like the voice of another, a singer's cant from the one with whom he had traveled upon the Plain, the one with the star-flung coat. What had been his name? *Summer Stars.*

The dark unicorn had no idea how long he had spoken, telling the unseen dragons and the shadowy Scouts before him everything about his people's history, how lying wyrms had defeated Halla four hundred summers gone, driven her and her small surviving band from the Hallow Hills. How they had come upon the Vale after long wanderings and taken refuge, there to grow strong and numerous again, in preparation for recapturing the Hallow Hills.

He spoke of his own life, how he had been reared by the king of the unicorns and, in his youth, faced a wyvern queen in her den. His hooves now struck sparks, his horn, hardened by wyvern sorcery, grown keen and hard enough to pierce even the toughest wyvern bone. He had dwelt half a year with two-footed firekeepers, learning the secret of their flame. His folk all hailed him Firebringer. Forging alliances with gryphons and pans, he had made his herd proof against wyvern stings. This coming spring, they would leave the Vale and march into wyvern-held Hallow Hills to retake them in Alma's name.

He spoke of the king of the Vale run mad and of pursuing him across the Plain. He spoke of his mate, pied Tek the warrior mare, a singer, wondrously fair, firstborn child to the late king who, serpent-stung to death upon the Waste, left the Vale in his daughter's charge. Queen of the unicorns she reigned, though she did not yet know it. Mother to twin heirs, a filly and foal. The only thing he did not reveal was his own parentage, never naming himself Son-of-Korr or prince. Despite his oddly calm, loosened-tongued state, he could not bring himself even now to face the horror spat at him by dying Korr, that he and his mate shared a single sire.

The voices of dragons spoke no more. The Scouts of Halla listened rapt. When he spoke of Tek, they cheered. Jan had no awareness of the passage of time, speaking on as in a dream. Neither night nor day penetrated the depths of Queen Mélintélinas's Hall. Figures among the crowd came and went as he spoke. He felt no need for food or drink or sleep. At times, he realized, he had ceased to speak, and the Scouts of Halla spoke, or sang, or chanted their own history: the journey of their four ancestors over the Plain, across the Salt Waste to the Smoking Hills.

Here, from Queen Mélintélinas, they had learned the wyverns' secret past: that wyrms had stolen dragonsfire, seeking to seize these dark steeps for their own, only to be driven off at last by the red firedrakes who once had sheltered them. The wyrms had wandered then, surviving the Salt Waste and the wide grass Plain until they slithered into the Hallow Hills and lied their way into a truce with the unicorns who dwelt there — all the while planning to betray them and seize their lands as once they had striven to seize the red dragons'.

The voices of Oro and his fellows sounded through the cavern in long, resonant notes. While one singer chanted a melody, four or six others droned a background chord which changed as the song progressed. These airs — some solemn, but many lively — filled the chamber's vast expanse. Jan marveled how the great hall enhanced sound and channeled it, so it seemed, to all the depth and breadth of the Smoking Hills. He imagined his words and those of the singers reaching out along all the netherpaths to wash against the ears of dragons slumbering, or perhaps listening, far underground.

At last he became aware that all voices had ceased, his own and those of Oro and the rest. A silence pervaded the dusky chamber that was neither cold nor ominous. Jan felt suspended still, untouched by thirst, hunger, or fatigue. Once more Oro stood beside him near the great crystalline boulder. The shaggy throng of mountain unicorns that once had kept their distance had moved closer now. A new voice spoke, one the dark unicorn had not heard before: a dragon's voice.

"Well sung," she sighed, and the echoes whispered, "Sung. Sung . . ."

A murmur passed through the crowd. Jan heard gasps of "The queen! The queen!"

"Aye," she answered. "You have wakened me, and the song your words have woven has entered my dreams."

The dark unicorn heard Oro's delighted, breathless laughter, saw playful nips and gleeful chivvying exchanged among many around him, though all seemed mindful of decorum, at pains to maintain a respectful hush.

"Of one singer I would hear more," said the dragon queen, her strange voice penetrating yet mellifluous, "the outlander who calls himself Aljan. Oro, who escorted him on the netherpath, guide him, I pray you, to my chamber below."

Jan sensed a sudden change in the hall. The unicorns around him froze, caught in their breath with expressions of uncertainty, even alarm. He himself felt nothing, neither terror nor joy. Beside him, Oro tensed.

"Great queen," he began, as if straining for calm.

"Peace," she bade him, almost gently. "Has he not drunk the dragonsup? Would I send for him if to do so would bring him harm?"

Her words seemed to calm the Scouts, though glances still darted among the company. The young maroon swallowed.

"And I, great queen?" he asked, nearly choking as he glanced at the shallow, fluid-filled depression in the dome of the huge crystalline boulder beside which he and the dark prince stood. "Am I, too, to sup?"

"Not yet," she answered. Jan sensed amusement just beneath her tone, saw Oro heave a soundless sigh of relief. "Do but lead him as far as safely you may, then instruct him the way to journey's end."

The words rang briefly in the still chamber. A moment of silence followed. Then quickly, quietly, the crowd began to disperse. The scores, perhaps even hundreds of small, shaggy unicorns moved near silently, melting back into the shadows to exit the great hall, through what egress the dark unicorn could not see. Soon he discerned from an almost indistinguishable change in the soft echoes in the chamber that he and Oro now stood alone.

"We must depart," the maroon beside him breathed. "First we must climb a little, and then descend a very long way for you to reach the queen."

The roan stallion led Jan to the far side of the immense chamber. The dark prince spied an inclined path leading up the wall toward a tunnel above. Oro started up. Jan followed, pausing in the tunnel's entry to gaze back down at the vast chamber below. The scattering of huge jewels, the pale, pillar-like shapes all lying fallen, the great, reddish scales, and the enormous oblong, irregular boulder with the fluid-filled depression in its crown all altered suddenly in the dark unicorn's view.

They no longer appeared to lie in random, orderless scatter. They were, he realized, the scales and bones of some great animal, its flesh long gone, its spine forming a winding trail across the floor. Bones of four great limbs splayed to either side. Toppled ribs lay in between, among the jewels and scales which must have adorned the creature's hide. Its skull, Jan perceived with a start, was the oblong boulder, resting jaw downward, empty eye sockets the symmetrical, gaping hollows. The little pool gleamed darkly in the — apparently natural — depression upon its brow. Jan could not guess the source of the liquid forming there. Gasping, he gazed at the huge reptilian skeleton below.

"What is that?" he managed. "Whose bones?"

His guide glanced at him quizzically. "The bones of Mélintéli-nas, late queen of the red dragons. Did I not tell you this be her lair?"

"Late . . . ?" Jan shook his head, trying to clear it. He felt stunned, stupid still. "But is not Mélintélinas the queen who has summoned me?"

Oro shook his head, turning to travel on. "Nay. That be her daughter, the new queen, Wyzásukitán."

The Dragon Queen
★ 14 ★

The Hall of Whispers served as the old queen's audience hall,"
Oro panted, champing to moisten his mouth in the hot, dry air.
"It be sacred to the dragons, but we have always stood welcome
there. Our hosts tell us our Congeries honors the memory of the
queen they mourn still."

"Mélintélinas," Jan murmured. "To whom Halla sent envoys
four hundred autumns past?"

The other nodded. "The same."

"When did she die?" the dark unicorn asked. "I thought firedrakes lived centuries."

Oro nodded. "Queen Mélintélinas reigned twelve hundred year
and passed into eternity scarcely a hundred winter past. Her suc-
cessor, Wyzásukitán, be young — as yet unpaired — but very
skilled in dragonlore. . . ."

The walls of the tunnels through which they descended grew
warmer, their dull golden glow becoming brighter. Wafts of steam
curled by, passing in gentle gusts. Jan was aware of the heat, but
it did not truly reach him. He felt no flush beneath the skin, no
prick of sweat. His heart did not pound, nor his breath labor. It
seemed to him he could embody the very heat of the sun and
suffer no ill.

Beside him, Oro's thick roan coat ran with sweat. His ribs

heaved. His speech came short. Sometimes he stumbled. At last he halted, staring ahead down the sloping path. Jan halted beside him. The fog had dissipated. Below them lay a lake of fire. Air shimmered above it. Beneath, liquid spurts of yellowish white mingled with sluggish swirls of sunset orange and molten red. A series of small, black islands, very closely spaced, formed a kind of path across — if one were very sure of foot.

"I can fare no farther," Oro gasped. "Heat fells me. You, though, be shielded by the dragonsup. Forge on across the cinder isles. The hold of Wyzásukitán lies beyond the brimstone sea."

Jan bowed to his host, seeking words of thanks, but found himself unexpectedly tongue-tied.

"Farewell for the present, Scout," he heard himself say at last. "I trust to rejoin you shortly."

Oro also bowed, very low. "Fare you well, Firebrand," he answered gravely. "I and my folk await your return."

Abruptly, he swung and stumbled back up the trail. Jan watched the dark roan stagger, reeling almost, then rally and press on. Jan watched him disappear as the trail rose, curving away and passing into other, higher chambers. Oro's halting hoofbeats gradually receded. Motionless, Jan listened until they faded at last. Then he turned and headed down to the lake of fire.

The air about it shuddered with heat, the burning fluid Oro had once called dragonsflood, fiercely incandescent. The feather in his hair smoked slightly, fragrantly. Yet, he felt no fiery blast as he crossed the black and cindery shore. Near its edge, the glowing brimstone had ̶arkened and solidified into a fragile crust. A great gust of heat shook the ground, rumbling like the breath of some immense creature beyond the subterranean lake of fire. Its sun-bright surface wrinkled, rippling.

When the tremor had passed, Jan stepped out onto the first of the minuscule islands. Its pitted surface grated and clanged beneath his heels. Little showers of sparks fell into the radiant substance of the lake and disappeared. The dark unicorn moved cautiously, sometimes retracing his steps. The lake stretched on, its low, dark ceiling lost in shadow. Such must be the birthplace of the sun, he mused, whence mares of smoke and stallions of fire blazed forth to charge heaven.

He saw lake's edge ahead. At first it seemed but a far distant darkness upon the gleaming surface, but as he approached, Jan realized it was neither a cluster of islands nor floating slag, but the limit of the brimstone sea. He stepped from the last island onto the cinder shore, which rose gently toward a cavernous opening in the wall of rock ahead. The ceiling soared higher here, the gigantic cavern mouth smoothly oval in shape.

Another glow lit the chamber beyond, steady and reddish. Jan walked toward it, up the beach. Pale smoke trailed through the crest of the entryway in a steady, tendriled stream. Another great sighing, accompanied by rumbling and shaking. The smoky mist redoubled. The dark unicorn halted till the quake subsided, then moved forward again. The black, pitted pebbles crunched and shifted beneath his cloven heels. He reached the great entryway.

"Welcome, Firebrand," the creature before him sighed. "For you I gladly suspend my contemplation. Enter and be welcome. I have awaited your coming four hundred years."

The dragon queen sprawled, inestimably vast, filling the great chamber before Jan. She was long and sinuous and covered with jewels. With a start, the dark unicorn noticed huge leathery wings, red as the rest of her, draping her back. Puzzlement made him frown. Living as they did, so far underground, he would never have imagined the red dragons to be wingèd. The old lays mentioned no powers of flight, and the remains of the old queen, Mélintélinas, had borne no wings.

Wyzásukitán looked at him. Her head was wedge-shaped, the muzzle long and slim, with flaring nostrils through which her hazy breath steamed. Two long mustachios, like those catfishes bear, sprouted below each nostril. They floated fluidly on the air as the dragon moved and turned her head. Her ears were slim, like gryphons' ears. A row of spiky ridges ran from the top of her head down the back of her neck, along the spine and tail to the tip, which ended in a flattened wedge.

Her body was covered by a myriad of ovate, interlocking scales which shimmered, reflecting the light of the lake of fire. Innumerable round and faceted stones encrusted her scaly skin. Of every color, though red predominated, they caught and held the light, burning like distant fires. Her massive hind limbs bore immense, pardlike claws. Her forelimbs, smaller and more delicately made, sported taloned toes of a size to crush a unicorn in a single snatch. Her breath moving through her lungs and throat did so with a hollow rushing like surf.

Upon her forehead, above the great ruby eyes, a circular depression lay, like a shallow bowl. In size and shape, it exactly resembled the slight hollow in the enormous skull of the late queen, from which he had recently sipped. The natural dish in Wyzásukitán's brow gleamed, a dark, clear liquid pooling there. The firedrake kept her head perfectly level, he noted, as if on guard against spilling the precious contents. Jan bowed to her.

"Hail, Wyzásukitán, queen of red dragons," he said.

"Hail, Aljan Firebringer," Wyzásukitán replied. Despite the harsh susurration, her voice was surprisingly melodious. Her steaming breath smelled of resin and spice. "Before her end, my mother spoke of your coming."

"What word did Queen Mélintélinas say of me?" Jan asked, surprised. Oddly, he felt no fear.

Wyzásukitán exhaled another cloud of fragrant breath and lowered her head, turning it slightly, only very slightly, to one side. "She told me one of your kind would come from beyond, bearing news of my great enemy, Lynex."

The dark prince nodded. "Lynex the wyvern king was driven from the Smoking Hills by your mother, Queen Mélintélinas, four hundred winters gone." Jan recited what he knew. "He and his folk wandered the Plain until they reached the Hallow Hills, at that time homeland to my folk. Lynex inveigled his way into the good graces of my people's then-king, despite protests by his daughter, the princess Halla. When the wyverns slithered into limestone caves hard by my people's sacred mere, the Mirror of the Moon, Halla, her suspicions roused, sent scouts to find the Smoking Hills whence these white wyrms had originally come. Her scouts parleyed with your mother the winter's length. She kept two here and sent the third back with warning of the wyverns' teacherous ways. . . . But surely Halla's scouts informed your people of all these things," Jan broke in on himself, "when first they arrived four hundred years ago."

The huge dragon nodded, her breath swirling about her. It rose toward the chamber's distant ceiling. Jan guessed it eventually reached the surface of the hills to drift in the dense fog that gave the region its name.

"Yea," Wyzásukitán answered. "So they did. And the two who remained here at my mother's behest became founders of the line that dwells here yet. Their chanting fills our meditations with beautiful song. We have lain very still these last four hundred years, harkening it." One shoulder moved: perhaps a shrug. "In that regard," she breathed, "your Scouts do for us much as the wyrms once did."

"The wyverns were singers?" Jan exclaimed.

Again the red dragon nodded. "They patrolled our dens, kept them free of vermin. They ate our dead. But we prized them for their songs and the stories that they told, which nourished our dreams."

"They call themselves your cousins," the dark prince told her.

Wyzásukitán snorted. Her breath swirled. "They are no cousins of ours."

"What do the red dragons dream?" Jan asked.

The dragon queen sighed. "Much in the heavens and under the earth. We live a long time, by your counting, and have no need to hurry about our affairs. Much time we spend in contemplation, envisioning what will come and what is and what has already passed — but I stray. I was asking of Lynex. We have heard no news of him since your late princess's scouts arrived. Tell me what befell after the one who departed returned to the Hallow Hills."

Jan nodded. "He warned Halla of wyvern treachery. But too

late. The wyrms had already bred. Come spring, they attacked, killing most of the herd before driving Halla's small band of survivors away. These wandered until they found the Vale, which has sheltered us for forty generations. But our time there is almost out. My folk mean to return to the Hallow Hills within the year, to wrest them back from Lynex and his crew. We are told he lives and rules the wyverns still. In the way of his kind, he has grown more heads than the single one with which he started. We hear he is seven-headed now."

"And seven times more treacherous, to be sure," mused Wyzásukitán.

"Why do the red dragons hate the white wyrms so?" Jan ventured. "You lived in harmony so long. What trespass caused you to cast them out?"

"Harmony would be too strong a term," the dragon queen replied, voice darkening. "Suffice to say we dwelled without enmity until the advent of Lynex. Lynex was different from other wyrms. His tail bore a poison sting, unlike the blunt tips of his fellows. He used this barb to hunt live prey, including his own kind. He ventured aboveground to stalk the shag-haired goats and bred with others of his kind to produce more sting-tailed wyverns, killing those of his broods that bore no stings."

Wyzásukitán turned her head, remembering.

"He and his folk conspired many seasons, while we slept unaware of the plots fomenting around us. Lynex led his sting-tailed wyrms to kill or drive away all other wyverns. But we suspected naught until Lynex and his followers began to prey upon my people's pups, carrying off eggs from the nest and stinging to death the newly hatched, then dragging away their bones."

The firedrake's eyes smoldered, her beautiful voice growing tighter, more harsh.

"Lynex declared himself king of wyrms and cousin to dragons. Master of fire he styled himself, porting coals about in a golden bowl. My mother awoke at last and roused her kith to drive the wyrms away. Lynex fled, and all his poisonous tribe. We trusted winter's cold aboveground to kill them — but they huddled about their king's firebowl and escaped to trouble your tribe as once they had troubled my own. My dam held herself responsible for this wrong. It weighed upon her, and upon my people. Four hundred years have we lain in contemplation since, considering how best to fashion a remedy."

"Remedy?" Jan asked. "Have you discovered one?"

The dragon queen turned. "To understand that, Firebrand," she answered, "you must understand my kind." Again she shrugged, at once both languid and restless. "Behold my wings. My mother was already well into her prime, as we dragons count time, her wings long shed, when your late princess's scouts arrived."

The dark prince listened as Wyzásukitán's folded wings rustled softly, shifting.

"She had flown her mating flight a hundred years previous and would lay eggs from that tryst to the end of her days. She had no wings anymore, nor had any other of her kith, for as you may know, among my kind, only the queen and her consort ever breed. My mother's consort had long since flown. They always do, after the nuptial flight. Where a queen's consort flies, we do not know, for none ever return. We are a female race. A male is born among us only once in a thousand years."

Before him, the great dragon's voice warmed, gentled.

"They are black, these firedrakes, most beautiful to behold. My own consort is so much younger than I," murmured Wyzásukitán. "My mother hatched him only shortly before she died. He will not be ready to fly for three centuries yet. So darksome fair, he will make the perfect sire to all my progeny. My wings, how they ache from disuse! They are ready now, and I long to try them."

Realization jolted Jan. "Your . . . your consort," he stammered. "He is your sib? Your own mother's child?"

The dragon queen flexed her massive, bat-form wings. "Of course. It is always thus among dragons."

A bitter taste rose in Jan's mouth. He thought of Tek, his late sire's own uncounted daughter, Korr's first, unspoken child. Wary of offending the dragon queen, Jan swallowed hard. Yet such a union as she described was unconscionable among his own folk, even if his and Tek's pledge had been undertaken innocently, neither knowing Tek's secret parentage. Yet once done, it could never be undone: Dhattar and Aiony were the living proof. Shaken, Jan found his tongue.

"You say Lynex, too, bred with his own kin?" The thought repulsed him.

Again Wyzásukitán nodded. "As did your own scouts upon their arrival here."

"What?" cried Jan, shocked. "How do you mean?"

Ever so subtly, the dragon queen cocked her head. "There were only two," she answered quietly, "two that remained. They have had no contact with others of your folk these four hundred years. How did you imagine they had multiplied if at first sib had not pledged with sib?"

Jan's mind reeled. He felt his knees lock. How was it he had not deduced something so obvious? Inbreeding explained the striking resemblance among all Oro's folk: modest stature, stocky build, dark roan or dapple coats, those odd, half-standing manes. Jan shook himself, staggered. Numbly, he strove to collect himself, to bring his awareness back to the firedrake's lair. He opened his mouth to speak. But the dragon queen spoke first.

"Your thoughts return to your Vale, I see," she said, "and to those you cherish there. Come." She bowed her head to the chamber's floor. "Gaze into me, and you will see what is and is to be."

Jan breathed deeply, trying to clear his head. Shaken still, he approached the dragon queen. Her mouth was easily great enough to engulf him in a single snap, yet he felt no fear, only his own turmoil roiling within. Despite her reptilian shape, he doubted somehow that dragons ate flesh. Steaming, her fragrant breath enveloped him. Her enormous, ruby-colored eye watched him as he leaned to peer into the dark pool of her brow.

The King's
Uncounted Daughter
★ 15 ★

Tek stood in the entryway to the cave, gazing off across the Vale. Equinox was upon them. Brief summer had run its course. Soon days would last shorter than the nights. The tang of fall seasoned the air, though the grass grew green, not yet goldening, and evenings had not turned chill. Tek watched the long shadow of the Vale's sunward side advancing toward the far sunlit slope. Unicorns still grazed the hillsides, or ramped and frolicked on the valley floor.

The pied mare stood keenly aware that all she surveyed she beheld for the last time in season. Never again would she gaze upon the Vale on summer's ending day, autumn's eve. Come spring — whether or not her mate had returned — she and the herd must depart for the Hallow Hills. The creeping shadows overtaking the Vale advanced. Tek sighed, longing for Jan, heart filled with something akin to despair. Neither he nor she had expected his absence to stretch so long. Jan's chasing his crazed sire had only achieved what Korr had striven toward all along: to part her from her mate and him from her.

The pied mare set her teeth. She loathed the dark king with all her fury. Though as a filly and young half-grown she had enjoyed his high favor — exactly why, she had never known — she had always mistrusted him, kept her distance. About the time of his son's initiation, she and Jan had become shoulder-friends, and still the dark king had smiled his approval. Only when Jan had grown old enough to eye the mares had the king's mood inexplicably darkened — though never toward Tek, only toward his son. She had steered well clear of Korr then, never dallying with the young prince before his father's eyes.

Still, she never could have imagined the king's rage upon her return from the Summer Sea when he learned of the sacred pledge she and Jan had shared, a vow unshakable in Alma's eyes. The king had railed wildly against her then. When her burgeoning belly made plain that she was in foal, the dark stallion's ravings tipped into madness, and he had sought her death. Fleeing the Vale, she had taken refuge with her then-outcast dam, Jah-lila, who had used sorcery to defend her and midwive her young.

Again the pied mare breathed deep, the bare hint of a smile quirking her mouth. How the world had turned since then: now Korr was the hated outcast, Jah-lila the honored insider, advisor to the prince. Tek herself had returned in triumph, her eminence second only to that of her mate. Quietly, she studied the darkening Vale, which she had ruled all summer as prince's regent. The herd trusted her, gladly followed her word. She had won their respect on her own merits. That she was daughter to the red wych and dam to the prince's heirs only enhanced her station.

Tek's smile slipped, faded. A frown of frustration wrinkled her brow. Where was he? Where was her belovèd Jan? Weeks had passed since the scouts she had sent had brought back any useful news. At first, when summer had been new, she had waited. But when, after three days her mate had not returned, she had dispatched runners into the Pan Woods to look for him and his quarry. Her foster sisters, the young pans Sismoomnat and Pitipak, had set forth as well. All had returned with tales of Korr's senseless terrorizing of the Wood. It had taken weeks for Tek to reparley the peace with all the goatling tribes.

She had realized then that Jan dared not return unsuccessful. The goatlings expected — indeed had demanded, and she confidently promised — that the dark marauder be captured and punished for his trespass against the unicorn's allies. The pied mare shook her head. She had never considered herself a diplomat. She had none of Jan's glib grace, his quick understanding. Still, she had evidently succeeded, for the pans had held their truce and agreed to wait the outcome of the prince's quest.

Meanwhile, the prince's mate had learned, Jan had followed his sire onto the Plain. Again, Tek tasted despair. That limitless expanse gave Jan everywhere to search, Korr anywhere to hide. The herd's lack of ties with the Plain's few, scattered wanderers troubled her as well. For centuries her own folk had hated and feared these wild unicorns, believing them outcasts and rebels from the Vale. Tek knew differently, yet still felt the greatest unease at Jan's venturing among such unknown folk. Outside the Ring of Law, who knew what customs they might keep? That the Plain was also home to great, banded pards and savage grasscats filled her with dread.

Despite all dangers, Tek had found no dearth of volunteers to scout the Plain. The first to set out had brought back nothing. The Mare's Back was simply too vast for outlanders to track either friend or foe. She instructed her next scouts to seek out Plainsdwellers and ask their aid. But, as she had feared, the ones most of her own folk still stubbornly called "Renegades" shied clear of dwellers of the Vale — and again her scouts returned thwarted.

Her resolve only strengthened, she had called on Jan's and her own shoulder-companion Dagg to lead the next search, and this expedition had at last borne fruit. Dagg had encountered Plainsdwellers, and though he clearly lost no love for ones he considered Ringbreakers or descendants of such, he had approached politely as many times as needed to persuade them. In the end, he had learned what he had come to learn: that Korr had rampaged across the Plain. The Free People called him the dark destroyer.

Jan, too, apparently because of his similar coloring, had at first been mistaken for Korr and been shunned. At length, he had managed to gain the trust of a party of Renegades even as Dagg and his fellows now had done, and convinced them that he sought to contain the mad stallion, not repeat his crimes. Dagg had learned of the long chase Korr had led his friend, how Jan had sought and received aid of a seer or singer known as Alma's Eyes. But when Dagg had eventually caught up with this one, the young prince had already left him, vanished away into the Salt Waste on the trail of the king.

"It was odd," Dagg had said. "When first I saw him in profile, by moonlight, my heart lifted with joy. I thought he was Jan. They have the same legs and frame, the same muzzle and mane. Their voices, even some of their gestures, echo in the most uncanny way."

The dappled warrior had snorted then.

"Of course, by day, none could mistake the two. The seer is an evening blue speckled with stars. His manner of speech is that of the Plain. He is older than Jan, not quite Korr's age, and spent ten days in Jan's company."

Again the dappled warrior had snorted, remembering.

"After their parting, so I gather, this Alma's Eyes went among his people singing the history of Jan and the Vale. Jan, it seems, recounted a number of our lays to him, which allayed much of the Plainsdwellers' mistrust. Korr's acts clearly had stirred much ill feeling against our folk."

Dagg shrugged, sidled, seeming almost chagrined.

"I believe the links Jan forged during his sojourn upon the Plain will serve us well come spring. Jan, so it seems, made a fair enough singer to catch the ear of this Alma's Eyes, who recounts nothing like our own formal singers of the Vale — and yet, a kind of wild beauty haunts his song. His folk admire him, and through him, Jan."

Tek laughed quietly to herself, thinking of her mate. He had always revered her singer's gift, declaring himself reft of any skill. Yet she had always suspected he, too, harbored the bent. How he loved the old lays, remembered them flawlessly, remarking even the slightest variation from one recitation to the next. He spoke with ease before even the greatest throng. What if until now, his musical nature had manifested solely through fiercely expressive dancing? She had always known him to be as much a singer as he was a warrior, a peacemaker, a dancer, and a prince.

Someone moved beside her on the slope before the cave. She started, remembering belatedly that she shared this stony spot with Dagg. The dappled warrior moved closer to her. She did not turn her head, the image of his robust frame, pale eyes, grey mane, and yellow coat firmly imprinted on her mind. The grey spots flocking his withers and hindquarters thickened into stockings on all four legs. He rubbed shoulders with her companionably. She leaned, shouldering him in turn. Quietly, unselfconsciously, Dagg voiced her greatest fear:

"What if he does not return? What if Jan does not appear by spring? What then?"

She shuddered, sighed. "We must honor our pact with the gryphons regardless. We must leave the Vale and press on to the Hallow Hills."

"The herd will follow you, and gladly," Dagg told her.

Tek shrugged, smiled. "In Jan's name."

Here Dagg surprised her. He shook his head. "For your own sake. You are a great warrior. Our folk would charge with you into the wyverns' jaws for that alone."

She felt a little thrill of gratitude, of pride, tried not to show it. "Now that Jan's blood makes us all proof against their stings, such a charge should prove easier."

Dagg chuckled softly. "I doubt you delude yourself thinking our task will be accomplished with ease."

"First we must see the herd safe through winter — Alma grant us another mild one, I pray, for the sake of our fillies and foals." Tek frowned, thinking. "Kindling marks the opening of winter, and Quenching its end."

She gazed down at the valley floor where, in the lengthening shadows of evening, beneath a blue, brilliant sky, her twin offspring ramped whinnying along with Lell and with Dagg's firstborn, Culu. Barely a year and a half old, the suckling foal sported forequarters of intense, true yellow shading to brilliant salmon at the rump, exactly the hue of the sundog for which he was named. The pan sisters Sismoomnat and Pitipak chased the four colts amid much whistling and squealing. Ringing their swirl, Jah-lila, Ses, and Dagg's mate, Ryhenna, stood, shooing stray tag-players back into bounds.

Tek eyed the coppery mare, who, like her own dam, had been born outside the Vale to a hornless race, but who, upon joining the herd, had drunk of the sacred waters of the moon's mere deep within the Hallow Hills and been transformed into a unicorn. Ryhenna's coppery coat exactly matched the hue of her standing mane. Her tail fell full and silky. Like Jah-lila, she was beardless, lacking tassels to the tips of her small, neat ears and feathery fringe to her fetlocks. Instead of being cloven, her hooves were solid rounds.

Yet despite such differences, Ryhenna had been welcomed into the Vale even as Jah-lila now found welcome, hailed as Jan's savior for aiding his escape from her own captors, the two-footed fire-keepers. Ryhenna's transformation had been celebrated in myth and lay, her copper-colored horn admired, and with her mate's aid, she had set about learning the ways of a warrior with a will. Jan had declared her mistress of fire, and she presided over Kindling and Quenching, the herd's newly created ceremonies at winter's beginning and end, striking the sparks from which all the torches of winter would burn.

"By winter's end, before we march," Tek said to Dagg, "we must all harden our heels and horns that we may smite the wyrms' bony breastplates without shattering our weapons."

Dagg nodded. "Come spring, it will be time."

The game below had broken up. Tek watched the figures moving up the hill toward her, colts and fillies frisking still, the mares moving more leisurely. Lell pranced alongside Sismoomnat, the elder of the two pan sisters. The pied mare caught a snatch of their conversation as they ambled by, Lell tossing the milk mane from her eyes, Sismoomnat resting one forelimb on the dark amber filly's withers with a trace of a smile. Tek, too, smiled. Lell reminded her more than a little of Jan as a colt: hot-headed and passionate, fiercely intelligent but ruled by her heart.

"His wings were broad and green, and his voice so lilting sweet. He vowed to return to us, come spring, and accompany us to the Vale."

Sismoomnat nodded gravely as Lell halted and began to graze. The young pan bent to pull and collect grass seed in one upturned, hairless paw.

"You must introduce him to me when he returns," she murmured. Tek turned her attention back downslope. They were discussing the gryphon Illishar. Still. The pied mare marveled at it, that the green-fletched wingcat could have so captured Lell's curiosity. Nothing seemed to distract her from speculating when he would return, expounding the magnificence of his flight and the sweetness of his song. She would prattle thus to any who would harken until their ears well and nearly withered. Tek regarded Dhattar and Aiony, accompanied by Pitipak, the younger pan. The three of them had begun another game on the slope. She heard white Dhattar saying, "Nay, we'll not see him at all this winter."

Aiony added, "Save in dreams."

Pitipak made a small sound, as of sympathy. Tek's ears pricked, but she dared not interrupt with questions. Like as not, such would only quiet her offspring completely, or loose a torrent of observations too tangled for Tek herself to sort. Quietly, their dam eavesdropped.

"He talks to the one with the red jewels now," Aiony was saying.

"She's older than we," Dhattar laughed, "and goes about things very slowly."

Chasing him around Aiony, Pitipak nearly caught him. The black-and-silver filly dodged away now, as well.

"She's been sleeping a long, long time."

Tek turned her mind away, unable to follow their thread. Almost certainly, she knew, they were discussing Jan, but she lacked any context with which to make their words meaningful. Reluctantly, she contented herself with the assurance he was alive and hale. Ryhenna came up the hillside now, followed closely by her young one, Culu. With an affectionate nip, Dagg left the pied mare's side. The coppery mare whistled a greeting to Tek before nuzzling her mate. The little foal began to suckle. Jah-lila and Ses came up the rear. They, too, spoke quietly as evening neared.

"I have often wondered where in the wide Plain he might be found, but of late the more intensely," Ses was saying, head down, tone barely above her breath. "Then, on a sudden, to have news of him after so long, that he is well, a singer. . . . I had always suspected —"

Her words broke off as she and the red mare drew close to Tek. Schooling her expression to betray nothing, the pied mare listened in surprise. Ses spoke of Jan, of course — who else? Yet, despite her obvious strong emotion, her words rang somehow odd in reference to her son. Puzzled, Tek glanced away and harkened without seeming to.

"Both you and I have forfeited much for the welfare of our young," Jah-lila murmured to Ses.

The pied mare felt a telltale frown creasing her brow and dismissed it. Her own dam, she knew, had forgone a place in the herd for nearly ten years in order that her filly might be raised among them as Teki's daughter. Tek — and all the Vale — now knew that the stallion whose namesake she was had not been her sire. To this day, the red mare continued to conceal that one's identity. Some nameless Renegade was all the account Tek had ever been able to wrest from her.

Of her own dam's sacrifice, the pied mare was well aware. But what of Ses? Did Jah-lila refer to the public repudiation of Korr by his mate when, during that terrible winter, his madness had threatened even Lell? Yet Tek had the strongest feeling that Ses's unknown deed must have been to Jan's benefit, not Lell's. The pale mare's eyes were closed, as if in pain.

"I count the days till Jan's return," she whispered to Jah-lila. "Though I could do no other and keep my offspring safe, I have held this silence far too long. By Alma's eyes, Red Mare, I swear when next we meet, I'll tell my son the truth."

Jan felt himself returning. He became aware of the dragon's den again, of the awful glare of the pool of fire, of its intense heat. Neither troubled him, though he was vaguely aware that he should long since have swooned. Dimly, in the back of his mind, he tried to remember what had caused this strange imperviousness — dragonsup? — but his thoughts were fluid, shifting still, and the query refused to come to the forefront of consciousness. Instead, a new need suddenly kindled there, bright and imperative: to learn the meaning of his mother's vow. *I'll tell my son the truth.* He had no inkling what she could mean.

"What is this?" he demanded. "What have I beheld?"

Before him, the languid dragon stirred. Great lids slid down over garnet eyes, then up again. The pool upon her brow rippled and stilled. Her vast body stretched away across the chamber, enormous claws of her toes tightening. Her monumental, rose-colored wings flexed. The resulting gust fanned the steam of her breath in curling eddies about Jan. She chuckled very quietly, deep in her throat, at his sudden urgency, all trace of his former reticence gone.

"None but your home and friends, the unicorns of your Vale," she answered, chiding. "I should have thought you would have recognized them."

The dark unicorn let his breath out, chastened. "Your pardon," he offered, then tried again. "What I meant to ask is: is what I see upon your brow that which is, or are these images your own inventions, conjurings. . . ."

"Lies?" Wyzásukitán inquired mildly.

"Dreams," Jan countered.

Again the red dragon chuckled. "You see what is. I see it, too, but it is no dream of mine. We dragons do not dream, in that sense. We contemplate that which is. The only conjurer here is you, invoking upon my brow those things you most desire to see."

Jan frowned, unsatisfied. "But is it real?" he whispered. "Or only imagined by me?"

Wyzásukitán shrugged. Her massive wing moved, glittering. Her head remained perfectly still. "Does it feel real — or imaginary?"

"Real," Jan answered, unhesitating.

The dragon queen nodded, closing her eyes again and inclining her head almost imperceptibly. The strange water upon her brow lapped, smoothed. "Then trust it as real, for I believe the truth, however harsh, is what you long to see above all things, even above soothing lies. A courageous wish, and a most unusual one. Álmaharát-elár-herát, whom we call the Many-Jeweled One, or Her of the Thousand Thousand Eyes, has chosen you well for her purpose. You have seen what is and what has been. Come. Look again. I will show you now what is to be."

Kindling

★ 16 ★

Jan gazed deep into the dragon's pool. The Vale lay below him in a gryphon's eye view. He leaned closer, perception skimming lower through the air. Frost rimed the grass, brown stubble now. Wisps of snow sifted down, floating like feathers. Sky hung grey, early dusk drawing on. Jan watched his fellows gathering. When he spied the great heap of brushwood on the council rise, he knew the day could only be solstice, the start of winter.

His herdmates below looked well-fed, pelts thick and warm. Nearly all the many fillies and foals would be weaned by spring. *When the herd must depart,* Jan heard himself think, unsure if he spoke aloud in the distant dragon's den. *I must return by then,* he thought. *I must lead them.* The notion filled him with dread, not of the task itself, but of the other that must accompany it: disclosure of Korr's unspeakable secret.

Far below, Tek stood upon the council rise. She was a striking sight, bold black and rose, her particolored mane lifting in the slight, frigid breeze. The herd around her assembled joyously. How regal she looked, like a princess, like a queen. *She is their queen,* he thought. *Leader of the herd now that Korr is gone — and not as my regent, but in her own right: undeclared princess of the line of Halla all the time that I have ruled.*

Watching her, Jan felt terror and longing war within his breast.

He did not know, suddenly, how he would bear yielding his station as prince. For honor's sake, and out of love for Tek, he could consider no other course. Yet its taste rose bitter in his mouth — for another thing he must relinquish, too. And this he could not face at all: abandoning his mate, renouncing her. *Not Tek, my belovèd!* It was inconceivable.

Mounting panic took him by the throat. He gasped, shuddering. The image in the dragon's pool wavered, obscured by snow. Frantically, Jan strove to still his roiling thoughts. Gradually, his inner clamor quieted, breathing eased. The images in the pool clarified. He gazed into them deeply, desperately. The scene below offered distraction, lifted him out of his turmoil and pain. His last awareness of the dragon's den and his own identity faded as he grew wholly absorbed.

Tek spoke to the assembled herd, and they danced the great ringdance, trampling the snow. Much later, when the dance had ended, Tek again addressed the herd. Her foster father, Teki the healer, came forward and sang the lay of Jan's winter captivity three years past and of his eventual return, bearing the secret of fire in his hooves and horn. Impervious to solstice chill in their thick winter shag, the resting herd stood harkening, or lounged at ease on the frosty ground.

Teki's lay done, Tek called on Ryhenna to stand beside her on the rise. Dagg's copper-colored mate had fought at the prince's shoulder during his escape from the two-footed firekeepers. She too, like Jan, had trod upon the burning coals Jan had kindled that day, tempering her round, solid hooves to sparking hardness. Each year since the herd had acclaimed her its priestess, she had kindled the great bonfire that would burn all winter long.

Calling on Alma now, thanking the goddess for her gift of fire, the coppery mare reared and dashed her hooves against the stones on which the dried tinder rested. Sparks flew. Ryhenna rose and struck again, again. Whinnying, she cavaled, stamping her hind heels. All the herd whistled with her. More sparks. Some flew into the midst of the tinder and caught. Smoke curled up, then little tongues of flame. When the bonfire had become a blaze, Tek called members of the herd to come forward.

In twos and threes, unicorns approached the council rise. Each bore a dried branch clenched in teeth. Carefully, they dipped their brands into the flame, then raised them burning aloft. The fire-bearers sprang away at a gallop, ploughing through snow, seeking their grottoes before the firebrands guttered. Each grotto, Jan knew, housed a similar tinder pile beside a cache of stores. Here borrowed flames would burn all season, warming the herd, that none need ever again suffer privation from hunger and cold. Guardians would tend the great bonfire on the council rise until the birth of spring.

Jan found his viewpoint pulling back from the Kindling, buoyed like a gryphon on a rising wind. The images before him blurred, altering. He seemed to have traversed many miles in a single breath. Vague impressions of Pan Woods and Plain swept rapidly beneath him, then the rises and ripples of the Hallow Hills. He began to descend, rushing earthward. Below, he glimpsed the Mirror of the Moon, the unicorns' sacred pool, hard by the ex-panse of broken limestone shelves housing entry to the wyverns' dens.

The next heartbeat found him within. Long caverns twisted through the white limestone, all coated with a crystalline glaze. As the pale wyrms slithered, their tiny scales sloughed, volatile oils from their skin rubbing off, forming silvery trails. Over hundreds of years, the trails had thickened into layers which caught the lightwells' gleam, diffusing it, to lend a dim glow to the dens even in their deepest parts. The translucent patina had a resinous odor. Jan knew it to be fiercely combustible. One spark could set the whole warren alight.

Jan found himself in the deepest recess of the vast network of interlocking tunnels. A great wyvern lay curled in his lair, unaware of the dark unicorn's distant observation. This wyrm was the largest Jan had ever seen, larger even than the three-headed queen he had battled as a colt. Jan guessed that this creature must be very old, for wyverns grew throughout their lives. At the tip of his poison tail, seven barbs glinted. Two badger-broad forepaws, his only limbs, scratched absently at his vitreous belly, stretched taut by a recent meal. Old scars disfigured his breast.

The wyrm had seven heads. Realization seized Jan with a start. Each head possessed a hood, bristling whiskers and dozens of needle-sharp teeth. The eldest, central pate was also the largest. It lay dozing, long neck stretched along the ground. Other heads twined about it. Two were nearly half as large. These also slept. The rest were smaller, younger, wakeful. Of them, the final, seventh nob was a mere slip, whining and nibbling at its own gill ruff. Its three companions stirred restively, glancing about the room as if on guard. A firebrand smoldered smokily nearby, only the smallest stack of twigs heaped by for future fuel. Furtively, in whispers, the four smallest heads argued.

"Why must *we* always keep watch," the next-to-smallest complained, "while the large ones sleep?"

"Silence!" the fourth-largest head hissed. "You'll wake the One."

The complainer and its closest companion both hissed and turned to eye the largest pate, which slept on, unperturbed. The tiniest sniffed at a fellow's gills, parting colorless lips for a tentative nibble. The second-to-smallest spun and snapped at the tiny head, driving it back. The fourth-largest clucked at the other three, then cast about suspiciously, eyeing the egress to the wyrm king's den as if impatient for some visitor. The second-largest countenance, flanking the One, stirred. All four of the small aspects riveted their gazes upon it for a few heartbeats, then lost interest when it made no further move.

"Where in all the burrows is the kindling?" the fourth-largest demanded. "Our brand's near burnt out."

"Do you think it was the peaceseekers, waylaying the wood gatherers again?" the fifth-largest nob ventured.

"Peaceseekers!" the next-to-the-smallest growled, then spat. "Stingless grubs."

The tiny head hissed furiously, a tangle of sounds that might have been, "Stingless! Stingless!" Its three waking comrades ignored it.

"It was when our queen died, five seasons past," the fifth-largest muttered, "that was when our fortunes fell."

The next-to-smallest one beside it harrumphed. "They were wretched before."

"Hardly!" the fourth-largest snapped. "While our queen lived, she kept the barbless freaks in check."

"Verminous peaceseekers!" its companion, fifth-largest, snarled.

"We were never cold then; that I'll grant," the next-to-smallest face conceded.

"Peace! Peace!" the tiny head hissed as though it were a curse.

"Killed by those thrice-cursed unicorns," the fourth-largest head murmured.

Its slightly smaller companion added, "Our gallant queen. Priestess of the divine fire."

"She never let our torch grow cold," the second-to-smallest added.

The tiny head alongside hissed out, "Torches. Cold."

The gazes of the four small waking faces flicked between the egress and the guttering fire. The one largest pate dozed on, as did the two middle-sized heads that flanked it. The larger of those uncoiled its neck, turned upside down. Again the four small heads froze, silenced, until their medium-sized fellow again lay still.

"Cursed be the night-dark prince of unicorns," the fourth-to-largest whispered. "When he slew our queen, we lost our heirs as well."

"All those ripe eggs, ready for hatching," the fifth-largest lamented. "Tramped under his cloven heels."

"His and his shoulder-friends', the pied one and the dapple," the next-to-smallest added.

The fifth-largest continued, "Two dozen sharp-pricked little prits. Had they but hatched, they'd have quelled and mastered all these stingless freaks!"

"Eggs, prits," hissed the littlest head. "Freaks!"

"Yes, stingless," the fourth-largest head of the wyrmking echoed. "That's all the wyverns were before we hatched. When our folk slaved among the thrice-cursed dragons, none bore a sting. We, Lynex, were the first. We bred our line into a race of wyverns — independent, strong! — not those cringing wyrms our folk had been. We made our followers hunters, capturers of prey, no longer puling scavengers, eaters of the dead."

Another head took up the thread. "And for years upon years, our line bred true. We ourself sired most of the eggs our females laid. The stingless ones were few and easily destroyed. But now the One grows old and sires no more. The eggs the unicorns crushed were our last brood. Now stingless ones hatch nearly as frequently as those with stings! Some females refuse to eat such young, hide them away instead to keep them safe."

"The old queen knew how to find and devour them," its companion beside it interjected. "But she is dead now, and the One has lost interest. He dozes his hours away, content to let others address our woes. . . ."

"But others do not remedy as they ought," another interrupted. "The stingless peaceseekers are becoming a troublesome faction. They speak out against the spring hunting. They themselves seek only carrion to eat —"

"Carrion!" squawked the next-to-smallest head, and the fifth-largest spat, "Filth!"

"They refuse to take fellow creatures' lives!" the fourth-largest ranted. "Pledge not to hunt living prey!"

The voices of all four of the smaller heads had risen, becoming both louder and more shrill. They hissed and squabbled among themselves until the two middle-sized heads — flanking the largest, still-sleeping visage — jerked awake. Clear, crystalline eyes fixed on the smaller four, the middle-sized pair rose hissing.

"Stingless freaks," one crackled.

Its mate echoed, "Witless ones, more like."

"Still your prating tongues before you wake the One," the second-to-largest muzzle cautioned, reaching to sink its fangs into two of the smaller four in turn. All of the little heads leaned frantically away, but the necks of the middle-sized heads were longer.

"No more talk of peaceseekers and unicorns," the third-to-largest head commanded. "Such dross troubles the dreams of the One. Our late queen is gone, but our fire burns on."

"Hist! Hist!" the youngest head broke in. Behind, the fire was nearly out.

"Quick, lackwits!" the second-to-largest pate snarled. "Feed the flame. If it dies, the One will snap you four off at the chins and devour your brains."

"You were ordered to watch," its companion, the third-largest, berated. "A fine mess you have made of it, too. This torch is the last in all our dens, to be hoarded and tended with utmost care!"

Frantically, the four smaller heads snatched up tinder and twigs to add to the dwindling fire. At first it seemed they had smothered it, but then smoke curled up and bright tongues of red and yellow burst across the fuel. The two middle-sized maws snicked and snorted, the four smaller pates sighing with evident relief. Five of the wakeful, coherent heads turned to cast angry, hopeful looks toward the chamber's egress.

"Where in all the dens is the wood gatherer?" the third-largest demanded of the one beside it. "Could it be the stingless peaceseekers again? You know they preach life without reliance on fire."

The second-largest muttered. "Fire savages the blood. Fire first gave us stings and a taste for live meat. . . ."

All five watching the door continued to grumble. Behind them, the wyrmking's one great, original head dozed on. Meanwhile the littlest face watched the bright, short-lived flames consuming the last of the firebrand's fuel. For a few moments, the fire guttered, fizzing, then shrank still further. It became a blue flicker, vanished in a waft of pungent smoke. Sudden chill swept the room. The nostrils of the five other waking heads flared. Gasping, they wheeled to gape at the shadowed remains of the burnt-out branch. Not a sound broke the stillness but the tiny maw's whimpers.

The eyes of the one great head snapped open, stared for a moment at the newly darkened chamber. The only light now illuminating the den was a distant lightwell's feeble glow. Lynex's central head reared on its muscular stalk. All around, the other crania writhed, wailing, even the second- and third-largest. The great head ignored them, glaring straight at the empty fireledge, now nothing but ashes and char. The wyrmking's knifelike claws dug into his gleaming belly below his savagely scarred breast.

"Which?" he growled, voice deeper than any Jan had ever heard. "Which one of you let my fire go out?"

Jan felt himself in motion again, rising, pulling aloft. He left the crystalline dens of wyverns beneath the Hallow Hills and crossed the Plain, traversed the Pan Woods. He found himself hovering above the Vale once more. The snows had passed. Another ceremony, similar to the Kindling that had marked winter's onset, was now under way. Again unicorns circled the great bonfire, still burning. The air had warmed, cool yet, but with the promise of balmier days ahead. Some of the herd were already shedding their heavy shag. It had been another mild winter, Jan could see: thanks, no doubt, to the weather wych, Jah-lila.

After the dancing, Teki again ascended the council rise. This time he sang of Tek's flight from the Vale, how his foster daughter had carried Jan's unborn offspring through bitter snows and taken refuge in the wilderness with her then-exiled dam. He praised the pan sisters Sismoomnat and Pitipak who had delivered Tek and described the torrential floods that had overwhelmed the murderous warparty Korr had sent against her in the spring.

That had been the ending of Korr's power, if not his madness. Jan had returned from captivity among the firekeepers just as Tek and her newborns had made their own return. The lay ended with the reunion of mates and Jan's embracing his twin filly and foal. Many of the youngest listeners had drifted into sleep. The fire priestess, Ryhenna, addressed the herd, reminding them that once moon reached its zenith, the bonfire would be tended no more, its flames allowed to flicker out, coals left to cool.

This night, however, she added new words, urging all full-grown unicorns to sharpen their hooves and horns, then tread as she now trod upon the embers rimming the dwindling tongues of flame. Into these she dipped her horn, holding it in the swirl of fire that it, like her fire-hardened hooves, might toughen beyond all previous strength, the better to pierce the wyverns' bony breasts.

Eagerly, all of fighting age complied: newly initiated half-growns, seasoned warriors, elders, a dozen of whom formed the Council which confirmed all kings' judgments and granted each succeeding battleprince his right to rule. First Tek, then Dagg, then Jah-lila and Ses, followed by Teki and the rest, bent to run keen ridges of spiral horn against flint-edged heels, honing both edges in the same smooth stroke, then came forward to join Ryhenna.

Those colts and fillies and suckling foals still waking looked on with longing. Too tender for war, they were forbidden to sharpen their hooves and horns. At last, the long procession ended. Their elders, weaponry now tempered, returned from the council rise and lay down among their offspring to doze the weary night till dawn.

Jan watched the moon climb, pass zenith, decline. The whole valley lay silent, still — except for furtive movement atop the rise. Jan beheld his own sister Lell, barely five years old, not yet initiated, clumsily keening her hooves and horn. At last achieving a respectable edge, she crept forward, ears pricked and eyes darting. Gingerly, she stepped onto the bonfire's coals, dipping her young horn into the last red wisps of flame.

"I don't count what Ses says," Jan heard her muttering between clenched teeth. "I *am* ready. I'm not too young. I mean to be a warrior, and I might as soon begin by battling wyverns. She'll not keep me from this fray."

"Bravely spoken," a voice behind her quietly replied.

The timbre was a low, throaty growl like the purr of a hillcat. Lell jumped stiff-legged as a startled hare and whirled. Silhouetted, a gryphon sat on the council rise. Jan himself was amazed. He had not observed the other's approach, nor heard his wings. The tercel had alighted in utter silence, cat's eyes dilated in the blazing moonlight.

"Illishar!" Lell hissed, her joyous whisper just short of a shriek that would have wakened others and given them both away.

"The same, little one," he replied. "I bid you hail. Only lately arrived, I wished not to disturb your folk."

"You are most welcome," Lell answered fervently, then hesitated, casting a glance at her sharpened hooves, then over at the fire. "I beg you," she burst out softly, urgently, "do not speak of what you have just seen. . . ."

The wingcat smiled. "I see naught but a gracious filly who, waking at my approach, arose to welcome me."

Lell eyed him fiercely. "I mean to be a warrior," she said. "Jan would let me. I know he would! If he were here — I mean to join this fray against the wyrms."

The green-winged tercel nodded. "So I see. And now, little one, may I beg a boon? Fall back, if you will, a pace or two and allow me a place beside your fire. My flight this day has been long and chill."

Lell stumbled back from the bonfire hurriedly, allowing the gryphon space to move into the glow of the coals. He crouched, then stretched himself, forelegs laid upon the ground, wings not folded, but raised, the better to catch the fire's heat. Jan heard the deep, steady rumble of his purr. Lell stood awkwardly, seeming not to know what next to do. The gryphon beckoned her.

"Step closer, little darkamber," he bade. "Do not grow cold on my account. Rest and tell me of your warrior dreams. I, too, sought to join my clan's battleranks against great odds. I succeeded, as you see, and have won a perch high on the ledges beside my leader's wing."

Lell happily approached and lay down facing the green-and-gold tercel. Jan marveled at his sister's lack of fear. She treated Illishar as she would her own folk, appeared to regard him as no different from a unicorn.

"Gladly," she answered. "I welcome your company."

The gryphon bowed his head in a flattered nod. "And I yours, little darkamber, for I sense that like me, you mean to win your way to the ledges of honor among your flock."

Spring

★ 17 ★

Spring, Jan saw, and no longer first spring. A month or more had passed since equinox. Watching in the dragon's pool, Jan felt uneasiness. He saw the future Vale spread green below him, his fellows grazing its hillsides, their winter shag long shed. But he saw no sign of himself, no indication that by the time predicted in this foreseeing, he had returned. And he would need to be returned by spring if he were to lead the march to the Hallow Hills.

Jan saw his sister Lell high on the Vale's grassy steeps. She looked older, less a filly than a half-grown. Her legs had lengthened, as had her neck and mane, her horn no longer a colt's blunt truncheon, but a slim flattened skewer, pointed and edged. Standing on a rocky outcrop overhanging the Vale, she looked a young warrior. Illishar sat beside her. His feline form — huge almost as a formel — dwarfed his unicorn companion. Lell had not yet reached a half-grown's size, but she had attained the shape, leaving fillyhood behind. Within the year, Jan felt sure, she would be initiated. How soon, he wondered, before she joined the courting rites by the Summer Sea?

Breeze lifted Lell's mane, her face grown longer and more slender, a young mare's. Beside her, Illishar's raised wings cupped the breeze, one curving above Lell's back. He and she watched a group of warriors sparring far below on the valley floor. Jan spotted the black-and-rose figure of Tek directing the exercises, the dappled yellow and grey of Dagg alongside her. Lell tossed her head.

"They won't let me join in," she said. "They say I'm too young. Jan would never exclude me so! So every day I watch them, then steal off and practice by myself."

Illishar stretched to let breeze riffle his feathers. "So, too, did I in my youth — until I had won me a spot among the formels. They would not grant it willingly. I had to prove myself beyond all quarrel. They called me a little, useless tercel squab, keen enough for hunting, perhaps, but never so much as considered for a perch beside the wingleader or for serious war." He laughed his throaty, purring laugh. "I proved every one of them wrong."

Lell turned to him. "We don't do that. Among my folk, we don't discount our he-colts. All half-growns are expected to become warriors. Besides, with unicorns, it is the stallions who are heftier."

Again Illishar laughed. "I know! Such an odd and fascinating flock. Though Malar did not deem my joining your war a savory task, I relish it, for I have learned more of your folk in one short moon than ever I could have done in a lifetime otherwise."

Together they watched the maneuvers below. Tek and Dagg's shrill whistles reached the heights. Jan had never seen the warriors so crisp. He felt a surge of pride, gratitude to Tek and Dagg, then regret that he was not to be among them. He shook it off. The herd need fear naught from lack of practice or skill when they met the wyrms. He could not have trained them better himself.

"You see? You see?" he heard Lell whispering. "The left flank doesn't swing fast enough. They must wheel more sprightly if they're to close the trap ere wyverns flee. When Jan arrives, he'll chase them into step."

Beside her the green-winged tercel nodded. "My flock employs similar stratagems, but ours are all airborne."

"Will you teach me?" Lell asked him. The other laughed, eyeing her wingless shoulders. Lell sighed heavily. "I wish I could fly."

"Become a gryphon, and you shall," her companion teased. The darkamber filly whickered and kicked at him.

"I want you to teach me another lay!" she cried.

"What?" the tercel reared back in mock surprise. "I have already taught you Ishi's Hatching. It is the talk of all your flock. Next they will say you are my acolyte."

Lell shook herself. "I would not mind a bit. I want to learn every song I can ere you must go." Her tone abruptly saddened. "After we fight the wyverns, you'll return to your mountains, and I'll not see you more."

The gryphon folded his wings, some of the feathers just brushing Lell's back as they closed. "No fear, little darkamber," he told her. "My pinions are strong. We gryphons do not let friendships lapse. But touching on your coming war, is it not high time your herd departed?"

Lell nodded, her eyes on Tek far, far below. "We all hoped Jan would have returned by now. But he has not come. So Tek waits. But I heard her telling Dagg we can bide no more than another fortnight before we must begin our trek. I think we should wait! Yet all the herd champs to face the wyverns. We have been waiting four hundred years."

Jan felt himself rising away from the Vale. The air around him thinned and darkened. His view dimmed. He had the brief sensation of hurtling through stars, then of sudden descending. He became aware of himself underground once more, beneath the Hallow Hills. Lynex the wyvern king lay in his barren chamber, all seven snaking heads wakeful now. Despite the absence of fire, the den was lighter than it had been. Illumination from the lightwells had the warmer intensity of spring. The wyvern heaved his scarred and bloated form upright to stare at the charred fireledge. The single greatest head among the writhing tangle of necks pulled transparent lips back from splintery fangs.

"First these stingless peaceseekers," it snarled. "Then my queen slain. Now the last of our fire burnt out." Its voice was deep, all gravel and broken flint.

The tiniest head struck out at nothing, flattening its hoodlike gill ruff, hissing, "Burnt out. Burnt out!"

"No thanks to *you*," one of the middle-sized pates muttered, glaring at the smaller ones.

The little nob turned, spat at its companions. "You!"

"Silence!" roared the one great head.

Five countenances flinched, but the sixth, the tiniest, turned and hissed. The large head snapped savagely at the little thing. With a shriek, the tiniest nob ducked. The great head eyed each smaller one in turn.

"I hold you all responsible," it snarled. "I might still cull the lot of you and rear a new crop of secondary skulls — ones with brains this time!"

The last words were a shout. Again the smaller heads cowered. None spoke.

"If only my queen lived still, she would know what to do. Winters have been so cold. Our torch dimmed, and the stingless freaks thwarted the wood gatherers. How they must have celebrated when they learned the torch was out. 'Devour them all!' my queen would have said."

The great head turned away, muttering. The half-dozen subsidiaries watched, all turning in unison as their leader wove. Jan was reminded suddenly of pacing among his own kind, or the random pecking of nervous birds. The wyvern shifted from one thick, badger-like forepaw to the other. Knifelike nails bit into the chamber's crystalline floor.

"So many of them now," the great head continued peevishly. "Their mothers hide them from me. They even breed. Whole nests of stingless offspring from stingless progenitors! There must be a way to find and seize them."

"A way," one of the two middle-sized heads echoed warily. The great head ignored it.

"Perhaps we should command loyal followers to hunt them,

harry them from one end of the warren to the other," the companion middle-sized pate suggested softly.

Two of the other nobs nodded vigorously. "Harry them! A clean sweep."

"Yes," the great head mused, picking at the ancient scars on the royal breast. "Yes. A sweep." Abruptly the One frowned. The smaller pates tensed. "But not all with stings can be relied upon. Most have nieces or nephews who are stingless, sisters or brothers, even daughters and sons! Some have gone so far as to begin to believe the ravings of those . . . those barbless lunatics."

"Ravings," the tiniest maw fizzed. "Lunatics!"

"How do they stay alive?" the wyvern king's largest pate exclaimed. "They will not hunt living prey. They must eat carrion!"

"Carrion!" the littlest head spat.

"What sort of existence is that for a wyvern?" the largest nob growled at a middle-sized head.

"No existence at all," it responded hastily.

Preoccupied, the large one turned away. "They are reverting to what we once were, when we dwelled among the thrice-cursed red dragons: stingless rubbish clearers, eaters of the dead!"

"Never again!" one of the small pates echoed.

Its fellows joined it: "Such indignity."

"The degradation."

"All our woes are the unicorns' doing," one of the middle-sized muzzles ventured. "Had they not deprived us of our queen, the stingless ones would never have multiplied."

"We must wreak revenge against the unicorns as well," the other middle-sized nob added.

The largest, central head considered. "That we must," it murmured. "But they only come in spring, and only a score or two, to keep their nightlong vigil by the wellspring atop the limestone steep. Truth to tell," he mused, "they come a few weeks after equinox. It is that time now."

The wyvern king reared suddenly. The other heads jerked in surprise.

"The stingless traitors can wait," Lynex's oldest pate said sharply. "We'll arrange an ambush for the unicorn pilgrims instead. My loyalists shall have the meat — and I'll know my supporters by who agrees to taste this living prey. Once we have feasted, time enough to fall upon the stingless and their collaborators!"

"Yes! Yes!" the other nobs rejoiced. "We'll lie in wait for unicorns along the path to their vigil pool. They will never sip its healing draught! We'll rend the flesh of our enemies, then devour our own kind — stingless cowards and any others not wyvern enough to use their stings."

The seven-stranded laughter of the wyvern king echoed through the limestone hollows. Again Jan felt himself lifted, drawn up through tons of earth covering the wyverns' dens, out into the light and air again. A blur of motion, the momentary feel of rushing. He found himself hovering above the Vale once more. Spring had advanced another half moon. Tek stood upon the council rise. Dagg and Ryhenna, Teki and Jah-lila, Ses, Illishar and Lell flanked her. Once more the whole herd stood assembled.

"He is not yet among us, but he will return," Tek told them. "We have waited as long as we dare. To delay more would betray his vision. I doubt not that Jan will rejoin us, but our march must now begin. We have just-weaned colts and fillies among us. This trek will last the remainder of the spring. It will be new summer when we reach the Hills, where wyverns wait our hooves and horns!"

Shouts of approval rose from the press. The cry of "Jan, Jan the prince!" went up, while some — more than a few — shouted, "For Tek! Tek, regent and prince's mate!"

Aye, Jan thought with sudden bitterness. *They* should *cheer her, for she is their rightful battleprince, not I.* Regret seized him, and envy. *Would that I were wholly other than who I am,* he thought, *some Renegade, even, not the late king's son. Sooth, I could gladly give my office up if only I might keep my pledge with Tek.* He shoved his painful thoughts aside. It was all hopeless. Below him, Tek cried: "Away, then. To our homeland! To the Hills."

She sprang from the council rise, her mane of mingled black and rose streaming. Her companions on the rise sprang behind her: red Jah-lila, painted Teki, dappled Dagg and his copper mate, Ryhenna, darkamber Lell with the milk-pale mane, and her mother, Ses, the color of cream with a mane like crimson fire. Illishar rose into the air in a green thrashing of wings. Sunlight flashed on his golden flanks. Beneath, the herd surged after Tek, all eager to depart the Vale, hearts bound for the far Hallows.

Jan became aware of an echo, oddly hollow, as though originating deep underground. His view of the herd climbing the steeps of the Vale shrank, grew distant. Before them, he knew, lay the Pan Woods and the Plain. Once more he pulled back, traveling at speed. It seemed that darkness fell, until he realized he had merely come to himself in the vast and sunless dragon's den. Glare of the molten firelake flickered across the pool of water in the red queen's brow. The chanting that had drawn him from the Vale echoed somewhere overhead, in the caves above. Awareness of himself and of Wyzásukitán once more faded as his mind floated upward to the source of the sound:

"Now fare we forth, far Hallows bound. . . ."

Jan beheld the Hall of Whispers, burial crypt of Mélintélinas. He saw the Scouts of Halla dispersed among the old queen's bones. Oro stood by the great skull with its pool of lustrous, dark water. He led the chant, bidding his comrades come forward one by one, take a single sup from that pool, which seemed never to run dry. Having sipped, each shaggy unicorn filed away across the great chamber, disappeared into shadows beyond the gleam of the dragon's jewels. Their recitation never faltered.

> "When time betides, a way be found.
> Afar, ancestral comrades call.
> We answer ably, ardent all. . . ."

Their words puzzled Jan. They moved with orderly determination, as though embarking upon some quest. *Far Hallows bound* — could Oro's fellows truly mean to cross Salt Waste and Plain? He distinctly remembered the dark maroon telling him no egress led from the Smoking Hills. How, then, did the Scouts intend to leave? Though the unexpected possibility of allies buoyed Jan, his skin prickled — for even if Oro and the rest managed to win free of these mist-enshrouded mountains, how would they avoid deadly wyvern stings?

Unease swept him. He struggled, but found himself unable to rouse from this dream of the future unfolding before him in the dragon's brow. The Scouts of Halla vanished from view. Lost in the underground caverns of the Smoking Hills, their chanting diminished, finally ceased. Darkness awhile. Then he beheld the Plain rolling before him, drenched in the sunlight of middle spring. He had no inkling how much time was to have passed.

Before him, two groups of unicorns converged. The first, led by Tek, her particolored rose and jet unmistakable among the orange reds and sky-water blues, the occasional grey or gold. Narrow at the head, flaring, then tapering toward the rear, the herd flowed across the green grass Plain. Young occupied the center, flanked by their elders on every side. The steady, deliberate pace, Jan observed, enabled even the youngest to travel untaxed. Halfgrowns frisked and sparred along the fringes. Plainsgrass around them rippled and bowed.

The vast warband of the Vale moved toward another group, far fewer, but much more widely spaced. The foremost of these stood dark blue with a silver mane. Jan recognized Calydor with his starbespeckled coat. To one side stood the seer's niece, Crimson, and her pale-blue filly, Sky. Crimson's belly looked heavy and round, in foal again. Her companion, Goldenhair, was nowhere to be seen, but Jan spotted her father, Ashbrindle, on Calydor's other side. Numerous Plainsdwellers flanked them. They stood awaiting the Valedwellers' approach.

Tek whistled the herd to a halt. Dagg flanked her, Ryhenna a few paces behind. Her mother, Jah-lila, stood at her other shoulder with Lell, Teki the healer, and Dhattar and Aiony with Ses well back of them all. Above, Illishar circled, his shadow passing over them from time to time.

"Hail, Free People of the Plain," the pied mare called. "I am

Tek, regent and mate to Aljan Moonbrow, our prince. We come in peace and seek no quarrel."

"Hail," the star-strewn seer replied. "I am Calydor, singer and farseer among my folk, who call me Alma's Eyes. Some here have met your mate. I bid you safe travel."

"We seek to pass through your lands on our way to our ancestral home, which we mean to wrest from treacherous wyverns," Tek continued. "Have we your leave to pass?"

Calydor tossed his mane. "Though your goal is known to us, none here may grant you leave — for the Plain is not ours. We lay no claim. Rather, 't claims us, the People of the Plain. Pass freely, as we do, and ask no leave."

The pied leader of the unicorns bowed her head. "I thank you, Calydor, and all your folk. I pledge my herd will not trouble yours as we pass. My mate has come before us and told our tale. Should any among you care to join our cause, my folk stand eager to accept allies. Once we have won back our Hallow Hills, all who fought alongside us will be welcome to share our newfound home."

Snorting, stamping, and a tossing of heads among the Plains-dwellers followed. Jan's ears pricked, but he could not be sure he had heard a whicker or two, quickly bitten off. Solemnly, Calydor shook his head.

"I thank you, Regent Tek, for your generosity. I know of none among my folk who would join you. We of the Plain are not reft of homeland. We stand content. Any of my fellows are, of course, free to embrace your cause. Perhaps in time some will make such wishes known. But we do not generally savor war. The vastness of the Mare's Back settles our disputes. If others offend us, we leave them. But we wish you well for the sake of your mate, who impressed me greatly as an honorable wight."

Watching, high above them in dreams, Jan warmed to Calydor's praise. Yet he sensed consternation among his own folk at the Plainsdweller's reply. Most of those from the Vale, Jan suspected, had simply assumed these ragtag vagabonds would rush to join the herd's battle march, praising Alma for the privilege. That their herd's sacred quest might be viewed with cool detachment by out-siders baffled some. Jan himself could only smile. He admired Tek's calm, collected response.

"So be it," she said warmly. "We welcome any who join us and bid fair weather to the rest. One other favor I would ask. My folk have traversed the Plain many times on yearly pilgrimage to initi-ate our young. But those bands numbered only warriors and half-growns, no elders or weanlings or suckling mares. The host before you moves far more slowly. We need guides to show us shelter from wind and rain, help us ward away pards and find sufficient water. Would any among you consent to the task?"

Jan sensed interest stirring among the Free People of the Plain. Calydor stepped forward.

"I myself will gladly escort you," he answered. "I wot these parts well. Many of my companions may choose to accompany. We are, I confess, most curious, having heard many rumors of you, but rarely met Moondancers face to face.

Tek nodded. "Very well," she said. "Let us share path for as long as may be."

With mixed eagerness and hesitation, the two groups merged, colts and fillies boldest, half-growns boisterous. Full-growns and elders on both sides approached more warily. Yet the two groups did mingle, exchanged tentative questions, greetings. Only one among the Valedwellers did not stir, Jan noticed presently. One mare poised motionless. Others eddied around her, yet she re-mained rooted, eyes riveted on the star-strewn seer who, joined by his brother, niece and niece's daughter, stood treating with Tek, Dagg, Ryhenna, Teki, Jah-lila and various Elders of the Vale.

Calydor caught sight of her suddenly. She stood not many paces from him. Glancing up, his gaze fell upon her. He froze. He had not marked her before, Jan realized. She must have stood screened from his view during Tek's initial greeting, or perhaps the pied mare had held the seer's whole attention. But he glimpsed the other now. Jan saw the silver-flecked stallion's eyes lock on hers. Half a dozen heartbeats, the pair of them stared mute. The mare's fiery mane, red as poppies, beat against the pale ivory of her pelt.

With a start, she wheeled and loped away. Not a word or a whistle, not a backward glance. Unnoticed by the others, the stallion's eyes yearned after her. Plainly, he could not desert the parley. But why, Jan wondered, had the mare not joined them? As one of the youngest of the Council of Elders, she was entitled, indeed expected. Jan's brow furrowed. The pale mare's conduct baffled him. He would have thought her eager to speak with Calydor, learn all she could from the seer of the time he had spent with Jan. But she had fled away. The young prince could not fathom it. For the red-maned mare had been Ses, his own dam.

Oasis

★ 18 ★

A passage of time. Jan knew not how long. He had lost all awareness of the dragon's den and of his own body, wholly absorbed
in visions of events to come. He knew only that time had elapsed
between the last future scene he had observed and the new one
now beginning. The Plain still, but night shadowed. A brilliant
moon shone down. Tall grass swayed and whispered about a series
of meandering waterways and interconnected pools. Jan spied unicorns of the Vale camped all around, most lying up near the largest
waterhole. A few Plainsdwellers mingled with the herd. Others lay
off in the tall grass or under trees flanking the fingerling pools.

Sentries, both Valedwellers and Plainsdwellers, stood alert for
pards. The fillies and foals lay surrounded by elders. Jan harbored
no fear for them. Scenting the slight, sighing breeze, he found it
free of all odor of predators. Nevertheless, he was keenly aware
that this oasis — so vital to his folk — formed a maze of rills and
rises, troughs and groves and irregular pools. Despite the sentries'
diligent watch, almost any creature — even one large as a unicorn
or pard — might steal past undetected if it moved stealthily and
luck ran with it.

Shadows, movement among the trees. Far from the main camp,
which lay barely within view through the close-spaced trees, Jan
detected motion. Two small figures fidgeted among the treeboles,

one black-and-silver, well camouflaged by mottled moonlight and shade, the other wholly white, pale ghostly as a dream. With a start of surprise, Jan recognized the tiny pair: Aiony and Dhattar, his own filly and foal. They stood taut, listening, straining to see through the moonblaze and shadow. Jan heard rustling.

"Here she comes," Aiony whispered to her brother. He nodded with a little snort.

A third figure emerged from the trees, larger than the first two, but still much smaller than full-grown. For a moment moonlight glanced across her. Jan was able to discern the darkamber coat, the milky mane of his sister Lell. For a moment, Jan thought he sensed another presence, something larger than all three of them, moving behind Lell in the darkness of the trees — but the moment passed. No scent, no sound, no further hint of motion from that quarter. Lell shook herself.

"There you are," she hissed. "It took me best part of an hour, stumbling about dodging sentries, to find you."

Jan saw his son's legs stiffen, his coat bristle. "We told you the pool shaped like a salamander."

Lell snorted. "They're *all* shaped like salamanders," she answered, exasperated.

Dha's mouth fell open as though to make some reply, but his sister murmured, "Peace. They come."

The darkamber filly and Dhattar both turned, moving closer to each other and to Aiony.

"I'm not sure this is wise," Lell muttered, her sudden caution surprising Jan.

"You wanted to see wyverns," Dhattar responded.

"Aye, but in secret?" his young aunt inquired. "Years from now, when we tell the tale, no one will believe us."

Aiony nodded, rubbing her cheek against the older filly's shoulder. "They will believe us, rest sure."

"Should we not inform Tek? As regent . . ."

"She deserves our loyalty and trust," the younger filly finished. "Aye. No doubt. Had we informed her, she would surely have kept her head and acted well."

"But what of others?" Dhattar picked up his sister's thread. "The herd's hatred of wyverns goes back centuries. Even now we march against those still loyal to Lynex who hold our homeland from us."

Lell's gaze turned inward, considering. "You fear if we told Tek, she might not believe us?"

Aiony laughed softly. "Not that. Nay, never that."

"If we told her," Dhattar replied, "she must consult the Elders. Others would learn of it. Soon all would know."

"You fear Tek might not be able to restrain our folk from falling upon these wyverns?"

Dhattar shrugged. "Perhaps. These wyrms are defenseless, after all."

"Not all of them," Lell countered. "You said some of them have stings."

"To which we are impervious," Aiony replied. "Nay, theirs is the greater peril. Our mother rules by the herd's goodwill. Why strain her regency by inviting strife?"

Lell set her teeth, deep in thought, and cast one furtive glance over her shoulder as though searching for something behind them in the dark. Jan detected nothing. Evidently neither could Lell. A moment later, she returned her attention to her young nephew and niece.

"Well enough, then. I will watch — but mark me, I'll raise the alarm if they offer the least . . ."

She did not finish the phrase. Across the narrow finger of water, a form appeared, translucent as ice. Blazing moonlight cut through its reptilian shape, illuminating sinews, suggestions of organs and the shadows of bones. The oily, fine-scaled skin gave off a rainbow sheen. Long-necked, the creature's body sported two wide forepaws before tapering away into a lengthy tail. The form was joined by another of its kind and another still. The nostrils on their long, tapered muzzles flared at the scent of water.

Standing just at trees' edge on the opposite bank, the three colts stood motionless. Scarcely the length of a running bound separated the three wyrms from them. Clearly parched, the newcomers hesitated only an instant before slithering toward the pool. Two bent eagerly to drink, but the third caught sight of the young unicorns reflected in the water. With a little shriek, it jerked upright. Its two companions did the same.

"Unicorns!" one hissed. "Warn the others —"

"Peace," Aiony called, her soft voice carrying easily in the still night air. "We mean you no harm."

The three across the pool hesitated, clearly torn between two terrors: that of remaining and that of fleeing without tasting the precious water. The middle one, slightly larger than the others, seemed to rally.

"What do you mean?" it demanded. "Are your folk not enemies of my kind? How is it you offer peace?"

"We are Lell Darkamber, king's daughter," Aiony replied, nodding to the filly at her side, "and Aiony, princess-to-be, and my brother, Dhattar, prince-to-be. We war only against followers of Lynex, who will not yield our rightful lands."

"We are seers, my sister and I," Dhattar went on. "We know you have deserted Lynex and fled the Hills, and that you hold him as much an enemy as do we."

Across the pool, the three wyverns gaped in surprise. Jan discerned all at once that they were younglings, far from fully grown. *Of course,* he reasoned. *They would have to be.* The only stingless ones to have survived among the wyverns had hatched since the death of the wyvern queen.

"It is true we are no friends of Lynex," another of the white wyrms admitted. "He sought to destroy our kind. Now he lies in wait for your pilgrims along the moon lake's path. We fled rather than join that treachery. We are done with Lynex and his stingtailed ways. We long only for a peaceful life which harms no one. We seek new dens in a new homeland."

"Show us your tails," Lell called. "We must be sure."

Unhesitatingly, the wyvern trio held up the blunt, stingless tips at the end of their whiplike tails. The darkamber filly nodded, satisfied.

"Well enough," she said. "Drink and go your way. We three

will not harm you. But mark you take all pains to avoid our sentries, for if you draw their notice, my companions and I cannot pledge your safety. Few of our fellows distinguish wyrms with stings from those without."

The three wyverns hesitated a long moment. Sheer fatigue seemed to decide for them, and they dipped their muzzles to the pool, drawing the water in desperate draughts. At last, the eldest raised its head.

"We thank you," it offered. "We have long suspected our legends calling your kind lackwits and fools to be untrue. Till now, we have had no truth with which to dispel them. Rest sure that our talespinners will remember this deed, how unicorns spared us and offered us water, allowing us to journey on unscathed."

"The rest of our number must drink," another of the wyverns hissed urgently.

"Fetch them," Lell replied. "We will stand watch."

Quick as a flinch, the smallest of the wyrms vanished into the trees. Of the remaining two, the younger spoke.

"Five summers gone, your warriors slew Lynex's queen and gave our kind the chance we needed to multiply and grow. Unwittingly, perhaps. Still, we owe you that."

"Our sire and dam slew her," Dhattar told them, "with their shoulder-friend, Dagg. They only did so because she meant to kill them and would not let them go."

"Our flight from Lynex has succeeded," the other wyvern replied, "solely because he dare not send loyalists to hunt us down while marshaling his forces to ambush you. We knew we must seize this, our one chance of escape, lest he fall upon us and devour us as he means to do with you."

Aiony and Lell glanced at one another. "He may find himself surprised instead," the older filly answered.

"But where will you go?" Aiony asked the two wyrms suddenly. "You must find shelter by summer's end."

The pair twitched in despair. "We know nothing of the world beyond our dens. We knew only that we must flee or die. We cannot guess where our trek will lead, only that it must be far from Lynex and his murderous kind."

"Hark me," Aiony replied. "My sib and I have seen your destination in dreams. You must circle back the way you came, for no haven lies before you. Travel north and west instead, and you will find dens in plenty by summer's end. This I vow. You must trust our word. Had we meant you harm, we had raised the alarm by now."

The two wyverns gazed at her uncertainly until a rustling behind made them turn. Other wyverns emerged from the trees, heads darting cautiously. Catching sight of the pool, they hastened to the bank, drank eagerly and long.

"Look into the water," Dhattar murmured to Lell. "I'll show you the wyrmking in his lair."

Lell looked deep, and as she did so, Jan felt his perception merge with hers. Through Lell's eyes, he saw the moonbright pool, its still surface disturbed by the touch of many wyverns. Lell heard their soft lapping, the rustle of bodies, quiet hissing of breath. Jan watched her reflection ripple in the pool beside Dhattar's. Their images pulled apart and re-formed into new shapes: Lynex's den, shot through with moonlight. The white wyrmking towered above a cringing, single-headed underling.

"Gone?" the central, largest pate demanded, and its secondary heads echoed, "What do you mean, gone?"

"Escaped, my liege," the messenger whimpered. "Fled to the Plain. Not a stingless one remains in all our dens."

"Fled?" the great head of Lynex raged. "They had no right! They were mine. My subjects. Mine to banish or destroy. So hungry — I have grown so very hungry, waiting on these unicorns. Where now is my feast?"

The messenger cowered before Lynex as the wyrmking's half-dozen smaller aspects ranted, "Hungry, hungry! Longing for the feast!"

Jaws snapping, heads writhing above the scar-laced breast, the iridescent white form reared up, roaring its rage. Suddenly the

great central head whipped around, returned its gaze to the messenger now creeping away.

"Halt," Lynex spat. "You do not have leave to go. Did you
not mark your king hungers?"

The other gave a terrified cry. "No, no, my liege! I am but a
messenger. Mercy. Mercy, I beg you! . . ."

Frantically, the little wyrm dashed for the den's egress. Quicker
than thought, the wyverns' seven-headed king lunged. Brilliant
moonlight from a lightwell glanced across him, breast scars gleaming between the stumpy forepaws' powerful, extended claws, teeth
like broken fishbones, all seven mouths agape. Sickened, Lell
heard the messenger shriek. Dhattar set his hoof down in the pool,
breaking the image.

"We needn't watch more," he told her softly.

Jan felt his sister's silent sigh. She shook herself, heart thumping
inside her ribs, voice tight with outrage.

"He's evil," she whispered. "He eats his own kind."

Dhattar nodded, then glanced away. The stingless wyverns had
finished drinking. Jan observed them: all were noticeably plumper,
more nimble, less weary. Aiony nodded gravely to the foremost
among them. Apparently they had been speaking softly for some
time.

"We will not forget, little black-and-silver. Seeking these dens
which you describe, we will praise your name, and think no more
ill of unicorns."

"Have a care how you depart," Aiony answered. "All the herd
does not feel as we. One day, perhaps, we will pledge truce with
stingless wyverns — but for now, this must be but our own, privy
pact. Avoid our sentries and depart in peace, guided by Alma's
eyes."

Softly as running water, the wyverns slipped away. Jan marked
only the barest rustle of grass as they withdrew. That, too, faded.
Lell looked at Aiony.

"They're smaller than I thought."

Dhattar nodded. "Those were but youths, and stingless. The

ones with stings are older, far greater in size. Our warriors will have no easy task."

"Truth," another voice behind them murmured, a deep, throaty purr like a grass pard's thrumming.

Dhattar and Aiony jumped and wheeled. Lell did not, merely cast a glance over one shoulder at Illishar just emerging from the trees. His massy, wingèd form was as graceful moving along the ground as it was in flight.

"You unicorns are a fearless lot," he chuckled. "I wonder you don't all perish before you're grown."

Aiony laughed, nipping the tercel gently on his great eagle's foreleg. "You move very silent, Illishar."

"And you are not quite the all-seer you think yourself, little moonshadow."

"We're young," Dhattar answered matter-of-factly. "We'll see more clearly in time." With one curving talon, the gryphon pulled a wisp of grass from the white foal's mane. Gently, Lell champed her nephew by the crest of the neck and shook him, then did the same to Aiony.

"I thought best — since you'd sworn me against informing your dam — to bring a warrior fierce enough to defend us at need."

Jan felt relief flooding him to realize Illishar had guarded the young trio the whole while.

"Come," the gryphon said, turning. "Night grows late. Were we to stay longer, we would be missed. Let us see if we are as clever at slipping back through the sentries as we were at slipping out."

Dhattar and Aiony on either side, Lell bringing up the rear, the three colts followed. The shadow of the grove swallowed them. Before them, barely in sight, the main body of the camp lay off across the tall grass. No sooner had the four companions vanished from Jan's view than two new figures emerged from the trees. These, too, had apparently concealed themselves and watched. Deep cherry red, Jah-lila shook her standing mane and turned to her fellow, the star-covered stallion Calydor.

"Sooth, their power astonishes," he remarked, "and in view of their age — foaled but three summers gone?"

The red mare nodded.

"This deed bodes weighty for their folk."

Jah-lila smiled. "When it becomes known. But that will not be for some seasons yet."

"Only three years in age." Calydor shook his head in disbelief. "The Sight runs strongly in their blood."

The red wych eyed him wryly, murmured, "On both sides. Now ask me what you will."

The star-marked seer snorted. "Will you aid me? Will you do as I ask and arrange a meeting? She will not converse with me in others' sight, or even look on me. She flees when I approach. I must speak with her. I must."

The red mare's black-green eyes grew merry. "Have I not always brought you word of her whenever I traversed the Plain? Let you know she was well and had borne two healthy colts and fared happily among her folk?"

"You told as little as you could," Calydor snapped. "You never told me her station, that she had pledged as prince's mate and borne him heirs."

The red mare shrugged, gazing off into the trees in the direction Illishar and his three companions had gone. "I had my reasons." Her gaze turned back to the other. "Tell me, now that you have met, what think you of Jan?"

"A fine young stallion, deft dancer, gifted singer — as different from the raver that sired him as I can imagine."

"And Ses's other child?"

"Brave as a pard, that one," Calydor exclaimed. "She'd make a fine 'Renegade.'"

Jah-lila whinnied with laughter. "High praise."

The blue-and-silver stallion shifted impatiently. "Enough chat, Red One. Will you aid my cause? Will you persuade her to meet me, in secret if she must?"

The red mare turned, eyeing him fondly and shaking her head.

"No need, old friend. Ses has already come to me, entreating me to devise this tryst. Wait a little. She will come."

Jan saw the blue-and-silver stallion start, frame rigid, eyes moonlit fire. Jah-lila nipped him affectionately and meandered away into the trees.

"I'll leave you to her." Her words floated softly back over one shoulder. "And wish you best fortune."

The shadows took her. Her form vanished. Ears pricked, breath short, Calydor gazed into the moon-mottled grove. The hairs of his pelt lifted as though he were cold. Night breeze blew balmy. His long, silver whisk tail swatted one flank. He snorted, tossing the pale forelock back from his eyes, and picked at the loose soil near the riverbank with one hind heel. Before him, a figure coalesced, a mare of moonshine and smoke. With a curious mixture of purpose and hesitation, she moved forward. Unseen, many leagues distant, Jan recognized her instantly. The star-lit stallion called her name. Turning toward him, Ses halted. He drew near, choosing each step.

"Too long," he breathed. "Too long, my one-time love."

She eyed him sadly. "Perhaps," she murmured. "I, too, have felt the years."

"Why did you not come to me," he entreated softly, voice scarcely steady, "as once I begged? Were your Vale's walls so high, so fast you could not win free till now?"

Again, her sad-eyed gaze met his. "I had a daughter and a son to rear. A mate with whom to keep faith."

"A mate who betrayed you, and all your folk," the seer rasped, "who nearly destroyed his own herd, then tried to do the same to mine."

Ses cast down her eyes with a bitter sigh. "He was not always mad," she breathed. "I loved him well. Why did you not come to me, if you were so determined?"

Her words were a plea. She turned, unable to look at him. He gentled, drew closer.

"Knowing my coming could spell death for us both?"

She moved away. He gazed across the dark, motionless pool, every lumen of the sky mirrored there.

"The Red Mare brought me word of you," he murmured. "At long, odd intervals: that you had borne fine foals, that you seemed happy. She would not bear my messages."

Ses gazed at the shadows. "Jah-lila never told me she had found you — I suspect she knew I could not have borne such news. Parts of my life in the Vale brought me great joy: my children, aye. But always there was regret."

The cream-colored mare with the poppy-red mane turned to face him.

"I never dreamed she brought you word. She did not speak of her journeys to the Plain. I never asked her to find you or speak of me. I thought you had forgotten me."

Again he moved nearer. "I have spent my life remembering you." This time she did not draw away. Still he only gazed, as though not daring to touch lest she vanish, a dream. After a time, he said, "She bore me only bits and snatches, as though hearsay, claiming she was exiled from the Vale and did not know more."

"She was exiled," Ses murmured. "But she is a seer and knows far more than what her own eyes tell her."

The silvered midnight stallion sighed. "I, too, am a farseer. A fine one. Yet I could never find you in my dreams. Still all these years, I never lost hope that one day you would come to me."

The pale mare's laugh was bitter. "I asked Jah-lila to contrive this rendezvous that I might appeal to you to keep your distance. None yet know the fate of my mate. . . ."

"What of it?" Calydor cried, voice hoarse with astonishment. "You cast him off! Three years hence. The Red One told me this."

"Because his madness endangered my child. That does not leave me free to pledge another. We of the Vale do not treat lightly the swearing of eternal vows."

Calydor whickered, in bafflement and despair. "Here we make no such pledges. You could leave your folk. . . ."

"Do not say it!" Ses hissed. "Not while my youngest remains a child. Calydor, do not tempt me."

"Your herd poises on the brink of war," the farseer replied. "Of course I will tempt you. I will tempt all your folk. Do not go! Do not hazard your life. Remain with me upon the Plain and what need then for your hallowed Hills? Let the wyverns have them."

The pale mare's countenance hardened. "You forget the wrong done my people so many years ago."

"Centuries. To unicorns who are all long dead."

"Lynex of the white wyrms is not dead," she answered. "He holds the Hills in triumph still. For the righting of that ancient wrong my son was born."

"Had you but left your folk and come with me," Calydor besought her, "then he had been *our* son."

Ses started, turning. "Ours?" she whispered, barely audible. "Do you not . . . ?"

But the other ran over her words. "A dozen nights and days Jan and I spent in one another's company, trading our peoples' tales. All I learned of him I have sung across the Plain. What goodwill you find among us now is due largely to news of his peacemaking. Sooth to look at him, save for his color, one would never guess him to be scion to that warmongering sire. Would he *were* my son!" Calydor exclaimed. "Would ever I had sired a son so fine."

The pale mare stared at him for a long, long while. Her chestnut eyes revealed nothing. At last she spoke:

"Rest sure that once this war is done and Lell is grown, I will turn my thoughts to the Plain and to you. I promise no more. Until then, I beg you, keep clear."

The blue-and-silver's reply was quiet and full of pain. "Here we stand on the verge of summer, just three days' journey from the Hills. On the morrow, Tek and her warriors press on, leaving behind colts and fillies too young to fight, elders too frail, nursing mares and the halt and infirm to shelter with us at oasis till your messengers return. This much my folk have promised yours. And if a few hotheads have joined your lackwit crusade, as many among your own ranks mean to desert: those who have lost their stomach for this war or who, like us, cannot comprehend its end. You could be one of those, my love. The pair of us could be away before your sentries were aware."

Firmly, the pale mare shook her head. "Not while my son lives. Not while Korr's fate remains unknown. Not while my daughter is yet too young to fend for herself."

Calydor smiled. "That last will not be long," he mused. "A precocious one that."

"Like her brother."

"She reminds me of the bold young filly in the lay of the mare and the pard."

Ses's head snapped up. "Mare and pard?" she inquired testily. "What mean you by that?"

The farseer only smiled, reciting offhand. "'She who saw her enemy couched in the grass, and loved him for his beauty and his grace, and charmed him there, despite himself, and lived to tell the tale.' You might do well to keep one eye upon your fearless daughter, love," he said. "Young as she is, I think her heart already stolen, and the thief yet unawares."

A little silence grew up between them. Moon moved across heaven and the waters ever so slightly. The sky rolled a hair's breadth, tilting the stars.

"How can you go?" he asked. "How can you fly to war with your son not even here to lead the fray?"

"Have you seen him?" she queried. "Have you seen Jan in your dreams? If Jah-lila sees, she will not say. The twins see him, but all they can say is that he speaks with one all covered with jewels, deep within the earth or sky. I know not what they mean. Do you?"

Calydor shook his head. "I have not seen him."

Ses snorted. "Fine seer you."

The star-strewn stallion tossed his head. "I foresaw the dark destroyer, and the peacemaker who followed. I foresaw you, so many years ago. And I have seen much of weather and of pards that have threatened my people over the years." He shrugged. "I know not why I cannot see your son. One viewer cannot behold everything. I am but one among Álm'harat's many thousand eyes."

Ses gazed at the camp, dimly visible through the dark line of trees bordering the pool. "I must return," she sighed. "Three days' hard travel lies ahead, and beyond that, battle. The twins vow Jan will return at need. I trust soon to see my son again." Already she was moving toward the trees. "Go hale and safe, Calydor, that we may meet again after this war."

"Swear you will come away with me then," he whispered, "so I may bear the wait."

But she said nothing. Only wind murmured. She vanished into the dark of the trees. Calydor discerned no trace. As though a haunt, she had turned once more to mist. The Plain lay utterly silent save for the faintest breath breeze. Somewhere in the distance, he heard a pard cough. Above him, the moon, silvery gibbous, blazed like the greatest of Alma's eyes among the summer stars.

The Scouts of Halla

★ 19 ★

Gazing into the depths before him, Jan realized it was not near-summer sky he saw, but the darkness of the waters on the dragon queen's brow. Glimmers there were not stars but gleams reflected from the lake of fire. All view of future events faded. He knew himself to be in the den of Wyzásukitán. How long — an hour, an evening? He had no sense of time. Still he felt neither hunger nor fatigue, thirst nor intensity of heat. He had not been with the dragon long, surely. No more than a few hours at most.

The clear fluid of the pool before him trembled, sudden ripples traversing its surface, shaking apart the stars. Dragon's breath swirled about him like fog as Wyzásukitán sighed, lifting her head. The dark unicorn fell back a pace as the massive reptilian queen now gazed down upon him from a great height. The long muscles beneath her taut, jeweled skin flexed. Her wings and limbs and tail arched, rid themselves of stiffness. Again she sighed, and her white breath shot out like jets of cloud.

"What troubles you, prince of unicorns? I sense your disquiet."

Jan gazed up at her steadily, refusing to let her vastness overwhelm him.

"I am grateful for this foreseeing which you have granted, great queen," he answered, "but uncertainty chivvies me. Is what I see before me only that which *can* be — or that which *will* be, which *must* be?"

"I grant nothing," Wyzásukitán murmured in her measured, guarded way. She sounded quietly amused. "You behold only what you yourself are capable of beholding."

Abruptly, she fell silent. Jan waited a long moment. When she did not continue, he made bold to say, "You have not answered my question, great queen."

The red dragon betrayed not the slightest affront. She seemed only interested, perhaps approving. "You must answer it yourself, dark prince. What is it you see?"

The dark unicorn hesitated. "What I see has the feel of truth. . . ." The words trailed off. The dragon waited. "Yet if what I see has not yet come to pass, then it can be neither true nor false."

Wyzásukitán's mouth quirked, suppressing a smile.

"Oh?" she asked, so softly he almost did not hear. "Is it the future that you see?"

"Aye," he answered tentatively, then with conviction. "Aye. It *is* the future — no mere dream."

"Ah," the red dragon queen sighed. The steam of her breath rose toward the ceiling in roiling columns as she drew the long syllable out. "What troubles you, then?"

Jan felt a sudden crick of frustration. Was she toying with him? Suddenly he wondered, then shook himself. Nay, truth, he was sure she was not. He suspected her of being deliberately obtuse, while at the same time certain there was no malice in her. She was not questioning him merely to amuse herself, though he sensed his answers somehow amused her. Quashing a sudden urge to reply in kind, he drew breath and tried again.

"I wish to know if what I see is possibility or certainty. Do I see but one of many paths the future may take, or do I see the surety of what will without question come to pass?"

The dragon's jewel-encrusted browridge lifted. Her nostrils flared. "Consider. If what you saw were mere possibility, why should that trouble you?"

Jan thought a moment before replying. "If mere possibility, why bother to observe it?"

Wyzásukitán's great shoulder shrugged ever so slightly. "To spy a goal toward which to strive — or a warning of perils to avoid?"

The dark unicorn frowned. "Perhaps."

"Now consider this," the red queen continued: "if what you saw were indeed predestined, unalterable?"

Jan shifted uneasily. "Then I am most troubled."

She watched him. "Why?"

"Because I do not see myself in these scenes-to-come. Where shall I be? Am I not my people's Firebringer? Must I not journey among them to the Hallow Hills and lead their preparations to battle the white wyrms?"

"Must you?" the dragon replied. "Is that indeed foreordained? Are you privy to the last step of every dance set in motion by Her of the Thousand Jeweled Eyes?"

Her look grew suddenly less detached. Inquisitive. Penetrating, even. Jan felt his discomfiture grow. "Nay," he answered. "Alma reveals little of her plans. What I learn I invariably glean in snatches, glimpses."

"Yet always she has guided you?"

He nodded. "Even when I myself remained unaware."

"Then what uneases you?"

Jan frowned, trying hard to frame the words. "I sense somehow, gazing into your brow, that time slips away. That I should hasten back to my folk before their hour of need."

"You believe that the hour does not yet betide," answered Wyzásukitán. Doubtfully, Jan considered. Nay, of course not. Why caval so? None of what he had foreseen had yet come to pass. All lay in the offing. Ample time remained to rejoin the herd. Ample time. Did it not? The dragon queen shrugged. "Perhaps you do not see yourself among your folk because you do not wish to be among them."

The dark unicorn gazed up at her, baffled. The dragon gazed down.

"Might your absence have less to do with inability to rejoin them than with your refusal to do so?"

"Refusal?" Jan exclaimed, astonished. Outrage pricked at him. "Refusal to rejoin my folk — to accept the destiny toward which I have striven all my life?"

Wyzásukitán evidenced no surprise. Gently, she said, "Another thing troubles you, Firebrand. A duty unbearable holds you back from your folk."

Jan stared at her, her great gleaming form vast and beautiful above him, the light of the lake of fire winking and glancing off her jeweled skin like a thousand summer stars. He felt his unease collapse into terror.

"I don't know what you mean," he stammered.

She looked at him. "Indeed?" she asked. "You do."

"Nay, I . . . ," he started.

"Say me no nays," she answered curtly. "It is your mate, is it not? Tek, the rose-and-black mare who leads your herd. You love her. You long for her. Yet you fear reunion. Admit why that should be, Aljan of the Dark Moon. Tell me why you refuse to rejoin your mate."

Jan's head whirled. The cavern seemed to tilt. He felt himself falling helplessly through infinite space.

"It is not . . . not Tek," he managed, lock-kneed, swaying. The careening chamber steadied, stilled. He breathed deep. "Not Tek I fear, but what I must do when next we meet. What I must tell her. . . ."

The dragon inclined her head. "That is?"

Words choked him. "That she is Korr's heir before me, my own sister by half, sired by my sire, the king's secret firstborn daughter, queen of the unicorns."

He scarcely believed he had gotten it all out. He stood panting, unable to look at Wyzásukitán. He stared off across the huge chamber toward the lake of fire. It rippled, shimmered, not silent, but making low roarings from time to time, its thick, molten flux moving at crosscurrents. Hissing sounded, fiery vapors venting, and the thick fizzing of spattered drops. Blaze and shadows played against the chamber's walls. He felt his whole being in a state of tumult like the lake.

"Trust what you feel," the firedrake told him. "What rises in you at this news?"

Anguish. Fury. Nausea. He could admit to none of them. "I don't know."

Above him, Wyzásukitán turned her head to one side and eyed him askance. "Do you mean to renounce your kingship to Tek? To renounce her as your mate?"

"I don't know!"

He had no inkling what he intended to do. He had lived all his life believing himself to be prince, only to discover the office belonged to Tek. He had no right to rule. Tek deserved the truth. Deserved her birthright. The love he bore her was so great he felt his heart might burst. Yet how was Alma's prophecy ever to be fulfilled if he renounced his leadership?

But deep within his inmost soul, he knew that none of those considerations really mattered. What appalled him most was that in revealing Tek's parentage, he must lose her. Despite vows sworn by the Summer Sea, no matter how unbreakable in Alma's eyes, regardless the fruit of that innocent pledge, how could such a union be allowed to stand? What joy to rejoin the herd if nevermore might he claim Tek as his mate? That their bond, meant to last a lifetime, must now end was what he truly could not face.

"I don't know," he told Wyzásukitán, his voice a ghost. The great dragon was bending down again. Her huge head came to rest on the chamber floor before him.

"Then gaze once more into my brow," she replied, "and find your answer there."

The dark water drew him, shot through with images. He moved toward it, unable to resist. Below, he saw the dark, rilled expanse of the Smoking Hills, their cinder-black tors thrust up like antler tines. Snow dusted the peaks and the deep crags which never saw the sun. Slopes sheered away into dragon's breath. Valleys opened below. Jan could not understand how he himself had breached these barrier cliffs. No egress seemed possible for any wight devoid of wings.

He heard their chant before he saw them, strung out single file like an endless line of roan-colored ants. They moved in unison, hooves all falling at the same time, till the black stone rang with the beat of their song:

> "So soon the Scouts of Halla, we
> Fare forth to fill our destiny:
> On hardy wyrms to hone our horns,
> Unite in arms with unicorns
> Who march the Mare's Back; thus we must
> Endure the deadly Saltland dust
> As firedrake allies ope the way,
> Behold our Firebrand's battle day. . . ."

The chant rolled on and on, each step bringing the winding train of unicorns closer to the impassable ridges. Jan distinguished Oro at the head of the lengthy queue, which seemed to consist solely of brawny half-growns and warriors in their prime. The dark prince of the Vale recognized them instantly as a warhost. But where did they intend to go? Surely they could not mean to join Tek's host trekking across the Plain, for how could they hope to escape the Smoking Hills?

Yet as he watched, something caught his eye. Oro and the others moved almost as in trance, impervious to cold. Though their movements were measured, their expressions remained alert. No somnolent marchers, these. Was it only their singleness of purpose which made them appear invulnerable? Higher they climbed and higher, more shaggy goats than unicorns. Steadily, unhesitatingly, they scaled nearly vertical steeps and descended precipitous slopes. Jan marveled at their tirelessness, traversing the sheer paths in their snaking file hundreds of unicorns long.

Even so, he surmised, they were approaching a spot where they could proceed no farther. Oro and the front of the line had already reached it: a flat plateau falling away into a deep canyon, overlooked by a tall pinnacle. For the unicorns now assembling on the plateau, no means existed to move forward. The drop into the adjacent vale was sheer. No way to skirt the rift, for it was hemmed by unscalable scarps, the tallest a conical peak poised at one end of the canyon. Its sharp yet massive point rose above the others like a thick, curved horn.

How did the Scouts mean to cross, Jan wondered? When all had assembled, Oro stood near plateau's edge, his back to the steep, unbridgeable valley. Jan could not make out his words, though the others all listened attentively. They stood in perfect stillness, so utter as to seem preternatural. Not one so much as stamped a hoof for warmth. Oro turned to gaze at the rift before them, then at the pointed peak rising to one side. Jan noted the cone's asymmetry, the side facing the valley undercut, so that the pinnacle seemed to hang above it, tons upon tons of incredibly hard, black rock.

A faint tremor shook the ground. Jan felt its thrum even in the air. The mountains seemed to mutter almost imperceptibly, then subside. Oro and the others drew back from the plateau's edge. Another tremor, more forceful this time. Echoes and sharp reports as of a great cracking and straining rebounded from the far side of the valley. Oro's band crowded tightly together in the center of the plateau. Again, the tremor stilled. Silence then, save for the cracks and groans, as though the fabric of some immeasurably vast tree, twisted by wind, were slowly, ever so slowly, breaking apart.

None of the warriors upon the plateau whinnied in fear. None cavaled. They all watched, Jan realized, eyes fixed on the tall peak leaning above the valley. Jan stared at the peak. It was vibrating. Slightly at first, then more and more insistently, it created a shudder in the air. The shudder grew, like a wind slowly building, until it buffeted but made no sound. The groaning started again, so low it was nearly below Jan's range, a deep, thunderous keening like nothing he had heard before.

The next tremor, when it came, was so sudden, so violent, even Jan, floating bodiless above, flinched. The black, snow-covered cone tore from its base, plunging down into the deep crevasse with a concussion that seemed to rock the world. A gout of smoke or steam shot up from the base of the shattered peak, which appeared to be hollow. A hail of cinders and dust rained from the sky.

The valley swallowed the peak and ceased to be as the fallen mountain filled the rift from edge to edge. Thundering rubble continued to quake there, shifting and seething. The broken peak's conical base, which had not fallen, now rumbled and broke apart. Explosive blasts of earth and smoke. Jan glimpsed something moving in the heart of the disintegrating base, a huge shining thing, reddish in color, crawling or flowing along like a slow river, or the side of some immensely vast creature in motion under the earth, a creature that had lain dormant so long it had grown larger than its original tunnel, a creature shifting in sleep, or waking and stretching sleepily before moving off in search of more spacious dens.

Oro and the Scouts of Halla were in motion, too. As soon as the first force of the blast had passed and the rubble now filling the former valley settled, every unicorn waiting upon the plateau sprang forward. They dashed headlong across the quaking new stretch in a sweeping charge while smoking grey cinders pelted out of the sky, covering them with a dusting of grey.

The Scouts of Halla were across the rift. As they reached the far side, Jan realized with a start that the hills were gentler here. Beyond, he saw, lay the waterless Salt Waste. Wind blew in the direction of the Waste, pursuing the sprinting unicorns. Cinderfall grew heavier, the ground's trembling more ferocious. Had Oro's band not surged forward precisely when they did, Jan saw, they would never have managed to cross. Brightness infused the ashfall. Some of the cinders glowed. Some were not cinders at all, he grasped, but droplets of dragonsflood.

A bright fountain spewed from a rift in the ruin of the fallen peak's broken base. Beneath welled a molted tongue of red that spilled slowly to the shallow depression's floor. Once the fiery flood had wound across, all passage would be blocked, at least until it cooled. How long would that take, Jan wondered — days? Weeks? The Scouts of Halla fled on toward the Salt Waste across the foothills of Dragonsholm. Their heels raised a cloud which mingled with the falling ash.

Battle

★ 20 ★

Summer. The suddenness of transition startled him. One moment Jan had seemed to be wheeling over the snow-capped Smoking Hills, air obscured by clouds of dust and smoke. The next, he found himself leagues upon leagues away, the wide, green Plain rolling beneath, a clear cloudless dawn sky above, the Hallow Hills before.

Unicorns of the Vale lay in the tall grass, gazing toward their unreclaimed homeland. Tek, flanked by Ryhenna and Dagg, couched at the crest of the rise. Jah-lila, Teki, and Ses waited close behind. The rest of the band reclined below them, well hidden. No colts lounged among the band, no ancient elders or suckling mares. Warriors only made up the great warhost, nostrils flaring to scent the breeze, ears swiveling to catch every sound. Thick haze hung low in the sky far to the east, its source beyond horizon's edge. It tainted the sunrise orange-red, a fiery light bathing the Hallow Hills. The dappled warrior beside Tek shifted.

"No sign of him," he muttered. "Where is he? He set out an hour since."

"Grant him time," Ryhenna soothed in the strange, lilting cadence of her former tribe, the *daya.* "Dawn breaketh only now."

The pied mare turned, called softly. "What is that haze in the east? Can you tell?"

Below her, the red mare lifted her head. "Naught that will affect us here. It comes of the Smoking Hills."

"A blood-bright dawn," Teki the healer beside her murmured. "Will the weather hold?"

"Aye," the red mare told him. "It will."

"Blood-stained but beautiful," the pale mare, Ses, beside them whispered. "Its red light illumines the hills. So they appeared on the eve of my initiation, years ago."

"When thou sawest thy vision of the Firebringer?" Ryhenna inquired.

Ses nodded, wistful. "And other things."

Tek turned back to the Hallow Hills, glowing crimson in the dawnlight still. "Where is Jan?" she barely breathed. "Why has he not returned?"

A shrill cry fell from above, piercing as a kite's. The pied mare started, felt the warhost behind her stir. Her gaze darted skyward. A moment later, his shadow passed over her, and she was able to glimpse Illishar, his hue so well matched to the green sky he had approached unseen. Circling, he began to descend.

"At last!" Tek heard Dagg exclaim. "Once the wingcat reports, we can devise our best means of attack."

The wyverns lay concealed, hidden behind boulders and rocky outcroppings. The ravine formed a box canyon, its banks gentle at first, but whoever ventured its narrow passage found the sides soon steepened to precarious slopes. The wyverns often drove game here: deer and boar, bands of antelope that had strayed from the Plain. No game drives now since the first of the year. Instead, they had waited, king's loyalists ever on watch for unicorns, those thrice-cursed skulkers of the Vale who never failed to steal into the Hills sometime during the spring.

"What a ruin," the first of two wyverns sheltering behind a single boulder hissed. "This dawn marks summer's first day, and where are the unicorns? They never came."

"Nor will they," its companion muttered, smaller than the first, and more slenderly made. "They died out or gave up or lost their way. The sum is, they come here no more."

"Precisely," the first wyvern muttered. "We've frittered all spring on this fruitless task, when we might have been coursing young fawns and cracking their bones."

This larger wyvern was of a bluer cast than the more slender one. Its tail was longer, the sting upon it more wickedly barbed. A rudimentary second head was budding from one shoulder, no more than an offshoot, its features still indistinct, mouth sealed shut, the bulbous, bruise-dark lids of its nascent eyes not yet open. It writhed fretfully against the thicker stalk of the bluish wyvern's primary neck. With one blunt, badger-like claw, the ice-blue wyrm petted it, humming.

"This ravine makes a fair enough game-trap," the slimmer, more pearl-colored wyrm was saying. A summer hopper flicked through the air. With a snap, it downed the long-legged thing. "I've run down onc and springer here, even a Plainscalf once."

Its two-headed companion nodded impatiently. "As have we all. But now we must let game pass unmolested, lest we spook any phantom unicorns that might wander near."

"The king has lost his wits," the pearl-colored wyvern murmured, sniffing the grass in search of other hoppers. "Ever since the queen was slain."

"*There* was a wyvern," the elder wyrm exclaimed. Its rudimentary nob slumbered now against its collarbone. It scratched its main pate's gill ruff with one knife-nailed badger claw. "She'd have thrown the king down and taken his place, had the unicorns not finished her."

A scarlet earthworm wove through the grass. The bluish wyvern stabbed after it, but missed. Its companion studied a yellow butterfly fluttering about its head.

"Then we'd have fire still," it answered. "She'd have shared it among us again. It was only the king's edict — and his fear — that forbade each of us keeping our own fire, as we used to do. All those winters lazing beside a burning brand! That's what made us strong. It's lack of warmth caused all those stingless prits to hatch."

The yellow butterfly fluttered near. The pearlescent wyvern clapped its jaws, but the next instant spat, shook its head and pawed its muzzle to dislodge the clinging yellow wings. "Uch! It tastes of saltclay and sulfur."

Its companion chuckled. "No doubt. What you say of fire is true as well. Now that the king's let his own brand die, our last flame is gone. Unless we find another source, no more stinging wyrms will hatch of our broods. Mark me."

"The stingless ones," the pearly wyrm added. "You heard they fled? Aye, across the Plain. Six days ago."

Its bluish companion turned. "Fled? I thought they were in hiding."

"Nay," the slender wyvern assured it. "Yet not one stinging loyalist was sent in pursuit — lest we miss the unicorns! Time enough to track peaceseekers once we've dealt with His Majesty's unicorns — what is this sudden fascination? He says he sees them in his dreams. Says he feels them watching him."

"Unicorns," the bluish wyvern scoffed, glancing at the ravine's grass-covered slopes dotted with boulders and slabs of exposed stone. "We'll never see another. . . ."

"Hist!" his companion snapped, suddenly alert. The pearl-colored wyvern's gaze was fixed downslope. The larger wyrm heard grunts and whiffs of surprise from fellows massed behind other boulders on both their own and the facing slopes. Only those hiding lower on the near hillside were visible to the bluish wyvern. They, too, had become instantly attentive. Alongside, the pearl-colored wyvern breathed a single word: "Unicorns!"

Downslope, filing into the canyon, came a party of unicorns. Late morning sun blazed down. The breeze sighed balmy, just a bare trace cool. A robust young stallion led, his yellow dappling into grey along shoulder and flank. Only a few others in the band appeared, like him, to be warriors in their prime. Most seemed youthful half-growns. They traveled cautiously, eyes darting, ears up-pricked. The wyverns waited in fevered silence until the last of the band, a slim, coppery mare, had entered the confines of the sloping ravine.

"Now!" the pearl-hued wyvern screamed, rising to plunge down the slope in a streaking slither. "Drive them deep into the canyon. Trap and devour them!"

The bluish wyvern also lunged. All around, its fellows dodged from behind boulders and coursed toward the hapless unicorns, who wheeled and whistled in alarm.

"They're mostly striplings!" the bluish wyvern cried. "Helpless prits. Sting them to death and drag the meat to the king!"

It saw its own kind across the ravine, pouring down the opposite slope toward their prey. But what was this? Instead of scattering in terror, the unicorns were massing. Racing toward them, the two-headed wyvern heard the party's leader, the grey-and-yellow dapple, coolly whistling orders, saw the coppery mare and young half-growns beside her swinging to form themselves into an out-ward facing ring, horns bristling to meet the wyvern onslaught. Here was no motley band of colts. Those wyrms who reached them first were skewered and tramped, fell back with screams of surprise, hisses of rage.

"No matter!" the ice-blue found itself shrieking. "No matter they're warriors. We're larger than they. We outnumber them. Use your stings!"

Its own tail lashed to scourge the dappled stallion ramping before him. The unicorn braced for the coming blow, did not so much as dodge. He held his place in the outward-facing ring, hooves set, horn aimed.

"See how your blood burns at this!" the ice-blue wyvern shrilled, bringing its tail barb down like a flail.

The yellow stallion shuddered, shrugged the stroke aside, then lashed and lunged. The bluish wyvern drew back, surprised. All around, its snarling companions swarmed. None of the unicorns broke ranks. The blue wyrm saw them repeatedly stung, but though they flinched, they did not fall. The battle became a grunting, panting shoving-match, wyverns pressing in against the circle, horned warriors refusing to buckle.

"Our stings have lost their power!" the pearly one beside it cried, panic beginning to edge its voice.

"Our horns have not," the copper-colored mare beside the dappled stallion retorted, lunging. Her horn pierced the pearlescent wyvern through one shounder. It sank, writhing, colorless blood streaming down its pale hide. Its badger claws pawed ineffectually at the wound.

"I'm pierced!" it shrieked. "Pierced through the bone! The unicorn has rent me!"

"Our weapons are keener than once they were," the dappled stallion panted. One flailing forehoof landed a stunning blow to the wounded wyvern's skull. "And tempered by fire. Your fibrous bone no longer dulls and chips our skewers."

Beside the stallion, the copper mare bent to finish the fallen wyrm. With a shriek, the bluish wyvern beheld others of its folk struck down by these half-grown colts, these stripling warriors. It reared to flee. The dappled stallion sprang. The bluish wyvern felt searing pain cleave its breast. *Pierced,* it realized, stunned. *Riven.* Already its awareness ebbed. *Run through the heart.* The cartilaginous breastplate that had protected its kind for centuries worthless now. *Our stings, useless. Our king's fire, burnt out.*

Sky above burned impossibly blue, not a cloud or a wisp obscuring the sun at zenith. Something circled there. A kite? No. Too large. Too green. Not the right shape at all. This creature's lower half looked like a pard. The wyvern's thoughts evaporated. Dimly, it felt the dappled stallion pulling his skewer-like horn free of its breast. Faintly, it felt itself fall. Distantly, it heard the high-pitched cry of the pard-bird overhead. Around the dying wyvern, its companions began to flee.

New whistling arose, not from the ring of young unicorns in the heart of the ravine, but from elsewhere on every side. The wyvern's transparent eyelids sagged. Unicorns, many more of them, streamed into the ravine from the entryway. A pied rose-and-black mare charged at their head. Other groups poured over the tops of both slopes, one led by a black-maned, mallow-red mare, the other by a poppy-maned mare pale as flame. These two bands converged on the fleeing wyverns while the third, larger mass swept up from the ravine's egress.

Trapped, the dying wyvern thought, astonished still. *Trapped even as we had hoped to trap them.* Screams from the wounded. The concussion of falling bodies. The dying wyvern's eyes slid shut. Battle's din, ever more furious, receded to a gentle buzz. The wyrm felt, barely, as from a great distance, the tramp of heels and the slither of bellies passing over it. *Overwhelmed by innumerable, invulnerable enemies,* it thought. *The utter absurdity. The waste. When our king bade us lie here in wait for unicorns, we, too, should have fled.*

"It will be a rout, then," Jan whispered, gazing into the illuminated darkness of the dragon's brow. His conclusion startled, confounded him. "Who would have believed it could be so? I had always thought recapturing the Hills would be arduous, a mighty struggle. . . ."

He let the words trail away as Wyzásukitán stirred.

"Oh, a rout is it?" she asked him gently.

Her smoky breath flowed and swirled about him. Across the dark pool, fleeing wyverns fell beneath the heels and horns of the unicorn warhost pursuing them across the Hallow Hills toward their limestone dens flanking the cliffs where the sacred moonpool lay. The dragon queen turned her head ever so slightly.

"You think it will be a rout?" queried Wyzásukitán. "You suspect your folk can win back your Hills so easily they have no need of you?"

The dark prince shuddered, considering. Did he truly believe these predictions, then? Dared he trust the visions? Had he gradually, without realizing, come to accept the images as the sure and certain future? But were they, he wondered? Would the events portrayed here come to pass in time, regardless of his own actions or failure to act? Dared he relax into such a soothing complacency?

"Nay, I . . . ," he started.

"Watch," the dragon queen murmured.

The images upon her brow intensified, their colors deepening, becoming brighter. Jan felt himself drawn in the way that had become so familiar during his brief stay with the dragon queen. How long had it lasted — a few hours? Half a day? How far into the future lay the events that he observed? He ceased to wonder as the view pulled him back into its depths. As before, he merged with it and lost himself.

He floated in the air above the Hallow Hills. The wyvern warriors who had lain in ambush in the box canyon had all broken ranks, seeking to flee the steep-sided ravine. Unicorns pouring over the sides fell upon them without mercy, the whistled orders of Tek and Dagg, Teki and Jah-lila, Ryhenna and Ses sounding clearly above the din: shrieks from the wyrms, the clash of hooves and horns, groans from the dying, panting and snorts.

Bodies littered the canyon, impeding the long-leggèd unicorns. The wyverns, with their slithering gait, snaked over and between mounds of the fallen. Ineffectual stings forced them to fight with teeth and claws. The few who managed to escape the ravine flashed away faster than coursing rainwater. The unicorn warhost gave chase, managed to cut a fair number down as they fled across the open, rolling hills, through broken scrub and groves of slender trees.

The fleeing wyverns' screams had evidently been heard, for out of the limestone shelfland adjoining the moonpool cliffs poured fresh waves of stinging wyrms. Shrieked warnings of the invaders' seeming invulnerability only confused the rescuers, who attacked the unicorns in the traditional manner, with their stings. The battle changed from a chase to a series of pitched skirmishes as the two surging warhosts broke apart into dozens upon dozens of smaller assaults and combats.

Morning passed. Noon sun, coolly ablaze in the deep blue sky, declined to middle and then late afternoon. The great black stain upon the air to the east continued to grow, filling that quarter, and then that half of the sky. It chased the sun like a dark, enveloping mass. Watching it, the wyverns groaned. "An omen, an omen!" Jan heard some crying. "A darkness from out of the Smoking Hills. Surely it marks the end of the world."

Wyverns fell. Unicorns, as well — but far fewer than the wyrms. Repeatedly, small bands of a half-dozen unicorns maneuvered to surround one of the huge, stinging wyrms. More than a few had double heads, they were so old. The ring of warriors then pressed in on the wyrm, striking and slashing, pummeling with hooves and stabbing with horns, while the wyvern lashed ineffectually with its barb, snapped needle teeth, and raked what unicorns it could with the knifelike claws on its broad, stub paws.

Even seasoned warriors working in concert took a long time to bring down each large, fierce wyrm. And for every wyvern felled, it seemed another, fresh foe emerged from one of many entryways to the wyverns' subterranean dens. Jan glimpsed Tek and Dagg consulting, Ryhenna and Teki leading others to guard the larger entryways, prevent wounded wyverns from escaping back underground, and kill new wyrms as they emerged.

The strategy achieved only partial success. The crumbling limestone of the wyvern shelves made precarious footing for even the most agile of unicorns, and so many entries pocked the surface of the shelves that the guardians could not ward them all. Jan saw many more wyverns enter or emerge. Yet the pied healer and the coppery mare stemmed the flood of wyverns, slowing the pace of reinforcements and hindering safe retreat.

"Where is their fire?" Jan heard Tek crying to Dagg. "Why do they not use it against us?"

"And where is their leader, the wyrmking Lynex?" the dappled stallion whistled back. "Is he too craven to show his seven faces? Would he but show himself, and this whole struggle could be settled here and now!"

"Lynex, you coward!" Jan heard Tek shout down into the largest entryway. "I'd battle you myself, wyrmking. You stole these lands from the late princess Halla centuries ago. You have lived so long only that we unicorns might grow strong enough

to take our homeland back again. Show yourself! Come out and
face me if you dare!"

As if in answer, a low rumble sounded from the wyverns' dens.
The hollow, deep-throated sound rose from the depths like the
howl of stormwind. Thrumming followed, as of mighty limbs
pounding the earth. The soft swish of slithering bellies whispered
under the concatenation of noise. Startled, the unicorns fell back.
The next instant, two dozen of the largest, most powerful wyverns
Jan had ever seen rushed from the entryway, fanning out in a great
semicircle and beating their paws upon the ground.

The earth shook with their thunderous drumming. Barbed tails
thrashed like willow withies whipped by storm. In unison, the
white wyrms roared. Each was nearly the size of the huge, three-
headed queen Jan had slain years ago in his youth. Not a one of
them did not have double heads, and two had third heads sprout-
ing at the base of their necks. All around them, from other
egresses, a flood of wyverns poured, all enormous, unwounded
and unspent.

Late afternoon sun hung westering. Panting, their coats foam-
ing with sweat, Tek's warriors stared at the advancing wyrms.
Lines of blood streaked some of the unicorns, where wyvern teeth
or claws had found their mark. The legs of some trembled,
whether from tension or fatigue Jan could not tell. He knew none
shook from fear. They had fought full tilt for hours, since before
noon. Now, though they gave ground slowly before the howling,
stamping wyrms, not a one of them fled.

Suddenly from the entryway, into the half-ring created by his
score of gigantic bodyguards, another wyvern emerged, larger
even than they. His seven heads arrayed, all their gill ruffs fanned,
teeth bared like seven nests of thorny splinters. His long, seven-
stinged tail lashed, doubling back upon itself. Massive paws, their
nails like swords, impaled the air.

Lynex loomed above his own bodyguards. Gazing at the immense wyrmking, Tek gasped, appalled. Pale skin blazing opales-
cent in the afternoon sun, the scarred and ancient wyvern was

easily twice the size his three-headed queen had been. Turning his baleful, seven-faced gaze toward Tek, the wyvern leader snarled.

"Coward?" the largest among his seven pates rumbled. "Little unicorn, you misjudge."

The visages wove and intertwined, bobbing and slithering one against another as they spoke.

"Do you imagine me a doddard, an old spent thing?" the second-largest face demanded. Its companion, nearly as large, spat, "Think again!"

"Behold my personal bodyguards," the fourth-largest commanded. Beside it, another, only slightly smaller, added, "We have not yet even begun our battle."

"What matter our stings no longer fell you," the second-smallest countenance inquired, "or that our fire burnt out?"

The tiniest maw hissed and slavered, snapping frantically at nothing. "Coward. Doddard. Bodyguards," it gurgled. "Battle! Stings and fire!"

"I am old beyond counting, hungry and powerful," the monstrous central head roared. "I have waited a long time for you. Prepare to die, puny, brazen upstarts. Killers of my queen. We seized these hills from your ancestors centuries past — and we do not mean to give them up!"

With a shout like rolling thunder, the colossal wyrmking, his bodyguards and all his followers surged forward. Tek stood stockstill, as though riveted by indecision or fear. Steep, precarious shelfland rose before her, the cliffs of the moon's mere behind. With a jolt, Jan realized what it was his mate surely already saw: if the wyverns succeeded in driving the unicorns back against those cliffs, the wyrms could crush them there and devour them all before the sun had set.

Flight

★ 21 ★

Rally!" Jan shouted, voice echoing hollowly in the vast chamber of the dragon queen. "Tek, rally them — form the crescent and the wedge. Don't let the wyrms drive you against the cliffs!"

The image before him wavered and rippled apart. Jan's awareness wrenched back to his surroundings: the dragon's den, the impossible heat and wavering glow of molten fire. The dark unicorn blinked as Wyzásukitán abruptly moved, lifting her brow high above the young prince's vision. He stared at her, startled and angry that she should snatch his view of Tek and her peril away. Ramping, he opened his mouth to speak, but Wyzásukitán spoke first.

"Tell me what you have seen, dark prince," she bade. White smoke of her breath wreathed her whiskered muzzle.

"I see my mate and her band in jeopardy," Jan answered shortly. "I charge you, lower your brow once more. . . ."

The dragon queen eyed him, brow held regally above, not inclining her head the least measure. She studied him intently, gaze neutral, without malice, but no longer leisurely languid and amused. "Tell me your feelings, dark prince. What at this moment do you feel for your mate?"

"Love, longing, concern," Jan said without a moment's thought. "I see danger and would be there to defend her."

"So you would return to your mate?" Wyzásukitán asked. "And to your folk, whatever the consequence?"

"Aye, of course!" the dark unicorn cried, stamping. Sparks flew. The answer seemed so clear to him. He could not believe he had wandered in such confusion until now. He must return to Tek, rejoin the herd and accept whatever destiny Alma had prepared. The dragon queen looked at him.

"And will you tell your mate Korr's secret?"

Jan nodded. The answer did not come happily, but come it did and without hesitation.

"And your folk?" Wyzásukitán pressed gently. "You will tell them as well?"

"Of course," the dark unicorn answered. "I'll not live a lie, asking Tek to surrender her birthright that I might keep power not mine to hold."

"You will renounce your kingship?" the dragon queen sighed, white breath curling among her floating whiskers.

Jan nodded. "Aye, for love of her. And for Alma, who is what is: all truth, the Truth of everything that exists. Tek's parentage is what it is. So, too, my love for her. I must be true to both, and to myself."

The queen gazed down at him, her thousand thousand jewels glinting in the golden light of the molten lake that seethed beyond chamber's egress to the rear of Jan. He moved toward her, deeper into the chamber, his heart grown calm, at peace within himself.

"Why do you not ask that I lower my brow?" the dragon queen inquired. "Do you not wish to resume your gaze?"

Jan shook his head. "Nay. I wish only to return to my folk. I must winter with them their last season in the Vale, cross the Plain with them and join them as they fall upon the wyverns. It matters not that I may no longer serve as battleprince. Tek, as queen, must rightfully lead and rule them. Gladly will I march at her side, free of the silence and secrets Korr used to deceive us all."

"You would return, then?" the dragon queen asked.

He nodded. "Tell me what path I must take to depart these steeps and return to the Vale. All fall and winter lie before me. I must use that season to best advantage in broaching this terrible news to Tek and the herd by the time spring breaks and we cross the Plain to the Hallow Hills."

Wyzásukitán shrugged, flexing vast shoulder blades. Her huge, batlike wings lifted a trace, rustling, their crusted jewels dragging the golden ground.

"Aljan Firebrand," the dragon queen replied, "no pass leads from Dragonsholm to return you to your Vale."

Jan frowned. "Somehow I found my way here from the Salt Waste. A way leads out again. It must."

Slowly, carefully, the dragon queen shook her head. The dark water of her brow never spilled. "None you could ever tread again."

The furrow in the dark unicorn's brow deepened. "Given time, I could find it," he answered, moving closer. "With your aid, I could find it more quickly."

The dragon pulled back, turning her head to eye him. "The path by which you came exists no more," she answered simply. "The rills of Dragonsholm continuously shift as my kind turn over in their dreams. On rare occasions, one of us changes her den. Then the earth shudders for many leagues. Peaks fall; valleys open and fill; new ridges heave up. These Smoking Hills are in constant flux. The way you found endured but briefly. It is no more."

Jan felt cold. "How long before a new way opens?"

Again the dragon shrugged. "Impossible to tell."

"But I must return to the Vale," the dark unicorn protested, "while autumn's yet new. I would be with Tek before the snows and use the coming winter to accustom the herd to the news I bear."

Wyzásukitán lifted her great, lithe form higher from the ground. First she tensed, then relaxed her huge forelimbs, her hind limbs. Her long tail stirred. "Fall is flown, Aljan. Winter, too. And so as well the spring. This day marks the first of summer, Firebrand."

Jan stared at her, badly confused. "You jest," he cried. "No more than a few hours have passed since I came to you. . . ."

"Indeed?" she asked. "I never jest. And I tell you now, you

have stood with me all winter and all spring, and with Oro in the Hall of Whispers all fall before."

The dark unicorn shook his head. "Nay," he insisted. "It is but hours. I have not hungered or slept. . . ."

"You drank the dragonsup from my late mother's brow: all that remains of her waking dreams. It eased your hunger and fatigue, your thirst, your vulnerability to heat and cold. How else did you think, Firebrand, to stand before me in my den beside a lake of molten stone?"

Jan gazed up at the red dragon queen, speechless. She drew breath and sighed white clouds before continuing.

"I bade Oro and his warriors also sip before I sent them off, that they might gallop the whole way to your far Hallows, without pausing to eat or drink or rest. The hour grows short. Your people stand in urgent need, and time betides you to return."

"Time, time . . . ," Jan murmured. "How long have I stood dreaming here?"

"As long as it took the events which you witnessed to unfold," the dragon queen replied.

"Then what I saw, all that I saw . . . ," he groped.

"Was occurring as you watched," Wyzásukitán replied. "Your sense of time has been suspended by the water of my mother's dreams. You experienced these months as we dragons do, in a long, fluid reverie devoid of time."

"What I saw," Jan tried again, "the battle. . . ."

"Is no prediction," the firedrake answered, "rages even now, this moment, as we speak."

The dark unicorn felt his skin prickle. He demanded, "Tek's peril?"

"Is real. Is happening now."

A jolt like lightning coursed his blood. "Then I must go to her!" he shouted. "At once —"

He wheeled as though to dash from the dragon's den, recross the lake of fire, find his way to the surface again. The red dragon called to him.

"Hold, Aljan. What you saw in my brow was unfolding even

as you beheld it. How long, do you think, to reach her, even if you ran day and night, never resting?"

He pitched to a stop, heart dropping with a sickening plunge. "Too late?" he demanded. "Do you say I have come to myself too late? That the children-of-the-moon will perish or triumph without me, locked underground, leagues parted from them, my destiny failed, unable to save or even join them in their hour of gravest need?"

His last words were a cry of agony as he realized: he had tarried too long, lost in his own chaos. His mate would succeed or die without him, his people win back the Hills or lose them in his absence. He was destined to participate in nothing, contribute nothing to this pivotal juncture in his people's history. Even if he eventually escaped the Smoking Hills, how would he dare rejoin his folk? His colts perhaps half-grown by then, his sister already a wedded mare, his memory in the mind of his own mate dimmed, his people's recollection of him faded, his destiny forgotten, unfulfilled. He would be recalled only as the one who had failed Alma's sacred plan, her would-be Firebringer who had never managed to accomplish her end. The dragon queen above him was laughing gently.

"Too late?" she chuckled. "High time, more like. Time your charming Scouts trotted back to their Hallows. They are a sweet-voiced tribe in sooth. Their songs have raptured my fellows these many years. But we have lain too still for far too long listening, entranced, holding steady these precarious steeps."

Jewels flashing, no malice in her, she smiled at Jan. He understood then that she was laughing at herself.

"My sisters have all outgrown their dens. Even my mate-to-be. He is young yet, still wingless, not ready to fly — though my own wings ache. Time I ventured a practice flight. Exercise, so they say, strengthens the sinews."

Her great eyes blinked. She paused considering.

"I shall find my betrothed a plaything," she murmured. "Some pale exotic wyrm fetched from far lands, one that will live long and sing for his delight."

She glanced at Jan.

"We dragons, as you know, do not eat flesh."

Wyzásukitán rose to her fullest height. The curve of her spine brushed the chamber's ceiling.

"Too late, Firebrand?" she asked. "Too late to fill your destiny? Never, Dark Moon of the unicorns — not while I have wings."

Her great leathery pinions unfolded, spreading across the cavernous roof. The innumerable jewels of her dark reddish hide gleamed, brilliant as night sky crowded with summer stars. One huge forelimb reached toward him, her claws spread wide. Jan had not even a moment to flinch before her gigantic talons closed about him, impossibly strong. They could have crushed him in an instant, he realized, yet he felt no fear as they curled snugly about him and lifted him easily from the cavern floor. He sensed the last remnants of the green feather in his hair vanish in a blazing flash.

Wyzásukitán's huge hind limbs flexed. Her shoulders, braced against the chamber's ceiling of curving stone, shoved upward with a mighty heave. The cavern broke apart in a shuddering roar as the dragon queen leapt free of earth. Rocks and boulders showered around them as the dragon shot upward. Jan found himself cradled against her jeweled breast, sheltered from falling debris. The hot ichor that beat beneath her scales pulsed slow and steady as the heartbeat of the world.

As the mountain fell away around them, Jan felt the outer air. Below, the lake of fire fountained skyward, no longer contained by rock. Molten stone rained all about them like liquid stars. The dragon's vast wings stroked and oared the wind, rising with effortless power into the darkening sky. Jan saw the Smoking Hills far below, jagged and black and wreathed in white mist. Rivers of fire flooded the ridges as far as he could see. The mountain from which Wyzásukitán had just burst was only one such peak which spouted fire.

Sun had already set upon the Smoking Hills, plunging them into darkness save for the ember-bright glow of dragonsflood. Wyzásukitán veered in a hurtling rush toward the west, where dying sunset flamed scarlet still, a distant, unseen conflagration. Smoking cinders and flaming chunks of rock arced around them as they flew. Jan realized they were climbing higher, and higher yet, rising above the burning dust and ash.

The farther they rose, the more frigid the wind became. Though he felt its bite, Jan did not mind the cold, or the airlessness of atmosphere attenuated almost too thin to breathe. The dragon queen's heart hammered. Her great lungs labored even as her stroking wings maintained their powerful, even rhythm. She was soaring aloft, coursing westward, chasing the sun. The Smoking Hills raced far, far below. Tiny peaks burst and spattered fire. Crimson rivulets threaded the black landscape.

The Salt Waste rushed beneath them, racing along at impossible speed. The upper ether through which they lanced had grown so thin there scarcely seemed to exist any wind. The rising cloud of ash and dust fell away behind them as they flew. The world shrank. Above, the sky darkened, air thinning into nothing, stars beginning to prick through the crimson blaze that colored the sky. Slowly, it grew more tawny. They left the crimson behind. The Salt Waste receded and the Plain rolled underneath.

They were drawing nearer the western horizon, closer to the Hallow Hills. The vanished sun appeared, unsetting, rising above the western horizon as though it were the breaking dawn. Sunlight streamed across the Plain, turning the sky not scarlet, but gold. Time seemed to reverse as they sped westward from first evening into dusk into very late afternoon.

From high, high above in icy space near the limit of the air, Jan looked down to see a host of unicorns galloping far in the distance ahead, much closer to the edge of the Hallow Hills than he and Wyzásukitán. Members of the host were all dark in color: ink blues and reddish roans, charcoal dapples and deep-golden duns. A roan maroon led them.

They raced with the energy of warriors still fresh, newly embarked, yet Jan knew they had been traveling for — how long: hours? Days? He knew only that sipping from the late dragon queen's dreams had fortified them in the same manner it had fortified him. He wondered if they had any notion of passing time. Or did they journey in reverie, a blur, as he himself had journeyed through three-quarters of a year deep in the darkness of the dragons' halls?

He watched the late, late afternoon sun floating infinitesimally upward, growing gradually younger and brighter with each passing moment. Its strong yellow light illumined the distant Hallow Hills. He felt the rhythm of Wyzásukitán's wings change, descending now. The warband of unicorns far ahead and below had just left the rolling Plain. The Scouts of Halla were streaming into the rills of their ancestral land.

The wyverns pressed forward relentlessly, the white wyrmking at their head screaming his hatred for unicorns. Tek braced herself, determined not to be driven farther back. Already her warriors around her were dangerously bunched. They had no room to pivot and dodge, none to charge to one another's aid. The wyverns had them pinned against the moonpool cliffs, escape to either side so narrow that few unicorns could have survived a dash for freedom. The rest would have been overtaken and cut down. Better far to make a stand. Indeed, it was their only hope.

The pied mare glanced to left and right, surveying the battle. Dagg fought shoulder to shoulder with her, his mate, Ryhenna, on his other side. She spotted Ses farther back and to the left, the cream-colored mare with the flame-bright mane holding her ground in a press of other unicorns against the surge of oncoming wyverns. Tek searched the opposite way, glimpsed her own dam, Jah-lila, even farther distant, flanked by her foster father and namesake, the healer Teki.

The unicorn warhost stood spread in a long, shallow ribbon against the moonpool cliffs, more wyverns pouring from their holes and rushing toward them at every moment. Coldly, clearly, Tek grasped Lynex's strategy: with luck, he hoped to break through the unicorns' ranks and splinter them, then surround each smaller group and overwhelm it. Barring that, she knew, he planned to grind them against the cliffs until their line thinned and collapsed.

The extent to which her troops had allowed themselves to become stretched was not good, the pied mare saw. No helping it now. Her only viable tactic was to form them into an outward-facing crescent strong enough to resist the momentum of the wyvern advance. Then, carefully, she must pull the tips of the crescent inward, massing and thickening the formation before bulging its forward edge into a point. Perhaps, just possibly, she could then drive this wedge into Lynex's army, thus breaking it in two.

But they stood a long way from there yet, she acknowledged grimly, even as she whistled to rally the herd. She heard others take up the cries, pass them on in shrill piping that rose above the grinding noises of battle. Raggedly, the crescent began to form.

Scarred Lynex, amid his double-dozen huge bodyguards, reared at the heart of the onrushing mass, driving his followers with shrieks and threats. Despite all the foes her warhost had slain so far, Tek realized, as many more faced them now, fresher, larger, wilier and older than any they had fought earlier in the day. The new onslaught's force was tremendous. Again and again, Tek hurled herself forward, fighting furiously. Half a dozen wyverns fell before her hooves and horn. Dagg and Ryhenna protected her shoulder. Overhead, Illishar harried and stooped.

Others of her band did not fare so well. The pied mare spied places where the ranks of her defenders had grown perilously thin. The crush of fighters impeded reinforcements from reaching those spots. She saw Ses standing at one such point, nearly the sole defender. How much longer could she hold out? To the other side, Teki and Jah-lila worked feverishly, marshaling warriors to strengthen the line.

The crescent had stalled coalescing into the wedge needed to drive the wyrmking's hoard apart. Tek whistled the rallying cry again, again, but the exhausted unicorns were faltering. Before them, Lynex, three times the size of any other wyvern on the field, hooted his glee.

"Smash them, crush them!" his largest head shouted.

"Rip them, rend them," the two middle-sized pates flanking the main one cried.

"Snap them, slash them, bite and devour them," three of the smaller maws ranted, while the littlest nob gabbled and hissed: "Smash, rend, slash, devour!"

The wyverns were breaking through. Tek saw the line waver in two places. Ses leapt toward one of the weakening points, spurring on comrades with her whistles and cries. Ryhenna sprang to join her. On the opposite side of the pied mare, Teki and Jah-lila forged toward the other spot at which the warhost's ranks were in imminent danger of giving way. Too slowly. Defenders crumpled beneath the wyverns' teeth and claws. The crescent was staving in. Tek felt her own heart quail. The healer and the red mare would never reach the breach in time.

"Dagg, go!" she shouted, giving her shoulder-friend a slap on the rump with the flat of her horn.

The dappled warrior sprinted toward the buckling formation's edge, shouldering his way across the fray, whistling encouragement to those who still lived and desperately fought on. Tek returned to the struggle before her. She dared not follow Dagg's progress even a moment more. His absence and Ryhenna's created a gap in the ranks around her. She leapt forward to fill the breach.

The seven-headed wyvern king towered above her, his immense bodyguards writhing. They bore down on Tek like a mountain falling. Illishar swooped, dived, trying to strike at the wyrmking's heads, but his double-headed bodyguards battered the gryphon tercel off. The pied mare found herself unable to hold her ground. Notwithstanding her furious charges, she was being driven back, step by step. How many more before she found herself against the cliff? Her folk around her, she knew, found themselves in the same case: hemmed in, incapable of breaking free.

"To war! To war!"

The cry rang out from behind the wyverns whom they faced. Faint at first, it strengthened suddenly as the wind turned and carried the resonant war chant to the pied mare's ears full force. Unicorns. Unmistakably a warcry of unicorns. Beyond the wyrm-hoard, a raising of dust and a thunder of heels. The words grew nearer and louder yet.

"We be the Scouts of Halla! In the Firebrand's name we come. Aljan-with-the-Moon-upon-his-Brow has summoned us to your aid, Queen Tek. Wyzásukitán hastened us from the Smoking Hills. The wyverns! The wyverns! To war!"

A flood of unicorns crested the wyvern shelves. Smaller than the common run, all were dark roans, deep blues and greys, brick-red dapples, brindles of tarnished gold, their leader a young stallion of frosted maroon. The pied mare could only gape as the shaggy strangers stampeded down the limestone slopes like a cascade of maddened hill goats. Tek wasted not one moment of the wyverns' panic. As the white wyrms spun, shrieking, she whistled: "Forward! Strike hard, warriors of the Ring!"

Around her she saw, felt, heard her own folk plunge ahead with renewed vigor, rushing to meet these unknown allies who called her queen and claimed to come from Jan. The wyverns, caught between two closing pincers of unicorns, screamed in terror, their ranks disintegrating.

"A trap!" the deserters shrilled.

"Stand your ground, you bloodless fools," shouted the wyrm-king's central head. "We outnumber them still!"

In full rout, scattering for their lives, his troops ignored the command. The Vale's warhost, rumps no longer against the cliff, joined the newcomers in pursuing and skewering as many as they could. Few wyrms managed to clamber back into their caves, for the rush of newcomers had swept them downslope, away from their dens' entryways. For the first time since the arrival of Lynex, Tek began to feel — not just hope, but truly feel — that the unicorns might carry the day.

Upstart

★ 22 ★

Lell galloped across the Hallow Hills through the late afternoon light. Signs of battle lay everywhere. Strewn upon the summer grass, in the meadows and little stands of trees, upon the grassy, broken slopes and beside the streams, lay carcasses of the slain. Mostly wyvern, the half-grown filly noted with relief. Her folk were prevailing, then — or had been earlier. Sun hung low over the western horizon, its light a warm, golden amber, not yet deepened to crimson. She would have to hurry. Lell turned her eyes from the slain and galloped on.

She had left the oasis where suckling mares, weanlings too young to be initiated, the old and the infirm had remained in the Plainsdwellers' charge, there to await news of the battle's outcome. But Lell had not waited. Five years old, she was of age to join the warriors. Had a pilgrimage been made this year, she would have been initiated. But Jan had not returned and the herd been deep in plans for war. The harsh winter of three seasons past had slain every other filly and foal her own age. The herd would brook no pilgrimage of one.

What, then, the prince's sister fumed, was she to do — wait till she was a doddering mare and the sucklings at last grown old enough to join the Ring? She refused to wait! Jan would never have allowed such a travesty — and in his absence, she would not permit the most glorious battle of her people's history to pass her by. Besides, she reminded herself smugly, the twins had said she *must* go. They had come upon her as she had been preparing in secret to slip away. She had feared at first they meant to stay her, report her to Calydor, sound the alarm.

They had done no such thing, only said they had come to aid her, knew where the sentries stood and what path was best to avoid their eyes. They said they had come to tell her Calydor was occupied elsewhere and that now was the ideal time to slip away. He would not miss her for hours, perhaps until morning, if she went straightaway. Then they told her the route to the Hallow Hills, as glibly as though they had fared it themselves.

"But we *have* fared it," Aiony had told her, though Lell had breathed not a word of her thoughts aloud.

"Night past," Dhattar continued, "we followed the path of past pilgrims in dreams."

Lell had long since abandoned hope of grasping the twins' meaning when they spoke of their dreams. Instead, she had accepted their aid gratefully, tucking the course they described away into memory honed by Illishar, like the rhyme and meter of a lay. *This is what Jan would have wanted me to do,* she found herself thinking, a bit uncertainly — and then with more confidence, *at least, this is what Jan himself would have done were he in my case.*

And the way had not proved so very hard to follow, after all. She fared only half a day behind the warriors. They had departed the previous afternoon, she the following morning. Grass trampled and earth turned by their passing remained for Lell to follow. She pushed relentlessly, resting but briefly before pressing on.

Where was Jan? The thought beat at her unceasingly as she ran. *Why had he not returned?* She felt as though she must make up for his absence somehow, must go in his stead. None of the others could be relied upon, the twins cautioned, not even Calydor. Though a seer, he had not dreamed what they had dreamed. He would not believe them, they feared. And telling him would spoil Lell's chance to go. Tek would need *her,* they insisted, no other.

She must kindle fire. She must join the fray before sunset, must fly like the wind with the heart of a pard. She must not yield.

Lell set her thoughts aside as she came to a rocky rise. White limestone and black earth marked a difficult trail. From somewhere beyond, the amber filly heard, the din of battle rose. Her limbs trembled. She had run since dawn. It was not fear, she told herself, and began to climb.

The slope was steep and slippery. Scree tumbled continually from beneath her hooves. At times the hillside lay bare before her, devoid of scrub; at times it wound through trees. Choosing her footing, she climbed higher. Panting, she tried to scan the path ahead. Oddly, what she most feared was not wyverns, but her own folk, Illishar's airborne eyes, especially. That he might spy her before she reached the fray and swoop to thwart her only hardened her determination. Though she had often confided her intention to join the warriors, somehow she doubted he would approve so readily were he to encounter her here, now, preparing to fling herself into battle.

Panting, she reached the top of the precarious slope and ducked into cover of the trees. The noise of war seemed much closer now. Cautiously, she made her way through the grove toward it. The trees around her were odd, their aroma smoky and sweet. Never before had she seen trees with such scabrous, twisting trunks and bluish-silver leaves in the shape of crescents, hearts and rounds. The limbs were all sprouted in rose-colored buds, some already burst open into flower. Their odor was smooth, milklike, soothing. The most tempting thing she had ever scented.

Milkwood, she realized suddenly. The magical trees grew here alone, on the moonpool cliffs of the Hallow Hills. Jah-lila had eaten of these buds in her youth, Lell knew, when the red mare had first become a unicorn. Ryhenna, too. Their properties were marvelous. Famished, Lell sampled a spray of buds. She had barely eaten over the last days of hard travel, and not at all today. The savor of the buds was sweet without cloying, creamy as mares' milk. A cool tang ran through her. It made her both shiver and long to taste again.

The sounds of battle grew more insistent. The amber filly tore herself away and sprang on, trotting now, seeking the source of the din. Ahead of her, the trees thinned. She scented water. She found herself on the shore of a pool, perfectly round and perfectly clear. White limestone sand made up its bank and bottom, falling away into a blue spring that roiled and bubbled. Strangely, the surface of the pool lay perfectly still, mirror-smooth. Lell started, understanding where she was.

"The Mirror of the Moon," she whispered, naming the sacred mere about which initiates kept night-long vigils, into which they gazed to glimpse their own futures, and from which they drank in solemn ceremony, becoming warriors of the Ring.

Lell shivered again, parched with a day's waterless journey, and yet at the same time cold. Slowly, respectfully, she approached the mere. Bending, she drank — not the single, ceremonial sup of the newly initiated, but a great draught. The taste was sweet. The amber filly stared into the crystal waters, searching for some vision such as Dhattar and Aiony beheld each time they glanced into any puddle or stream. But she saw nothing. No fate. No destiny.

Lell skirted the pool's edge. The clatter of battle grew steadily louder. She reached the far side of the mere. Leaving the moon-pool behind, the amber filly hurried deeper into the trees. Presently, she saw grove's end, open sky beyond turning deeper and deeper gold with the advancing sunset. The milkwood plateau dropped away in an almost vertical cliff. Below lay the wyvern shelves, sloping in broken ledges to the south, toward the Plain. Caves pitted the soft, white stone.

Across this rocky expanse, the battle sprawled. Wyverns and unicorns clashed and charged across the crumbling surface. Lell saw unicorns pursuing wyrms, surrounding them. Hemmed by inward-facing rings of warriors, the captured wyverns reared and snarled, fighting with tooth and tail and claw. Horned warriors dodged and darted, feinted, struck. Others guarded entry to the caves.

Snorts and shouts sounded above the clash: shrill whistles of warriors, screams from the wounded, groans from the dying, curses, triumphant yells, the thump of heels upon the rock. A fine white dust hung above the fray, stirred by the ceaseless scritch of bellies and tromp of hooves. Sky was the color of goldenflower. Black shadow of the moonpool cliff crept slowly across the shelves.

Lell watched, mesmerized. Shaking, she was unaware of fear. She picked out the black-and-rose form of Tek below her, rearing and stabbing at a two-headed wyrm. Far ahead of the pied regent, the amber filly glimpsed the red mare, Jah-lila, and the black-and-white pelt of the healer, Teki. They seemed engaged in cutting off retreat to the south. Far from them, on the other side of the field, Lell saw Dagg's grey-dappled figure fighting alongside the coppery form of Ryhenna. They made up part of a ring surrounding a pair of wyverns, one of whom lay wounded.

To their flank, separated from them by a great distance, Lell saw her dam, Ses. The cream-colored mare ramped and reared, mane tossing along the curve of her neck as bright as poppies, as flame, despite the late afternoon's advancing shadow. Her mother's back was to the cliffs. Lell watched without the slightest qualm of being spotted. What troubled her more was how she was to descend that sheer, near-vertical slope and join the fray.

The gold in the sky was taking on a tinge of fire. Scanning aloft, she did not see Illishar. Fear seized her. Then she found him — on the ground, beak and one claw buried in the throat of a massive wyrm. He was dragging the lifeless form upslope. When he cast the slain thing across an entry, blocking it, the warriors that had been guarding that cave sprang away, freed to other tasks.

The field swarmed with unicorns the amber filly did not recognize: odd roans, all brick and slate, lapis and ruddy sienna. Darting and springing about like deer, they maneuvered the treacherous footing of the wyvern shelves undaunted, fighting with ferocious energy. One among their number, a dark maroon, fought alongside Tek. Lell caught his cry above the din:

"For the queen! For the queen, in Halla's name!"

Her own people's shouts were "For Jan, the Allmother's Firebringer!" and "For pied Tek, regent and prince's mate!"

Who were these strange little shaggy unicorns? Allies, clearly.

They bore down on the foe with a fury her own folk strove gamely to match. The white wyrms they fought twisted and struggled, lashing and sometimes bowling hoofed warriors off their feet with powerful sweeps of their otherwise useless tails. The amber filly, gazing upon the seething turmoil below her, had no idea how to interpret it. Were the unicorns winning? She hoped so.

Yet at the same time, she had the uneasy feeling the battle might still go either way, as easily tipping in the favor of the wyverns as not. Dusk was fast drawing on. What would happen at nightfall? Would the two sides fight on? Would darkness return the advantage to the wyrms? If they managed to slip safe belowground under cover of darkness, the amber filly reasoned, they could easily hide in the earth for as long as they chose. Would Tek dare risk leading a second assault down into the twisting maze that was their dens?

It was their sheer size, more so even than their numbers, Lell realized, which might determine battle's outcome. The stinging wyrms were easily three and four times the size of the youthful, stingless peaceseekers she and the twins had aided three nights before. These wyverns were old, toughened, loyal to their king. Some had double heads. Largest of all loomed their seven-faced sovereign, massive Lynex, unmistakable, far larger than the bodyguards that ringed him. Furiously, Tek, the dark maroon and others of the stranger-unicorns threw themselves against the wyrmking's protectors, trying to break through. Already three of the royal guards had fallen.

Lell came to herself with a start. Would her brother, Jan, have stood gaping so, like a witless foal, when there was a task to be done? Sky above was turning from golden to amber. She must kindle fire. No time to lose, for the twins had told her she must bring fire to the battlefield before the setting of the sun. Clumsily, Lell bent to strike the tip of her horn against one flinty heel. A spark leapt up, flared, then fell to earth and died. Nervously, Lell tried again. No spark this time. A third strike. This time two sparks glowed, but each snuffed out in midair before reaching the ground.

Tinder, she realized. She must use tinder to catch a spark, nurture it. Frantically, the darkamber filly cast about her for something dry and fine. Dead grass or shredded bark, anything would do. Below her, the battle raged on. Overhead, the sky blazed, the fiery tinge intensifying with every second that passed.

Wyrmking

★ 23 ★

The pale mare tossed back her poppy-colored mane and lunged again at another wyvern, piercing the fibrous breastplate beneath its skin and bringing it down. It writhed and thrashed, already dead. She felt its sting glance heavily against one flank. The wyvern's colorless blood ran down her horn, soaking her brow, burning. Ses slung her damp forelock out of her eyes and fought on.

The clatter of battle rattled around her. The sun hung low, already hidden by the limestone cliff overlooking the wyvern shelves. The Mirror of the Moon lay on that forested plateau, she knew. She killed another wyvern. Were the wyrms being routed? She did not know, fought the more fiercely to keep from having to think. She had kept her thoughts from many such thorny mires of late — quandaries such as what she would do after this war, when Lell was grown. When she was free.

What would she do if Jan never returned? Nay, he must! Alma had shown her in the vision of her initiation night that she was to bear the long-awaited Firebringer. Surely he would appear. The only mystery was when. But what then? Dared she tell him the truth, as she had sworn to Jah-lila she would do?

She thought once more of that secret she had hidden from him and all the world since before his birth. Why had she done so? Self-preservation, surely. And at the urging of the Red Mare, who had assured her over and over that Jan must be born unto the Ring and reared as prince-to-be. Her own status as prince's mate had meant little to Ses. She had kept silent to protect her son and to spare her mate, whom she had truly loved — hoping ever against hope that he would one day free himself of the dreadful guilt that had ridden him to his death.

And yet, more than for any other reason, she had held her tongue for Lell. On the night of her initiation, long before either of her children's births, Ses had seen not only her destiny to bear the herd a Firebringer, but another to come after him: a wingèd thing. What her filly's dream pinions might mean, the pale mare could not guess. But she had named her daughter Álell. *Wing.* Regardless of her firstborn's fate, the poppy-maned mare trusted her filly was safe, secure in the care of the Free Folk of the Plain, three days' journey from this war.

She fought on. The dust of battle rose all around, a white haze. The figures surrounding her seemed pale as haunts. Sky above now edged from golden into flame. The unicorns had secured most of the entries to the wyverns' dens, she saw, preventing retreat back under the earth. The wyrms lay slain by heaps and dozens about the shelves. Her own folk's losses, she noted with relief, were fewer than the wyrms'. The unicorns had formed a solid line, pushing the wyverns slowly, inexorably toward the Plain.

The wyrms' resistance was frenzied. After initial panic at the arrival of the stranger roans, some among the wyvern horde had rallied. Had they yielded, or rushed headlong with their companions for the Plain, Ses was certain Tek would have spared further bloodshed and let them go. But all who remained refused surrender. Seven-headed Lynex, surrounded by bodyguards, shrieked with multiple shrill voices at the remains of his horde to fight to the death and not to yield.

Where was his fire, the pale mare wondered? All her life she had heard of wyverns hoarding flame, stolen from the red dragons so many years ago. Yet the foe had not used the deadly stuff even once this day. In dousing the wyrmqueen's flame years past, had her firstborn robbed the wyverns of all they possessed? She could not say. She only knew Lynex wielded none as he towered above the wedge-shaped attack formation led by Tek.

His bodyguards writhed and reared, striving to keep Tek's warriors at bay, but one by one, the double-headed guardians were being seized and pulled down. Of the great scarred wyrmking's original score, only a dozen remained. The odd-colored strangers, who called themselves Scouts of Halla, rallied around Tek, aiding her assault against the seven-headed wyrm. They fought tirelessly, like creatures possessed. Their leader, a small maroon stallion, conferred with the pied mare and followed her commands, singing out to his followers in a ringing chant that was nothing like the piercing whistles Vale unicorns used.

For what did Lynex wait? Why did he still fight on? Ses could not fathom him. The golden-orange sky above grew more and more intensely flame. A sudden commotion interrupted her thoughts. She wheeled, half expecting to find wyverns had broken her fellows' ranks, gotten behind her somehow. Instead, she saw a unicorn stallion come charging around the cliffside onto the battlefield. He cast feverishly about with the look of one taking no part in the fray, but desperately seeking among the fighters.

He was tall and lean and long-maned. The gloom of the cliff's shadow muted his coloring. From the toss of his head, from his gait and stance, she thought for one wild instant he was Jan. Then the actual hue of his coat registered: midnight blue scattered with silvery stars. A shock went through her: Calydor! What could his purpose be? Like his fellows, he had refused to join this fray, agreeing only to ward those of the Vale too young or old or infirm to fight. Spotting the pale mare now, Calydor sped toward her.

"Ses," he cried. "Is she here? Is she with you?"

With the wyvern directly before her now dead, the pale mare turned to meet the Plainsdweller.

"What do you mean?" she panted. "Whom do you seek? Why are you not with Lell and the others?"

Searching still, the star-covered stallion pitched to a halt. "'Tis your daughter I seek! We discovered her missing the morn after your warhost departed."

"Missing?" exclaimed Ses. "What, how . . . ?" Her balance reeled.

"We combed the oasis, but found no trace — no pards," he told her quickly. "I am certain she followed the host. Did she catch you up? Have you seen her?"

"Come to enter the fray?" Ses cried, fear thudding against her heart. "My Lell is no match for these monstrous wyrms! She's but a filly — and each of them larger than a full-grown warrior. . . ."

Hastily, she, too, began to scan the battle. The wyrmhorde tee-tered on the brink of overthrow. In time, the unicorns' steady forward push would surely overwhelm them. But time, she real-ized, noting the brilliant color of the sky, might be what the uni-corns did not have. As soon as the sun sank away, all odds might change. If Lynex could hold on just so long. . . . Beside her, the star-strewn stallion spoke.

"You have not seen her? She is not among you here?"

"Nay," the pale mare gasped, nearly frantic now, aware that simply because she had not laid eyes on Lell amid the day's may-hem did not mean her daughter had not hurled herself foolishly into the fray. Even impervious to wyverns' venom, the amber filly could still easily have been torn to bits by their teeth or claws. Calydor's brow furrowed.

"Mayhap she did not last this far," he murmured. Ses wheeled to stare at him. He swiftly added, "She may have had sense enough to abandon her wild scheme, to turn back, and I missed her. By my reck, even with pards, she's safer on the Plain than amid this slaughter. . . ."

Sudden shrill whinnying caught their attention. Whirling, Ses saw one of the wyrmking's bodyguards deserting, thrashing to break free of the attacking unicorns and make its escape. Scouts of Halla fell upon it as it rushed by. Frenetically, it shook them off. Several gave chase while the rest sprang after Tek, who now pressed forward in a fury, fighting toward Lynex as the sunset sky caught fire. The wyvern king and his ten surviving guards cursed their fleeing companion.

The enormous wyrm was coming straight toward her, Ses realized with a start. A day of battle had dulled her wits. She felt Calydor spring past her to intercept the wyrm, moving with a grassbuck's strength and speed. Coming as it did from one who once so coolly championed flight over combat, his action caused her an instant's surprise. Then she saw that pressed as the pair of them were, so close against the limestone cliff, no room remained for flight.

Ses sprang after the blue-and-silver stallion. She dived at the great wyvern's tail, impaling its poison tip as it swung around toward Calydor. Her horn grated, sparking against the ground. It occurred to her what risk the singer had taken, venturing the battlefield in search of Lell, unprotected as he was from white wyrms' stings. As the pale mare pinned the wyvern's tail, the star-strewn stallion stabbed upward under its gaping jaw. Already the other of its two heads lay dead.

Once more realization came: Calydor did not possess fire-tempered hooves or horn, could not have pierced the bony breast-plate protecting the monster's heart if he had tried. She heard the wyrmking's guardian give a high-pitched scream. It stiffened. Calydor shook free, sprang away from the dying creature's flailing claws as it toppled. Ses braced herself, kept her horn firmly planted in the creature's thrashing tail lest the Plainsdweller be struck by a reflexive sting.

"Look to your leader! Hie, Tek! Tek," Calydor was shouting, sprinting suddenly toward the black-and-rose mare. Ses, too, leapt away, leaving the wyvern for others to finish. She had seen what Summer Stars had seen: Tek and her battlemates smashing through the ring of bodyguards at the weak point opened when the traitor fled. The Scouts formed a blunt wedge that shoved into the opening, forcing the guards farther and farther apart. The wedge then split, each half continuing to press outward, creating a corridor.

Down this corridor charged Tek. Bugling her warcry, she hurtled at Lynex like a striking hawk. The wyrmking caught sight of her, reared back, but with a mighty leap, the pied mare caught his third-smallest head in her teeth. She gave a savage shake, like a wolf pup snapping a rock squirrel's neck, then let go and dropped to the ground. There she half crouched, stance ready, horn aimed. The king of the white wyrms convulsed. A cry sprang from six of his throats. The third-smallest head lay limp, slain. The Scouts of Halla strove gamely to keep Lynex's remaining body-guards from closing ranks and pinning Tek inside their ring. Ses pounded across the corpse-strewn field, hot on Calydor's heels.

"Wretch! Wretch," keened the wyvern king. "A hundred years and more have I tended that head."

Tek's words rang boldly over the din of battle. Ses made them out with ease.

"I'll snap all seven like buds from a stalk," the pied mare re-turned. "Four centuries have my folk suffered exile because of your treachery! Now we mean to put that wrong to rights and drive the last wyrm from our Hallow Hills."

Another of the wyrmking's bodyguards broke from its compan-ions and strove to flee. The Scouts of Halla pressed to hem it in. It writhed and flailed across Ses's path. Ahead of her, Calydor's way was also blocked as he fought to reach the corridor and Tek.

"Hoofed grass-eater!" scarred Lynex shrieked. "Little whis-tling nit!"

"A warrior of the Ring am I," Tek threw back at him. Ses's ears pricked. The pied mare shouted on. "Mate to the prince and mother of his heirs. Regent in his absence, I am your fiercest en-emy. Scheming, deceiving tyrant wyrm!"

Once more she sprang, from a standing start, with a vigor that astonished Ses. About the great wyvern's central pate, his lesser crania darted, wove. The pied mare seized one of these in teeth, a nob larger than the first she had killed. It screamed and tore free. Tek landed, instantly sprang again. Lynex reared, lifting his faces above the reach of her teeth. Tucking her chin, she stabbed the injured head deep in its cheek. A sharp shake of her horn as she fell to earth reversed the slash into its eye. The wounded visage wailed, bleeding great streaks of near-colorless blood and entan-gling itself among the wyrmking's other necks and heads.

Again he bellowed, so loudly the pale mare's ears flinched. Ahead of her, Calydor had made his way around the knot of Scouts attacking the fleeing bodyguard. She strove to follow him. Now the star-strewn stallion fought forward through the throng of unicorns that had once formed the corridor allowing Tek in to reach Lynex. The crush of battle was closing that opening, warriors backing and sidling into one another. The blue-and-silver stallion hurled himself into their midst. Ses shouldered after him. Beyond them — not far, but almost unreachable because of the press — Tek faced the wyrm.

His rippling tail, like a mighty rapid, swept toward the pied mare, its seven-stinged tip brandished to flail at her. Tek overleapt it, slashing down in the same motion, and Lynex roared. One massive forepaw, broad as the mare's ribcage, swung its saberclaws. Tek ducked, dodged, twisted, and ran it through. The bladelike claws of the other paw scored her shoulders. She pivoted and sprang free, laughing. Ses saw blood welling into the wounds Tek did not even seem to feel.

The pied mare speared the wyrmking through the side. With a snarl, his great head swooped, sank its splinter-fangs into her shoulder. Tek struck him off with one forehoof, slashing a long, shallow wound across his throat. Ses watched his torn gills begin to bleed. The pale mare flung herself against the mass of unicorns grappling with towering wyrms. Calydor still forged ahead. She sought to trail just behind, squeezing through what gaps he managed before the surge of battle closed them. Beyond the shifting, near-impassable wall of warriors, the pied mare taunted the wyrms' seven-headed king.

"Surrender, Lynex," Tek roared. "Give up this fight. Swear never to return, and I will let your folk depart."

"Never!" the white wyrm shrieked. "Not while I live will I allow my people to retreat." He struck at her again with one massive forepaw. Nimbly, she dodged away.

"Your bodyguards desert you! How long can you hold them to certain death?"

"Where is your mate?" the king of wyverns snarled, his huge, main head darting to snap at her. Tek ducked and sidestepped, avoiding the clash of needle-like teeth.

"On errands more pressing than pricking at you, wyrmking," she answered. The unwounded maws of the great wyvern laughed. He slithered after her.

"Jan, who killed my queen — was he too great a coward to come himself, but must send his mate to face my wrath?"

"One warrior mare among my race is more than a match for you," Tek spat, lunging after one of two midsized heads flanking the main one, champed it by the gill ruff.

She got one foreleg over it, compressing its windpipe in the crook of her knee. With a squall of terror, Lynex tried to wrest his second-most-ancient head from her grasp. The pied mare held on with teeth and limb, her other legs braced. Ses saw the wyvern's near forepaw pinned against his body by the taut downward stretch of the captured pate's neck. His free paw tore at Tek but, too stubby and short, it could not reach around his scarred and bony breast. Tek dragged the head down, bowing her own head and leaning all her weight onto the forelimb that pinned it.

"Surrender," the pale mare heard Tek grate. "Yield, wyrmking, or you lose this head as well."

The huge white wyrm began to scream. His massive body rocked, trying to shake the pied mare free. Ses saw Tek let her standing limbs buckle, setting her down hard on the ground. The wyrm's secondary head remained pinned in her folded forelimb, gill ruff held fast in her strong, square teeth. Maddened with fear, the three auxiliary nobs as yet unscathed flung themselves high and wide, shrieking, while the main head swooped, attempting to catch Tek in its jaws. Teeth still clenched about the captured pate's gill ruff, the pied mare pointed her horn at the main head, keeping it at bay.

Off to one side, Ses became aware of flashes of copper and yellow-grey. Ryhenna and Dagg had seen Tek's danger. As Calydor and she herself did, they, too, were struggling to reach their shoulder-friend. Beyond, Ses caught another glimpse: Teki and

Jah-lila also fighting toward Tek. The maroon-colored leader of
the Scouts of Halla battled hard at the edge of the ring of bodyguards. All strove to converge on Tek's contest with Lynex — yet
none, Ses feared, would be able to reach her. The crush was so
great, finding space to plant a hoof, much less wedge one's body,
proved nearly impossible. Beyond, pied mare and wyvern king
fought in an open space. The sky above blazed like burning grass.

With a roar like stormwind, Lynex heaved. His massive body
undulated, then torqued. With a powerful wrench, the wyvern
king rolled. The force snapped the neck of his own head captured
in the pied mare's teeth. Unable to loose her grip in time, Tek
was jerked through air and slammed hard to the ground. She lay
a moment, motionless and stunned, as the wyrmking pulled free
of her, three of his seven heads now dangling uselessly. Slowly,
he reared up, paws raised, his dozen saberclaws bristling.

Ses heard the red mare shouting her daughter's name. Tek
stirred groggily. Clearly the breath had been knocked from her,
perhaps even ribs cracked. Hissing, Lynex swayed above her, savoring victory. The pied mare rolled painfully to her knees, shook
her head, then struggled up. She stood unsteadily. Ses whinnied,
barreling forward in Calydor's wake. To one side, Dagg's battle
yell rose above the tumult, echoed by Ryhenna's. Ses saw the pair
of them plunging toward the pied mare at desperate speed. Beyond, the pale mare glimpsed Tek's foster father, Teki, vaulting
over the fallen, her dam, Jah-lila, charging alongside.

Ahead of them all, at the battle line, the Scouts' maroon-
colored leader chanted orders to his troops. On every side, bodyguards toppled, pulled down. Unicorns hurtled toward their
injured leader like a thunder of forkhorns spooked by storm. And
none of them, Ses knew suddenly, with certainty, would reach her
in time. She saw that Lynex understood this. The congestion of
fighters and the piling of bodies around him was too great. The
pied mare was his. He was sure of it.

"Another moment, mare, and your flesh becomes my feast,"
he crowed.

Ses saw blood trickle from Tek's nostril and stain her beard.

Head slightly lowered, she gazed up at Lynex. She stood three-legged, favoring the forelimb she had used to pinion his second-eldest head. Ses saw her snort blood in a fine scarlet spray. Her limbs tensed, braced, almost crouching. Her mouth moved. The pale mare was never sure after if she had heard the words, or only understood them from the framing of Tek's lips and teeth and tongue.

"Well enough, wyrm," the pied mare snarled at him, green eyes leveled in a gaze of pure hatred, without a hint of resignation or surrender. "Try to take it, if you dare."

The wyrmking lunged. The black-and-rose mare reared to meet him. The sun set. Evening sky was the color of fading roses. A shrill cry halted everything. Or rather, nothing halted. It only seemed to halt. Ses felt herself frozen in time, still struggling forward like all her companions, the wyvern bodyguards falling around her, swarmed on and skewered by the Scouts of Halla. The high sound that had cut — was still cutting — the air was not a scream, the pale mare realized, but a whistle, a wild piercing battlecry shrilled by one younger and smaller than any other warrior on the field.

Turning — so slowly, it seemed as in a dream — Ses caught sight of her long-leggèd amber filly with the mane pale as milk galloping full-tilt down the cliffside above with a burning brand clutched in her teeth. The white limestone cliff rose nearly vertical. Showers of scree cascaded from Lell's hooves. The brand in her teeth flashed and crackled, its flame orange, its buds so newly lit that Ses could still discern their shapes: hearts and rounds and crescents for the leaves, five-petaled roses for the flowers. The milkwood's resinous sap popped, fizzing as it flamed, the smoky mingles of white and grey, smelling at once milk-sweet and tart as pitch.

Halfway down the precipitous slope, Lell sprang. The milkwood blazed as she hurtled, seemed almost to fly, sailing down toward Tek and the wyvern king. She came to earth far short, but she had gauged her leap to land her not on hard limestone but atop a heap of slain wyverns. The next instant, she sprang again, for the packed crush of living unicorns this time. Still piping her warcry, the amber filly dashed across their jostling backs, pounding hard for Lynex, milkwood brand flaming in her teeth.

Surprised, momentarily distracted, the wyrmking hesitated, turning his central head's gaze from Tek toward Lell. To one side of him, Dagg and the leader of the Scouts dragged down the last defender blocking their path. Ryhenna thundered after them. To the wyrmking's other side, Jah-lila broke through the wall of fallen bodyguards, her black horn slicked with wyverns' blood. Teki vaulted in her wake. Just ahead of Ses, Calydor struggled over the motionless form of another fallen guard. It lay within their power to reach Tek now, the pale mare realized.

The king of the wyverns seemed to reach the same surmise. He turned back toward the wounded mare. She ramped and feinted before him. Heaped bodies ringed them like a barricade. Ses saw that with her injured foreleg, Tek could not flee, could not hope to climb that mound of dead unaided. She could only stand defiant, pawing the air. With a howl, the huge white wyrm lunged. Ahead, as she scrambled upward in Calydor's wake, Ses saw Lell spring over the barricade of the slain, past Tek, swift as wind, light as wings, the firebrand blazing above her head. Full gallop, she scaled the belly and scarred breast of the king of wyrms and flung the firebrand in his face.

The wyvern leader roared, arching, knifelike nails clawing at his main head's eyes. The other three remaining heads screamed and strained as if hoping to tear free of the wyrmking's massive body, which tumbled backward, writhing. Lell plummeted to the ground as the scaly slope on which she had stood abruptly snatched itself away. Gaining the crest, Ses observed Jah-lila below seize the nape of her daughter's neck in teeth and haul her bodily away from thrashing Lynex as though Tek were a weanling filly. Teki shouldered from the other side, helping the red mare drag her daughter up over the fallen bodyguards. Dagg and the leader of the Scouts sprinted across to lend their strength. Among the four of them, they managed to half-lift, half-herd the injured mare to safety.

Lell, sprawled on the limestone near Lynex, was already scrambling to her feet. Ryhenna tried to go to her, but the furious thrashing of the wyvern's tail between them drove her back. The wyrmking keened and rolled, scattering the resinous firebrand into a thousand flaming shards. These were strewn by wind and the wyvern's looping, sweeping tail into a broad arc.

"My eye! My eye, you little, cursèd wretch," the king of the wyverns howled.

Sparks flew within the open space where he and Tek had lately dueled. Flames caught the wisps of summer-dry grass that sprouted in the crevices of the wyvern shelves. A semicircle of fire sprang up along the periphery of the open space. It stretched from far to Ses's left all the way to where Tek and the others had disappeared over the mound of the fallen. Spreading fast, the two ends ran around behind the wyrm as though seeking to join. Barely in time, Ryhenna sprang out of its path.

On the far side of the open space from Ses, beyond Lynex and Lell, the two running trails of fire met, completing a ring. The dance of fire, low enough in its initial seconds for a unicorn to have sprung over, rose almost instantly to above head height. Within its circle, the wyrmking flailed, his cries subsiding. Panting, he rose, collecting himself, tail coiling, one eye of his great head wizened shut. The other heads whimpered. He turned his one-eyed gaze toward Lell. With a cry, Ses plunged toward her filly. A curtain of flame roared before her, blocking her path. The pale mare pitched to a halt, ramped helpless on the mass of wyvern dead, gazing into a ring of fire in which Lynex and her daughter now both lay trapped.

"I'll see you rue saving your queen," the white wyrm snarled.

Lell backed away. "Not till you wyrms rue that ever you stole our lands from us."

The amber filly's voice was steady, her expression wary, but unafraid. Ses tried to call to her, bid her flee, but the crackling flames drowned out her voice. Lynex lunged at Lell. She dodged, sought to skirt him. Behind him the ring, newly joined, had not yet flared unleapable. The wyvern's tail swung, lashing, driving her back.

The amber filly struck at the stings, but they were far too swift and powerful. She had to spring away to keep from being bowled over. Lynex swept his tail in a leisurely arc, herding her. One badger paw extended to intercept her as she rounded the fire ring's inner curve.

Instead of dodging, Lell ran straight for the paw, then veered suddenly inward. Ses saw Lynex, lunging, lose his balance as he missed. His broad paw dipped into the fire. Howling, he snatched it out. Again Lell scaled the scarred slope of his breast. All four of his remaining heads bent to gape at her, but instead of fencing with her horn, she wheeled and kicked like a mountain calf, striking one of the smaller skulls smartly in the jaw. Shards of teeth fine as fishbones flew, glinting by firelight.

Sky above was the dark of flushed, sweet grapes. The burning ring lit the wyvern shelves in a yellow blaze. To one side, Ses saw Tek shouting, fighting to break past Jah-lila and Teki, Dagg and the leader of the Scouts, all of whom held her back from going to Lell. Within, the wyvern's newly wounded head slapped and flailed, preventing his other maws from striking. Lell flew like a woodshare away from Lynex. A woodshare with nowhere to go. All around burned the impassable wall of fire.

With a savage bellow, Lynex crushed his own wounded pate in the jaws of his largest visage. The little head ceased writhing. The great one opened its jaws. The smaller fell nerveless from its grasp. With a howl, the wyvern sprang, both paws extended. Lell ran for the wall of fire, as though she meant to dash headlong through it. The wyvern's tail swung round to prevent her. The amber filly skidded, avoided it, and leapt. But as she entered the wall of fire, the seven flails of wyrmking's tail coiled about her, plucking her back.

"Lell! My child!" Ses screamed as she saw her filly's coat catch fire. The pale mare sprang toward the flames. Calydor vaulted to block her path.

"Nay, my love! Don't sacrifice yourself. To save her would take wings!"

He would not let her by. Ses fought him, bit, pummeled wildly with her hooves. To no avail. He held his ground. She could not get past. Ryhenna had joined him. They were holding her back. Above the din, she heard Tek's desperate cries. Beyond Ryhenna and Calydor, beyond the curtain of fire, Ses saw her filly struggling to free her legs from the wyrm's long, twining tail, which only tightened, dragging her closer to Lynex's daggerclaws and gaping jaws. How much time had elapsed, the pale mare wondered — a heartbeat? Two? Was it possible Lell did not yet feel the fire? Her mane and coat blazed. The amber filly arched suddenly, a cry breaking from her. Ses cried out as well, as though she herself burned.

A sound that was like none she had ever heard before, half pard's roar, half eagle's scream, cut the night. From the darkness of fading sky above, a figure dropped, lit up by firelight, its great wings green as new-sprung grass. They beat about the wyrmking's heads, boxing, buffeting them. Ses saw the tercel's golden-furred paws slash into the wyvern's shoulder and breast. His eagle's claws closed about the throats of the two still-living smaller heads.

One of the wyvern's huge forepaws struck at Illishar. Powerfully thrashing wings kept it at bay. With a yell, the gryphon struck at the wyrmking's one remaining eye. The wyvern shrieked, contorted. Illishar leapt free of him and snatched Lell from his thrashing tail. She shouted, writhed, flame spreading from her to his feathers and pelt. His talons bit into her shoulderblades. Ses saw his pard's claws dig into her flank. She was nearly half-grown, at the very edge of his ability to carry.

Illishar, too, was screaming now, his burning wings battering the air, straining against a weight that nearly dragged him down. With furious strokes, he bore her up. Ses felt the wind of his wings, heated by flame, fanning the ring of fire. Wailing and squirming, the blinded wyvern tossed below. The burning filly writhed in the tercel's grip. He dragged her through the air, barely clearing the curtain of fire. Shrilling, keening, he fought his way upward, higher into the darkening sky. Flames licked across his belly and green-fletched throat.

The white wall of the limestone cliff loomed. He strove for altitude. Lell's screeches tore the night. She seemed to gallop through sunless sky. Fire ran all along their limbs. Illishar cleared the cliff, cleared the trees. He staggered low across the canopy of the milkwood grove, an erratic series of plummets and heaves. Far below, Ses lost sight of them. The light of their burning flickered, played eerily through the trees, lighting the air above. All at once, it vanished utterly, plunging the grove into darkness again as though the pair of them had, surrendering at last, fallen from the sky.

Endingfire

★ 24 ★

The darkness out of the Smoking Hills swallowed the last hint of dusk. Sudden night, devoid of stars, fell. The ring of fire encompassing Lynex lit the battlefield, upon which every creature now stood arrested save for the wyrmking, who floundered mewling. No sound save that thin, oddly vigorless wail and the crackle of flame. Tek leaned against her dam and foster sire, her off forelimb swollen, badly strained. That pang, and the ache of her bruised ribs and slashed shoulders was as nothing to the pain she felt for Lell and Illishar, who only scant moments before had disappeared beyond the clifftop, their terrible light abruptly doused. Grief crushed the pied mare's breast.

From the blackness above came a mighty rushing, as of wind. Tek felt a stirring reft of coolness, a waft as hot as sun-burned rock. Another noise now, louder than the ceaseless rush. This second sound belled like a mighty trump, calling, calling in long, clear notes that shook the earth. The notes drew nearer, nearer at incredible speed, as did the rush. The hot wind increased. All came from above, from the strange black cloud that had swept all day from the Smoking Hills and at last devoured the sky.

A blast of fire shot through the darkness overhead. The immense tongue of flame flared, subsided, was replaced by another, and another yet, each gout nearer. The unicorns, still motionless upon the battlefield, gaped. Their enemies, who also poised, craned upward. The darkness parted, and out of it, a dragon swooped. She was vast, vaster than any creature Tek had ever beheld, red in color, and embedded with thousands of flashing jewels which scintillated in the light of her fiery breath.

The dragon descended, impossibly huge, the size of a mountain. Each note she trumped was followed by a roaring spurt of flame. Without being aware, Tek found that she had recoiled, fallen back, as had every living creature around her, whether unicorn or wyvern. Only the wyrmking remained where he lay, rolling and moaning insensibly within the ring of fire. The rush of the dragon's wings as she approached scoured everything in her path. Tek slitted her eyes, tightened her nostrils, folded her ears against the hard, gritty gusts.

The mighty firedrake came to rest with a concussion that shook the hills. The heat of her drove both unicorns and wyverns back. Her jewels flashed and winked like innumerable stars or eyes. Her scales seemed to glow of their own accord. Her huge, membranous wings remained raised above her back, only half folded. One great foreclaw tightened upon the earth, tearing great troughs in the soft limestone. The other remained clutched loosely, cradling to her breast something Tek could not quite see.

Most of her immense form was lost from Tek's view by darkness and the rolling slope of the land. Forelimbs on the wyvern shelves, tail resting upon the Plain, she settled before the burning ring encircling Lynex. The dragon peered at the wounded wyrmking. Her magnificently finned and whiskered head was larger than his entire body.

"Lynex," she signed, expelling a billow of burning breath. "Lynex, do you know me?"

Her finished air swirled whiter than cloud, her words surprisingly melodious, despite the harsh susurration. Slowly, painfully, the wyrmking recoiled. Of his seven heads, only the central, largest pate still moved, eyes sightless and shattered. The other six dandled.

"Mélintélinas," he croaked. "Red dragon queen! I feel your heat."

The dragon shook her head. "Mélintélinas is dead," she whispered. "She did not live to see your end. It is I, her daughter, Wyzásukitán. Your queen."

"Wyzásukitán," hissed Lynex, dragging himself upright, sightless eyes questing fruitlessly to perceive her.

The great dragon's head nodded. "Aye. I am she who, four hundred winters gone, nearly fell victim to your jaws when, steeped in treachery, you decided dragon pups were fit food for your kind, that eating a living dragon's flesh could make you, like us, mistresses of fire."

She shifted, moving closer.

"Full-grown firedrakes, of course, you feared to molest. But new-hatched pups, these you stole and devoured while their nurses dreamed. Not even the royal nest was safe from your predations, for only the flesh of a queen's heir, so you determined, suited your own nobility."

The dragon's voice was hypnotic, her face impassive.

"So you sought to roll from the nursery that egg which housed my mother's heir. But the queen's sleep was not so deep as other dragons'. She woke. I hatched to find not nurturing attendants but a predator. I struck, defending my own life until my dam could save me. It was my tiny eggteeth and infant claws which scarred your icy breast."

The red dragon's enormous talons upon the ground tightened, crushing the powdery stone.

"You slipped my mother's traps and escaped the Smoking Hills. She ordered all your kind driven forth, expecting the lot of you to perish in the arid cold aboveground. But you had stolen fire and borne it with you. Thus were your kind able to survive and flee the Smoking Hills."

She turned. Ruby eyes studied him.

"Thus were you able to make your way across the Salt Waste and the Plain. You came here to trouble these unicorns, to steal their lands from them."

The firedrake's jeweled wings tensed, spread, stretching to their full extent.

"My mother, having flown her nuptial flight, had lost her wings and could not follow you. Nor could her earthbound sisters, since among my kind only unwed queens and their mates have wings."

Wyzásukitán hissed, her breath steaming.

"But I have always known what task I must perform before relinquishing my maidenhead. I have been a long, long time growing my wings, Lynex. Four hundred years have I contemplated this tryst."

The white wyrm rolled, sprawling, seeking to crawl away from her, toward the far edge of the burning ring.

"No," he groaned, then half shrieked. "Mercy! . . ."

"What mercy had you for a new-hatched dragon pup?" the queen of the red dragons inquired, her enormous presence glittering above him in the hot light of the fire. "What mercy did you show these unicorns, and their ancestors? What mercy did you grant any of your own kind who spoke out against your ruthless ways?"

She reached for him.

"Ah!" cried Lynex, shrinking and writhing as her great forepaw entered the ring of fire. "Let me go! Let me go!"

The queen of the red dragons shook her vast head. "Never," she answered. "My mother made that mistake. I shall not repeat it."

"What do you intend to do with me?" the white wyrmking shrieked, struggling uselessly against the dragon's grasp.

Wyzásukitán eyed him, and with a snuff of her strange white breath, doused the fire surrounding him. Flame jetted from her nostrils then, in steady, controlled spurts, illuminating the night.

"My mate-to-be is young yet," replied the dragon queen. "It will be hundreds of years before he is ready to fly. Till then, he needs a plaything. Something long-lived to amuse him as he grows." Lifting her head, she shot a great gout of fire across the sky, then bent to examine her prize. "Lynex," she inquired, "can you sing?"

"No!' the wyvern screamed. "No! No!"

His howls grew softer as she lifted him high into the air and turned her attention from him to her other forepaw, the one she cradled to her breast. Carefully, she lowered it to the ground. The enormous talons opened. A unicorn stepped free. Tek felt her own heart kick against her side. Jan! Her mate stood upon the limestone shelves, whole and unscathed. Scanning the battlefield, his eyes found her. Their gazes locked. Bending before him, the dragon laid her head upon the stone.

"Sip again, Firebrand," she urged. "One last dragonsup to protect you from your own fire."

Tek's mate bent his muzzle to the dragon's brow. The pied mare noticed for the first time the shallow depression, perfectly round, like a little Mirror of the Moon. Dark waters swirled there. She saw Jan drink.

"My thanks to you, Dark Moon," said Wyzásukitán, her white breath smoking, "for rousing me from my long sleep and guiding me here. Dance fire now through all the stinging wyverns' dens, that none may ever return to trouble you. Fare well."

Lifting her whiskered head, she scanned the unicorns. Around her, Tek saw her new-met, shaggy allies all stood with heads bowed. The dragon queen smiled.

"And fare well to you, proud Scouts of Halla, who lately dwelt among my kind. My sisters and I will miss your beautiful singing. We must find us other songs to haunt our dreams."

Her ruby eyes found Jan again.

"Firebrand, I take my leave. May the light of Her of the Thousand Jeweled Eyes illumine you."

Pulling herself upright into a crouch, the vast dragon sprang skyward. Her breath flared out in mighty bursts of flame, coruscating in the air, which hung thick and dark, full of particles. She coursed upward, as though to overleap the strange black cloud. Lynex's wails and cries receded. The darkness swallowed them. The great belling notes of the dragon's voice shot away to the northeast, back toward the Smoking Hills.

Tek stirred, saw Jan ramping, striking his heels and his horn to the ground. Sparks flew up, showering, setting the bone-dry wisps of grass ablaze. He dashed for the largest entrance to the wyverns' dens, the one through which Lynex and his bodyguards had emerged. A swarm of burning stars swirled in the wake of Alma's Firebringer as he disappeared into the cave.

Tek heard a roar, as of some resinous substance kindling all in a flash. Fire spouted from the mouth of the wyverns' dens, accompanied by roiling smoke. Tek saw smoke and flame begin to pour from other openings. Within moments, every lightwell in the porous limestone blazed with preternatural light. Crashes and rumbles, as of tunnels collapsing or bursting. The battlefield rocked. Tek heard those wyverns who yet remained screaming in fear.

"Let them go! Let them go," the pied mare shouted as the white wyrms slithered like stormwater toward the Plain. "Let the dogs and grass pards finish them!"

Her own folk milled, but held their ground. The shelves trembled and jarred. Pain in her side bit deep.

"That was Jan!" she heard Dagg beside her exclaim. "Jan, in the hand of the dragon queen."

"The holy Firebrand," Oro beside him whispered.

The dappled warrior turned to the shaggy stranger. "He's gone down into the wyrms' dens and set them alight."

Dazed, Dagg took a step in that direction, as though he half meant to go after his friend. The red mare Jah-lila called, "Hold. We cannot follow."

A dark grey ash began to fall. Tek realized for the first time that the mysterious black cloud was descending, enveloping them. It was made of cinders, tiny particles of soot. The stuff felt warm and gritty, feathery at first; then heavier and heavier it fell. It caked her ears and mane and the lashes of her eyes, coated her pelt and the pelts of her fellows. It covered the earth upon which they stood. Beside her she heard Teki the healer breathe,

"Álm'harat spare us. It is the end of the world."

The Son of Summer Stars
★ 25 ★

Jan's hooves sparked against the flammable crystal lining the wyverns' dens. As he galloped deeper through the twisting warrens, everywhere his heels touched was set alight. The fire ran after him through the caves, casting a blinding glare and billowing heat which did not trouble him, any more than had the airless cold above the ashcloud or the fever of the molten firelake. A tireless velocity carried him through all the length and breadth of the wyverns' dens, always faster than the fires he danced. Its flaring brilliance illumined his course.

He galloped through caverns and chambers, needing no guide. Alma showed him ever and always the way. All the dens through which he passed stood empty. He became aware presently that they were collapsing behind him, the superheated tunnels cracking and shattering, giving way in a series of terrible concussions. This would go on for a long time, he knew. Even after he departed these grottoes, they would burn for days.

The glory of Alma sang in his blood. Fire like the sun gusted beneath his heels. The moon upon his brow gleamed. He felt unbounded by physical body, unencumbered by space and time, keenly aware that before the new could be born, the old must be scoured away. He felt the agent of both that imminent demise and the coming rebirth, at one with all things, with Alma. It seemed the fire he danced was the great Fire, the One Dance that circled the world and the stars, the Cycle of All Things.

When at last his exultation waned, he understood that the dragonsup was ebbing, his divinity passing. Mortality returned. Time to make his way aboveground. He veered upward. As he emerged from the burning maze, air's coolness washed like a long drink of water against his skin. In the darkness of falling ash, he could not tell if it were day or night.

A dim, round orb that might have been either moon or sun gleamed wanly overhead. Canted off to one side, it threw only the slenderest of light. Ash lay thick upon everything, changing the look of the land, painting it grey ghostly as the realm of haunts. He found he was not lost, knew himself to be at the southernmost edge of the wyvern shelves, where they intercepted the Plain.

The Mare's Back, too, lay deep in cindersnow. He shook himself, dislodging a soft cloud of the fine, feathery ash from his pelt. Moments later, it began to coat him again. He turned northward, toward the Hallow Hills and the cliff beneath the milkwood groves where the heart of the battle had raged, certain that soon or late, if he followed this course, he would rejoin Tek.

Barely awake, Lell lay listening to the soft lap of the water supporting her. The world around her stood dark and very still. Ash was falling onto her half-closed eye. It piled in a downy heap on her eyelashes. She blinked, stirring. The water felt deliciously cool after the terrible sensation of burning that had troubled her dreams. She rolled, floundering, and found herself in shallows. Her folded limbs touched bottom, her knees and hocks in contact with coarse, shifting sand.

"Get up," she heard Aiony saying faintly, but quite distinctly, from somewhere nearby.

Dully, the amber filly struggled to untangle her disobedient limbs. A moment later, she was able to stand. The scent of milkwood blooms wafted all around her, their aroma heavy and all-pervading. She felt the tingle of the milkwood buds she had eaten, and the resinous smoke she had inhaled, suffusing her blood.

"Pull Illishar out of the water," Dhattar's soft voice chimed. "The moon's mere has seen to his burns, just as it did yours — but he's not awake yet, and it's time he came out."

Lell stood trembling, feeling the soft weight of ashfall. It clung damply to her pelt. There was no shaking it off. So thick were the cinders sifting out of the sky that the world seemed dark as twilight. Was that the moon shining above her, or the sun? She saw Dhattar and Aiony standing at the edge of the circular mere. The pure pallor of the white foal's pelt and the silver of Aiony's pied coloring seemed subtly, inexplicably, to glow.

"Where am I?" Lell muttered thickly, snorting to get the ash-mud from her nostrils.

"The Mirror of the Moon," Aiony replied, her voice strangely far-sounding, "where Illishar bore you to douse the flames. He knows naught of its healing powers, but he knew it was water, the closest to be found."

"Illishar!" Lell gasped, fully awake now, her heart giving a sharp, silent thump. "Where . . . ?"

"Behind you," Dhattar replied.

Lell wheeled unsteadily, spied the gryphon tercel floating half submerged in the clear surface of the mere, which was littered with milkwood flowers, she saw. The ashfall did not seem to affect the pool's clarity. Instead, inexplicably, the cinders appeared to vanish upon contact with the waters, which remained crystal clear, the mere's sandy bottom still snowy white, unsmirched. Its whiteness glowed almost as distinctly as Dhattar and Aiony.

"Pull him out," Dhattar was telling her.

Lell waded to the unconscious wingcat, bent to grasp one splayed, water-logged wing in her teeth. She backed toward shore. He drifted amazingly easily, supported by the mere. She managed to drag his head, neck, and most of his shoulders onto the shore. He twitched, sputtered, but did not wake. A bright silvery substance spattered his throat and chest. It coated most of his pelt and much of one wing. Curious, Lell bent to sniff. The fur and feathers there smelled odorless and new.

"What is it?" she stammered.

"The bright spots?" Aiony asked.

"Where the fire burned him and the mere healed him," Dhattar replied.

"Healed you as well," Aiony continued.

Lell glanced down at herself. She, too, was covered with patches of pale new hair. She stared at it.

"Burned?" she murmured, mystified. It had been a dream.

"The mere saved you both," Aiony replied, earnestly, distantly. "Illishar's scorched pinions and pelt have come back silver. Your own burnt hair has sprouted gold."

Lell turned to stare at the twin filly and foal. They stood quietly, only a few paces distant, still glowing softly, oddly in the dim ash-fall. Lell shook herself, felt the ash upon her pelt dislodge. None, she realized suddenly, was settling on either Dhattar or Aiony. It was falling through them.

"The ash . . . ," she exclaimed.

They glanced at one another. "It hasn't reached us yet," Aiony said.

"How are you come here?" Lell whispered, too stunned to think clearly.

"We're on the Plain," Dhattar replied, "with the Plainsdwellers and the rest. We're three days' journey from you still. The ash won't reach us for hours yet."

Lell could not take her eyes from them. Their translucent brightness fascinated her. "But where — how . . . ?"

Aiony shrugged. "We stand by an oasis pool, gazing into it. We see you and Illishar, the Mirror of the Moon."

"We watched the battle thus, earlier," Dhattar went on. "We only called you now to wake you, urge you to come out. It was time, and you were very deep asleep."

"The battle," Lell gasped, casting about her suddenly. "How goes the battle?"

"Peace," Dhattar answered. "It's won. Wyverns routed and Ly-nex borne away. Jan is returned. All's well."

Her mind a tangle, Lell half turned, but Aiony called, "List. You need not go down to them so soon. Rest. Illishar will want you by him when he wakes. Ample time betides. The Hills are won, the old age slain, a new age about to be born. Sleep. Regain your strength."

Her voice faded, retreating further and further as she spoke. Her image and that of Dhattar grew thin, finally vanishing alto-gether. Only ashfall drifted where the pair had stood. The amber filly felt her trembling limbs give way. How foolish to think she could have taken another step. Of course she must stay with Il-lishar, must tell him everything when he woke.

"Illishar," she murmured, bending over him. The slumbering gryphon stirred. Soft growling or purring sounded deep in his throat, but his eyes remained shut, limbs loose, his breathing steady. Her own eyes slid closed. She sank into sleep with one cheek pressed against his feathery breast.

The end of the world lasted three days' time. For all that while, the grey ash fell, gloaming the sun to a pitiful light weaker than the moon and stealing all warmth, so the days were cool and the nights chill dark. Cinders covered all the Hallow Hills and the wyvern shelves and the Plain beyond as far as any eye could see. And by the close of that period, these things had been achieved: Jan emerged from the wyverns' dens; Lell and Illishar awoke and descended from the moonpool to rejoin their folk; Ses gathered her filly to her with joyous cries, then bowed in gratitude before her gryphon rescuer.

Jan found his mate, and told her all — in confidence, away from others' ears. Still ignorant, his kith and folk and shoulder-friends embraced him, full of marvel and delight. He promised to give them the tale of his year's adventure as soon as the herd could be reunited and cinderfall had ceased. Meanwhile, the gloomy grit

sifted down and down, drabbing all hues, making ghostly the
world. Most of the slain lay beneath the milkwood cliffs, heaped
upon the wyvern shelves where fighting had been fiercest. Those
limestone hollows collapsed in a grinding roar of smothering fire
at close of the second day, consuming their dead. Other wyrms-
meat Jan and Tek ordered brought to the same spot to be burned.
The unicorn dead they carried to the ancient burial cliffs and laid
out beneath the sky.

By afternoon of the third day, the ashfall began to thin. As evening neared, the red mare Jah-lila stood upon a rise overlooking
the Plain and called in a storm. All night fell the warm, hard rain.
Sun rose undimmed on the following morning, the first real dawn
since the ending of the world. The Scouts of Halla gazed upon
their new homeland, admiring its splendor at the break of day.
Then they departed, pledging to return ere summer's end with
their elders and young, whom the red dragons had secreted safe
away during the late upheaval in the Smoking Hills. Oro bowed
low to both Tek and Jan, then turned and chanted to his band,
singing them into single file across the green and rolling Plain.

The Mare's Back, too, had been washed clean by recent rain,
free of the haunt-grey dust which had shrouded it. Calydor also
took his leave, along with Tek's runners, bearing news of the warhost's victory and summoning those of the herd awaiting at oasis.
On the twelfth day after the battle which had marked the close
of the Era of Exile and begun the Age of the Firebringer, the
herd's colts and fillies, suckling mares and their foals, ancient elders and the halt of limb entered at last into the Hallow Hills,
lush with verdant foliage and summer grass.

Jan and Tek greeted their twins, and Ryhenna and Dagg their
tiny son with relief and joy. The Plainsdwellers, to no one's surprise, evidenced little interest in the herd's newly won lands. Jan
suspected they now regarded the Hallow Hills as both battlesite
and gravelands, sacred and terrible, and not to be trespassed
lightly. Those who ventured the Hills escorting new arrivals took
their leave hastily, almost precipitously. Tek and Jan spoke their
thanks and let them go. Calydor had not been among them. His

absence puzzled and saddened Jan. But he had long since learned how strange were the ways of the Free People. They came and went capriciously, often as not without farewells.

Jan called the herd together on the fourteenth day, moondark, the time of portents and miracles. On the open meadow below the milkwood cliffs that housed the sacred mere, he sang them the lay of his journey through Pan Woods and across the Mare's Back in pursuit of Korr. He sang freely, in the manner of the Plain, of his travels with Calydor, his overtaking the mad king. His voice was strong and sure and omitted nothing, not dying Korr's revelation of Tek's parentage, not his own lost wandering across the Salt Barrens, not his encounter with Oro in the Smoking Hills, nor his sojourn belowground with the Scouts of Halla, nor his long rumination with Wyzásukitán.

Nothing he told his folk was by that time news to Tek or his closest kith. He had told them all in private, days before, starting with his mate. He had watched her hark to his news with tangled emotions: relief to discover at last her unknown sire, horror to find him to be Korr. And she had answered nothing, neither flying at Jan nor cursing, nor weeping, nor fleeing, nor falling into frozen gloom, nor any of the other wild responses he had dreaded. Instead, she had only stood beside him and nuzzled him, till he had cried out in helpless exasperation,

"And knowing this, what will you do?"

"I will think on it," she had told him quietly. "Come, love, let us bury our dead."

So they had done, while the cinders fell, till the rain of the mid-wife washed clean a world newly born of ashes and dust. Now Jan told the rest of his folk as well. Their reaction was stunned silence. Yet none cried out in condemnation against him or Tek. Any outrage was for Korr, and he was dead. Rather, his people heard Jan to the end. Doing so, he realized, because they loved him for his deeds alone. Prince or Firebringer mattered not.

Finishing his tale, Jan turned to me, Jah-lila, to verify my daughter's parentage. I did so, affirming that I had indeed loved the black prince of unicorns in his youth, a year before he had taken the pale mare Ses as mate. I had encountered him upon the Plain shortly after my escape from captors far to the south. Not yet then a unicorn, I had known naught of unicorn ways. Korr had pledged himself to me, but later broke the vow, deserting me upon the Plain and returning to his folk, sure I would be unable to follow him.

But follow I did, already in foal, and found him in his Vale. He pretended not to know me, to mistake me for a Renegade. I saw that should I attempt to lay a claim on him, he would declare me outlaw and cast me from the herd. So I called Teki, who sheltered me, my mate. In exchange for my silence, Korr allowed me to remain. I pledged never to reveal my knowledge of him until he himself had spoken. Still the prince's mistrust and fear begrudged me any peace. I left the Vale, exiling myself. When my daughter was weaned, I brought her from the wilderness and left her in Teki's care, that she might be reared within the herd and perhaps one day reclaim her birthright.

Jan bowed to me as I concluded, then turned once more to address his folk:

"A year ago, I knew nothing of these things. Until his dying words, I was ignorant of Korr's deception. When I succeeded him as prince, I did so in good faith, believing myself to be his heir. But I am not. Tek is the late king's firstborn. It is she who must reign now in his stead. Though I have been your prince, I cannot become your king. I call upon the Council to proclaim Tek queen. Would that you follow her as loyally as you have followed me."

The herd stood silent, like wights amazed. Plainly few had realized until this moment the import of Jan's revelation that Tek, not he, was the late king's heir. Slowly at first, and then more vigorously, murmurs of affirmation rose. They swelled, never quite becoming cheers — for Korr's treachery and the wrong my daughter had suffered could be naught to cheer — but serving as clear and unmistakable approval. The children-of-the-moon accepted my daughter as ruler in Jan's stead. The pied mare stepped forward.

"I accept with gratitude your acclamation," she told them

warmly. "Though Korr was my sire and I his eldest-born, I would not impose myself upon you without your assent. You and I have looked to Jan as our leader these last five years. I would not take him from you to advance myself. But if you will have me, then gladly will I serve as queen."

Her head came up, nostrils flaring, particolored mane thrown back.

"After four hundred years in arms, we find ourselves at last at peace, and sovereignty reverts from warleader to queen. But hark me. I'll not reign without Jan at my shoulder. Battleprince no more, consider him now harbinger of this new peace that we have won. Let the title he has so ably borne remain. As my first edict, with our Elders' leave, I proclaim him forever prince of the unicorns."

This time the cheers were thunderous. Members of the herd threw back their heads, pealed forth wild shouts, struck hooves to earth and drummed up sparks. The din took some little time to subside. That done, Tek bowed her head and stepped back, yielding once more to Jan.

"Know this as well," her dark prince bade them. "Neither Tek nor I harbored any suspicion of her lineage when we pledged one to another four summers gone. Korr concealed this knowledge from us, and Jah-lila bought her daughter's safety and place among the herd with a vow of silence to Korr."

Jan squared himself before his folk.

"For my own deed, I accept no censure. If trespass has been done, be it on Korr's head. With pure intent, I swore myself under summer stars, by light of Alma's thousand thousand eyes. Such a covenant cannot be foresworn. It is unshakable. I will not regret it now. Nor will I abandon Tek and the twin issue of our deepest joy."

Blacker than starless night he stood, head high, beard bristling in the wind.

"What has passed between us can be neither recanted nor denied. It is done. No word or feat can now undo it. Tek was my mate. She can be mine no more. Yet though we never again sum-

mer beside the Sea or bring forth new progeny, she remains the
only such love I will ever know. I'll seek no other in her stead.
Though I sire no more young till the end of my days, I will never
pledge my heart to another."

The herd stood speechless, thunderstruck. Not a murmur or a
snort disturbed the hush. Doubtless none had yet reasoned
through the full consequence of the blood Jan and Tek believed
they shared. Bemused or troubled glances, expressions of cautious
approval, rank distaste, even dread passed like wildfire among
members of the herd to hear Jan preparing to renounce his sacred
marriage vow and the reason therefor. My daughter came forward
to stand at Jan's shoulder again.

"I, too, concur," she announced. "Though I remain barren
from this day forth, I'll neither disown my past nor plight any
other suitor my troth. Can you accept this of me and continue to
call me queen? Will you honor the now severed bond betwixt me
and my one-time mate, who cherish still the offspring we once,
unwitting, bore? Can you spare ill will against our young and welcome them as my heirs? Among us all, their innocence is abso-
lute."

Again, silence. Then gradually, murmurs — not grudging, only
thoughtful. Beside the healer, Teki, who once to safeguard me
and mine had called himself my mate, Dhattar and Aiony chivvied,
the black-and-silver filly snorting at flitter-bys, the white foal
scrubbing his young horn against one knee. They paid no mind
to anything else, as though unaware or unconcerned or, perhaps,
already certain of the day's outcome. Acknowledging them as
their future princess and prince, the children-of-the-moon could
feel no hardness of heart. In muted tones, but without cavil, the
herd assented. Tek closed her eyes. Jan touched his cheek to hers,
then drew breath.

"So be it. Tek, I therefore renounce. . . ."

I gave him no time to complete the phrase.

"No need!" I cried. "No reason to abjure your vows, no need
to wonder at the welcome of your heirs or forgo future young."

The young prince stumbled to a halt. Frowning, so puzzled I

could not hold back my joyous laugh, he and his queen turned
to look at me.

"Children, forgive my holding tongue till now, for I meant all
the world to know your mettle. Aljan Moonbrow," I declared to
him, "called also Firebringer and Dark Moon, you have spoken
earnestly in the belief that Tek is our late king's firstborn child
and you, his secondborn. The former is true. The latter, not. You
are *not* half brother to your mate. She is not your sib. You and
Tek are no kin whatsoever to one another. No blood ties you.
Henceforth let none ever question your union or your offspring
already born or as yet unborn."

Jan stared at me like a sleeper startled from his dreams. Beside
him, his pied mate shook her head as one kicked smartly in the
skull, half stunned. Jan roused.

"What?" he murmured, hoarse. "How can that be?" His voice
gained strength. "What do you mean: Tek and I share no blood?
Have you not confirmed her as Korr's heir? How is she then not
sib to me?"

Smiling, triumphant, I held my peace, for it was not mine to
answer now. I glanced toward Ses, who flanked me on that meadow's slope, and as we had already agreed, she stepped forward to
face the prince, her child.

"Because you are not Korr's son, my son. My mate who reared
you was never your sire. You are not king's get."

Her voice was collected, decisive, clear. Before us, the whole
herd rippled, some shying in surprise, others sidling, snorting. I
heard whinnies, whickers of disbelief, manes tossing, tails slapped,
hooves stamped. Ses waited them out. A look passed between her
and Tek, the young queen's so intent, it was almost a plea. When
the pied mare spoke, though, her words were calm.

"Tell us how this may be."

"I loved another," the pale mare said. "The summer before I
swore myself Korr's mate. He was one of the Free Folk. We met
and loved upon the Plain after their custom, without exchange of
any vows, and then we parted."

She met Jan's eyes.

"That autumn, when I pledged to Korr, I knew not then that I carried a foal. I meant my pledge. I intended to be his lifelong mate and bear his heir. It was not to be. I bore you to my lost Renegade come spring and carried you to term. You did not drop early, as others thought."

The pale mare glanced at me, then down, away.

"Except the midwife, who understood. When I guessed her secret in turn, each of us held silent after, protecting our own and one another's children from a capricious ruler. In time, I brought Lell, too, into the world, sired by my mate, the king."

She found Lell with her eyes. The half-grown filly, her dark-amber coat merled now with gold, stood pressed against the shelter of Illishar's folded wing. Like hers, his sandy pelt was brindled now, his grass-green fletching silver flecked. Amazement lit Lell's gaze, but she watched her dam without condemnation or grief.

"I will tell you this," continued the poppy-maned mare, addressing her son once more. "Though I spoke no pledge to my wild love of the Plain so many years ago, his memory has haunted me. Korr's death pains me deep. I loved him well. Had he renounced his madness and deceit, willingly would I have returned to him."

Her gaze lifted, skimming the assembled unicorns toward the unseen Mare's Back beyond.

"But Korr did not. Now he is dead, and I am free. The Hallow Hills are won, and my daughter grown beyond colthood faster than I could have dreamed. I find my thoughts straying to the Plain, ever and always, night and noon. There, the one I once loved awaits me still."

Her voice grew quiet. I had to prick my ears to hear.

"I long for him I so lately found again, who guided us across the Plain, shared battle with us, and begged me to depart with him, as I nearly did so many summers past when instead I chose otherwise, returning to the herd to swear my pledge to Korr."

Watching her red mane furl and toss, I could only approve the coolness with which she spoke, shirking none of the blame, but neither shouldering any not hers to bear. My daughter leaned against her mate, still staring at Ses. Beside her, the pale mare's son stood dumbstruck, as did all the herd before them. I thought the jaws of some might brush the ground.

"Korr not my sire?" he whispered, stammering as one struggling against a gale. "If not Korr . . . , then who?"

"Calydor," his dam replied, "whose name means Summer Stars."

Aftermath

Such, then, were the things that befell that day, so soon after the dawning of an age, the re-beginning of the world. Ses bade her young daughter and her son brief farewell, departing for the Plain in search of Calydor. She swore to return often, and she has kept that vow. Jan, too, vowed to venture forth upon the Mare's Back before next summer's end to find them both and learn more of the stallion that had sired him. This the dark prince did, sojourning time and again in the company of Summer Stars, who taught him more of the lay-chanter's art, so that Aljan Moonbrow is renowned among you — O dwellers of the Plain — as a singer of tales. But I thought you should know him as his own folk do, a warrior prince and a peacemaker.

For accords with the gryphons and the pans were but the start of his alliances. He traveled far across the Plain as Tek's envoy, forging pacts with many tribes. The unicorns are done with war. My daughter's reign has been a long, lazing dream of peace. Truly a new world her Dark Moon has made, and is making still. For though I am ancient, very near to Alma now, the world is young. Aljan and his mate are but elders. Many seasons lie ahead before they ascend the starpath to merge with the summer stars.

Thus the Battle of Endingfire initiated the passing of the old and set in motion the new dance that is still becoming, even as we speak. No more than a moon after, Jan stood upon the moon-pool cliffs, gazing up into dusky heaven thick with distant suns. The infinite expanse of the void encompassing those myriad stars seemed to enter him, pervading his senses and filling him with a deep, lulling wonder. He became aware of a presence, vast as the starry sky. Only a moment passed before he knew her.

"Alma," he whispered.

The presence answered, "Aye."

"Where have you been?" he asked her.

She laughed gently, silently, within his mind. "With you," she answered. "Always. Even when you do not know it."

Inwardly, he felt his ears prick with surprise. "Your voice sounds like the dragon queen's."

"I am many voices," the goddess told him, "that never cease to speak."

He turned to her within himself. "Why did you not tell me?" he asked. "Why did you let me believe myself prince?"

Again, amused laughter. "But you are prince," the presence replied.

"By acclamation," he retorted, "not by right. Prince at my mate the queen's behest."

The goddess answered nothing, only smiled.

"Why did you never give me any inkling Korr was not my sire?" Jan demanded, stung.

The other's air of tolerant amusement never faded. "Why should I concern myself with that?" she asked indifferently. "Have I not said before I do not make kings or rings of Law? Those things are yours to make or to unmake, exactly as you choose."

Jan held his silence.

The deity asked, "Is being my Firebringer not honor enough?"

The dark prince flushed, chagrined — then let it go, unable to muster true affront.

"Aye: born out of a wyrmqueen's belly," he murmured, re-counting the old prophecy, "foaled at moondark, and sired by the summer stars." He paused, considering. Alma's eyes burned very bright all around. Finally, he said, "I did not lead the battle against the wyverns."

The goddess whispered, "Did you not?"

Jan shook his head. "Tek did. Nor did I carry the brand against Lynex. That deed was Lell's."

The goddess nodded. "But you wakened the dragon that bore him away and danced fire through all the stinging wyverns' dens, expelling them from my Hallows forevermore."

Still troubled, Jan felt his brow furrow. "What sets me apart?" he breathed. "All the fire I ever found, I gave away: now my people's heels can all strike sparks. Their fire-tempered horns have grown as keen and hard as mine, their blood as venomproof."

Again the other nodded, laughing. "Of course. Did you think I had intended otherwise? Flame is not the only fire." Her tone turned almost stern. "You have brought your folk another spark far greater than any flame. You have opened their eyes to the world, Aljan, shown them lands and peoples formerly beyond their ken. You have whistled them out of their cramped, closed, inward-facing ring and led them into my Dance, the Great Circle and Cycle encompassing all."

She seemed to sigh, not with sadness but with joy.

"Such has always been my plan for the unicorns, that they dwell in harmony among my other favored children. You drove the followers of Lynex out because they would have none of that peace. Nay, flame has not been the greatest of my gifts to you. Knowledge, Aljan, that even now remakes the world. Knowledge is the fire."

Dusk had wholly faded now. Sky above had darkened to true night. The full moon, barely hidden by horizon's edge, was just beginning to rise. He knew he must return to his folk for the dance, and yet he did not stir. Gazing heavenward, he felt the goddess recede, not departing, merely withdrawing from his uppermost awareness. She was everywhere, he knew, in the heavens, in the stars, in dragons and unicorns. In him. He could not lose her. The knowledge warmed him to the heart.

See how I have whiled the night away! My friends, I never meant to keep you all so long. I thought my telling of Jan's tale would fill but two short nights. Instead I have talked each of three long evenings into dawn. Forgive me. I am an old mare, much given to prattle. In this age of peace, with no foes to conquer, no battles to plan, each day unfolds free of war and woe. What is there to do but talk, dream, love, and dance in celebration of this new age I midwived in by birth of the Firebringer at moondark under Alma's thousand thousand eyes?

Hail, dwellers of the Plain! I will let you go. Your kindness goes beyond counting to have harkened to me so long. Close cousins to my adopted herd, you know so little of us still. Hostilities between our two tribes have long since ceased, yet we see you too seldom, though your kind may pass as freely into the Hallow Hills as members of my herd now cross the Plain. Ere Jan, such amity could never have been. Yet he was not always the great peacemaker and singer you esteem. In his youth he was a battleprince, by Alma blessed: a warrior, a dancer, a bringer of fire.